PENGUIN BOOKS

OPEN-HANDED

Chris Binchy was born in 1970. He studied English and Spanish at University College Dublin and later graduated from the master's course in creative writing at Trinity College Dublin. He worked as an embassy researcher, painter and hotel manager, and later trained as a sushi chef. His first novel, *The Very Man*, appeared in 2003 and was shortlisted for the Hughes & Hughes/*Sunday Independent* Irish Novel of the Year award. His second novel, *People Like Us*, was published in 2004. He lives in Dublin.

Open-handed

CHRIS BINCHY

PENGUIN BOOKS

PENGUIN BOOKS

Published by the Penguin Group
Penguin Books Ltd, 80 Strand, London WC2R ORL, England
Penguin Group (USA) Inc., 375 Hudson Street, New York, New York 10014, USA
Penguin Group (Canada), 90 Eglinton Avenue East, Suite 700, Toronto, Ontario, Canada M4P 2Y3
(a division of Pearson Penguin Canada Inc.)
Penguin Ireland, 25 St Stephen's Green, Dublin 2, Ireland (a division of Penguin Books Ltd)
Penguin Group (Australia), 250 Camberwell Road, Camberwell, Victoria 3124, Australia
(a division of Pearson Australia Group Pty Ltd)
Penguin Books India Pvt Ltd, 11 Community Centre, Panchsheel Park, New Delhi – 110 017, India
Penguin Group (NZ), 67 Apollo Drive, Rosedale, North Shore 0632, New Zealand
(a division of Pearson New Zealand Ltd)
Penguin Books (South Africa) (Pty) Ltd, 24 Sturdee Avenue,
Rosebank, Johannesburg 2196, South Africa

Penguin Books Ltd, Registered Offices: 80 Strand, London WC2R ORL, England

www.penguin.com

First published by Penguin Ireland 2008
Published in Penguin Books 2009
1

Copyright © Chris Binchy, 2008
All rights reserved

The moral right of the author has been asserted

Set by Rowland Phototypesetting Ltd, Bury St Edmunds, Suffolk
Printed in England by Clays Ltd, St Ives plc

Except in the United States of America, this book is sold subject
to the condition that it shall not, by way of trade or otherwise, be lent,
re-sold, hired out, or otherwise circulated without the publisher's
prior consent in any form of binding or cover other than that in
which it is published and without a similar condition including this
condition being imposed on the subsequent purchaser

ISBN: 978–0–141–03622–9

www.greenpenguin.co.uk

Mixed Sources
Product group from well-managed
forests and other controlled sources
www.fsc.org Cert no. SA-COC-1592
© 1996 Forest Stewardship Council

Penguin Books is committed to a sustainable future
for our business, our readers and our planet.
The book in your hands is made from paper
certified by the Forest Stewardship Council.

For Siobhan and Michael

I

A smooth midsummer evening. Two-thirds full. Four-hundred-and-fifty-euro rack rate, two hundred minimum for a walk-in, although depending on who was around there might be room for negotiation. The open space of the lobby was shushed by the thickness of a sand-coloured carpet and populated by the kind of bodies you would expect – solid, expensive, a mix of foreign and local. Nobody out of place, all familiar, everywhere. Middle-aged. Tanned. Jackets and ties. The smell of heavy perfume. Here for a couple of drinks. Mid-week dinners that cost real money. Occasional mad blowouts that everybody would enjoy, remember, never regret. But not tonight. Quiet tonight.

Just walking through the door would let you know you were safe here. The cool air, the smell of lilies and freesias. The width and depth of the couches. The low lighting, hushed conversation, a tinkling water-feature. The benevolent portrait of a smiling Turkish-looking man who had some unspecified significance in the hotel's history.

Piano music, some cliché of easy-listening, drifted down like cigar smoke from the caged, dark-wood bar. Two girls were behind the desk at Reception, pretty but within reason, blonde but not too much. They stood a couple of feet apart, smiling blankly out across the open space. From any kind of a distance you wouldn't notice, but they were having a conversation. Their lips barely moved. Occasionally one or other would vibrate with contained laughter. The next shift was coming on and the girls were giddy with the anticipation of finishing. They weren't going anywhere, weren't doing anything. Just down to the car-park, into separate cars, a quick wave to each other and home. But it was the end of the day and that was always something. One of them flashed a look around, then, coast clear, checked the time on her watch and the other laughed again. State of you. Oh, who cares? We're finished now.

The night manager, nervous and thin, had arrived and was in the back office setting the daily audit in motion, a computerized process that would click and grunt and warble through the night. A hundred pages of data would print out and tomorrow an administrator would split that report into sections and pass them on to a more senior administrator, who would record the information, file it and then ignore it. Three weeks into the job the night manager was moving quickly from unfamiliarity into edgy boredom. The reality of what he would have to do was beginning to reveal itself, the unhappy prospect of long slow time that would need to be served. When he sought some source of comfort in his future, he could think only of sleep.

The night porters arrived, three of them together. Ray, Tommy and George. Clean-shaven, ironed shirts and dark uniforms. Everything in place and all as it should be, but still, somehow, they looked wrong, ghoulish underground creatures who didn't belong to the day, too addled and distracted to thrive in the night. Personal histories that you could see in their faces and that you would turn away from. They went to work in silence, checking stock and floats and the messages of the day in the book left for them by the day shift, a well-oiled routine that came from years of working together. The newest recruit, a young Polish fellow, shiny-faced and blond-haired and smiling, arrived last. The night manager watched him come, nodding in a curt way to acknowledge his over-familiar greeting, his friendly wave. It was a bad start for this guy. In the night manager's last place of employment people turned up before the appointed hour. Here it just seemed to be a loose guideline. Ten past. Twenty past. No apology or explanation.

But there was no point in making a fuss. Not on a quiet mid-week night with rooms to spare, only two guests left to check in and the bar emptying. The first wake-up call wasn't until six o'clock. If they kept their heads down and said nothing, they might get away with it. The night manager let the girls go. They walked off together, linked at the arm. The further from Reception they went the louder their talk became. The door opened into the inner workings, then closed on their conversation and they were gone.

An hour passed. The last of the bar crowd cleared out. Just before midnight the quiet was broken by the sound of a car horn, beeped twice. Two porters went out. After a moment a man in a polo shirt and chinos came through the revolving door, talking over his shoulder to his companion. Their conversation could be heard clearly. They were discussing the plant out in Celbridge, how far it was and how long they would need to get there in morning traffic. 'What do you think?' the first man asked the night manager, as they arrived at the desk. 'To get to Celbridge for eight?'

'Forty-five minutes should do you,' the night manager said. 'Maybe an hour.'

The two men talked back and forth, then agreed to meet at six forty-five in the lobby. They arranged alarm calls, the first guy for six and the second for five thirty. One of the men talked to Ray on the porters' desk about a place that might be suitable for jogging in the morning.

'Along Sandymount strand would be your best bet,' Ray told him.

'Is it far?'

'It's far enough. A mile maybe.'

'That sounds okay. How do I get there?'

'I can book you a taxi.'

The night manager smiled. He was entering the men's details on to the system, hopeful that this would be it. Most of the people staying that night were Germans on bus tours. Middle-aged and elderly at a rate that was too low, but they were no trouble. Their days were too structured for them to run riot at night. Not the done thing anyway. Bad for the group dynamic.

The two guests crossed the lobby to the lift and waited, talking idly to Tommy, the rise of a laugh from all of them, the ping of the door opening and then, with a clunk, silence fell again.

'That's us done,' Ray said to the night manager, as he passed the desk. 'We may relax.'

'I hope so,' the night manager said back.

'I'll get the dinner on,' Ray said, and headed towards the kitchen. He disappeared through the doors and the manager was left alone.

But Ray didn't go through to the kitchen. Instead he went down a set of raggedy stairs, their rubber edges flapping, walls dented and scraped by porters and housekeepers carrying new furniture, special beds for special people, outsize plastic figures for sales conferences, rolls of blackout blinds for the sensitive eyes of soft-rock giants, humidifiers for the vocal cords of country-and-western legends, every extra little something to make the day or night special. He walked out into the car-park's warm dead air. The floor and walls were concrete, the ceiling low and obscured by a network of pipes, plastic and metal, some with insulation, others raw and brassy. The sound of liquids purging and flushing and draining just inches above his head made him nervous. There were bunches of cables, tufts of fibreglass, holes and plasterboard patching jobs along the walls, storage cages, electricity stations, and then the grotty open area lit with fluorescent tubes that showed the way to the staff changing rooms, the laundry and another stairway up to the hotel. Water was dripping everywhere, the ground covered with puddles of varying colours, and as he walked across he watched to keep his feet dry. The air smelled of detergents and cleaning products mixed with car exhaust and rotting rubbish, a sweet, distant reminder of where he was. Extractor fans roared in the background. At the edges of his vision there was always something moving that wasn't there when he turned. He was sure there were underground creatures that resented his presence but weren't big enough or numerous enough to do anything about it.

Guests' cars were parked in a separate area close to the entrance. The guests never came down here but still the divide was always maintained – cleaner, clearly marked spaces with no pipes or tubes running above. The cars sat there, proud, shining, untouchable, all facing out. The porters parked them that way for a quick, tip-friendly exit. They stared across the puddles at the smaller, older, more decrepit staff cars, parked at varying angles to each other, a mix of fronts and backs.

He turned a corner and walked straight into someone, a short, hard body that pushed him back. In his surprise he shouted, an involuntary yelp. When he saw who it was he spoke: 'For fuck's sake, Dessie.'

'I was coming up to you.'

'You nearly gave me a heart-attack.' He put a hand on the other man's arm. When he got his breath back he laughed and handed him a key card.

*

Tommy was giving the new fellow instructions for the night's work, moving a silent Hoover back and forth over an already clean floor. 'Like this. Yeah? And when you finish here,' he said, his arm waving across the expanse of lobby carpet, 'do the bar and the terrace and then the toilets. Later on I'll show you how to do the cards. Are you all right with that?'

'Okay. Yeah.'

'Good man.' He turned quickly and moved off before the gimp could start asking questions. They came anyway.

'Sorry, Tommy.'

'Yeah?'

'What toilet is it?'

'The public toilets. The ones in Reception. Across there.'

'I hoover that?'

'No. You clean that.'

'This is job for porters? Is not job for cleaners?'

'Is job for you,' Tommy said. 'Talk to Ray if you're not happy.'

'What are you doing now, Tommy?' the boy asked.

'Are you really asking me that?' Tommy walked back slowly towards him.

The boy smiled, showing no sign that he understood Tommy's intention, as if his tone was lost in translation. He was a good-looking fellow, not without charm, but Tommy wasn't having it. He came and stood a foot closer to him than was necessary. 'Why? What's it to you?'

'If I need to ask you something, I will know where you are.'

'I'll be on room service. In the kitchen. On the phone. Okay? What would you need to ask me?'

The boy shrugged. 'Cleaning questions.'

'Ask George. He loves those. Knows everything about cleaning,' Tommy said, as he walked off again.

'No problem. And when will I do room service? Tommy?'

'Soon.'

'Soon is good,' the boy called after him. 'Maybe tomor-row?'

'Maybe,' Tommy called back. 'Or maybe fucking never, you smart cunt,' he said, into the middle distance, as the noise of the Hoover started up behind him.

Ray crossed the other side of the lobby to the porters' room. He took a key from a hook, walked over to the lift and looked across towards Reception. The manager was out of sight in the back office. He pushed the button on the lift and waited. When it arrived he stepped in and put the key into the security lock under a panel, turned it and pressed B. He felt the moment of hesitation, a shudder, then heard the gentle groan of protest from a lift expected to do something out of the ordinary. He went down two floors to the basement and came to a rest. It took a few seconds for the doors to open. When they did a man was waiting and Ray stood neatly into the side.

'Good evening,' he said, and nodded without making eye contact.

The man stepped in and said nothing. He stood behind Ray and watched him press the button for the fifth floor. The doors closed and they took off. The two of them watched the numbers on the display above the door, counting up. A ding. A mechanical voice with an English accent spoke – doors opening. The man stepped out. As he passed he reached out and, without looking, pressed a small wad of notes into Ray's hand. 'Thanks,' he said. Ray said nothing in return. The doors closed and he took the lift back down.

As he walked over to Reception the night manager called out to him: 'What's for dinner?'

'Stew.'

'Again?'

'You never get tired of stew,' Ray said.

'Apparently you don't.'

Ray smiled. 'Any time you want to cook, you can decide what we have.'

'It wouldn't be right, Ray. Not the way it's supposed to be.'

'Indeed,' Ray said. 'A gentleman like you couldn't be seen cooking for the scum.'

'I'm joking,' the night manager said.

'So am I,' Ray said. He headed back to the kitchen. Alone in the still-steamy heat of the empty kitchen, he checked to see that the money given to him was correct.

Five of them, four porters and the night manager, had dinner on a raised lounge area of the lobby. During the day business people met there and polite, tidy women drank tea and ate small cakes. The working party sat in darkness and shadow so they could see if anybody came to Reception without being seen themselves. Spread on the low glass tables in front of them were plates, a large casserole dish sitting on a kitchen cloth, cans of Coke, pots of tea, cups, ashtrays. They ate off their laps, mostly in silence. When they were finished they lit cigarettes, ignoring a law that they felt shouldn't apply at night, and drank tea. They talked about what was left to be done – who would get the breakfast cards, who would do the papers, the rest of the hoovering and the ballrooms. It was a conversation that had no resolution, just spirals of good-natured recrimination and grievance, same conversation every night. The new guy would end up doing the bulk, whether he realized it or not. The night manager listened to it again, then interrupted and asked about the Americans from earlier: 'How much did they tip, those two?'

'Nothing,' Tommy said. 'Fuck all.'

'Well, which was it?'

'Couple of quid. For six bags. Suits. The whole fucking lot of it. Taken out of the car, the car parked, everything brought up. For two euro? No use. Waste of space.'

The revolving doors began to turn. Every one of them looked over. A girl emerged into the lobby. Young, dressed for a night out, small bag on her shoulder. The only thing unusual about her was that she was alone. She walked straight across the floor of the lobby to the lifts. The night manager stood up as the others kept smoking, drinking, sitting. He took a couple of steps and stopped. In the darkness it was hard to see where any of them was looking. 'No use at all,' Tommy continued. 'The Americans are getting worse, you know. They've got it into their heads that you don't tip in Europe. How much would a porter in America get for what I did, Ray? Five dollars?' The doors of the lift slid open and the girl disappeared.

'More like ten,' Ray said. The night manager turned back to face them, pointed vaguely in the direction of the lift.

'Twenty, yeah. And yet they come here and think two euro is appropriate? They'd be run out of the place in New York.'

'Run out of it.' The night manager tried to speak over them, hesitated, then sat down again. Ray got up after a minute and lifted the empty plate from in front of him. 'How was that for you?'

'Very good,' the manager said.

'You see, I know what I'm doing,' Ray said. 'That's the difference.' The manager wasn't sure what he was talking about. 'We'll get this place cleared and then we can start organizing things.'

'I could sleep for a week,' said Tommy.

'After the work,' Ray said. 'But you have a rest there now,' he said to the night manager. 'If anyone rings or comes in we'll look after it. We'll be around. You sleep and we'll wake you when we're going down.'

The night manager looked up at him in a moment of clarity. 'Tell me everything's going to be all right,' he said to Ray, smiling now. Easier. Conspiratorial, but admitting nothing.

'It'll be fine,' Ray said, smiling back. 'We'll look after everything. The work will be done. You get yourself rested. I'll wake you if you're needed. But you won't be. Just relax.'

'Okay so,' the night manager said. He stretched out on the couch and got himself comfortable. This was how they did things. He could spend his life worrying about everything that went on. He could dig around and find out and nobody would thank him for it. Things worked, and he didn't need to know how. A place like this was too big for any one person to handle. Any staff member, any room, any guest could lead you into a quagmire, if you chose to poke around. Night manager? He was a clean man in a suit. A figurehead. The porters understood the dirty mechanics of it all. Let them at it, he thought. If I wake and the place is still here then I've won. He closed his eyes and was lulled to sleep by the distant sound of someone hoovering the women's cloakroom while whistling to himself.

2

It was easy for Gavin. He just put them in these uniforms and watched the punters pile in all week, standing three deep at the bar on a Wednesday night. Agnieszka knew what it had been like before and how it had changed since he'd been to that bar in Riga and had seen the future. It wasn't a difficult concept. All the staff, mostly girls, some boys, dressed in tight T-shirts and jeans that pulled and stretched, rode up and down and hid nothing. Nobody had been hired for their experience. She had seen him do the interviews, sitting in a booth and talking slowly to young girls, one at a time, keeping the questions simple for the really beautiful ones, getting the tone slightly wrong. Asking them to perform – 'Do a little twirl for me' – as he shifted in his seat and scratched himself and said things like, 'Oh, that's lovely,' and 'Superb.'

Could it be legal? She thought not, not here in the West, with its EU directives and honesty and cultures of excellence that must surely prevent employers making girls bend over in interviews, inspecting their haunches and teeth as if they were horses. But for the Eastern Europeans who came in droves through the door in response to Gavin's *Herald* ads, none of that mattered. They would take their minimum wage and occasional tips and be happy. Until they began to realize, as she already had, that it cost more than they'd thought to survive here and that the work was hard and sweaty and uncomfortable, and that €7.85 an hour was a cheap price to sell your arse for. All that groping, petting, patting, touching, brushing, sidling, passing, miming. The filthy comments they would gradually begin to understand. The threats and promises and wet entreaties panted into their ears. The casual sense of ownership that the guys had when they were in groups, goading each other to take it one step further before the manager could cop what was happening. But the manager didn't care. This was what they were all here for. She watched the new girls smile through it and then, as the weeks passed, she saw how their smiles faded and how the ones that lasted toughened up.

She was supposed to be a bar-worker, mixing drinks and opening bottles for a fun-loving, sophisticated crowd. But the crowd weren't as sophisticated as they thought they were, and as the night went on their sense of fun faded into incoherent abrasiveness. Before she had started she had negotiated a higher rate because she had experience and references from home, and once she'd proved herself she'd negotiated again. She was too quick, too reliable and too good-looking for Gavin to let her go. So now, at least, she was well paid to put up with it all. She tried not to let the staring and the hammered slow declarations of something that just wouldn't come out get her down. The pointlessness of it all. The repetition. What's your name? Where are you from? Do you have a boyfriend? You're a beautiful girl. You're sexy. You're a fucking ride. My friend really likes you. When do you finish work? Will you marry me? Will you come home with me? Will you fuck me? Will you let me fuck you? The moon-faced drunks that draped themselves across a busy bar taking up space to tell her something that required her to lean in close to them and wait, while they tried to put the words together in an order that she might find persuasive. She didn't stop for them any more, just shook her head. It happened this night and she just said no.

'What do you mean no? You don't know what I'm going to say.'

'You've had enough. Any more and I'll get you put out.'

'But I love you.'

'So does he,' she would say, pointing at Besim, one of the Albanian bouncers who just happened to be close by. Not the biggest guy but he definitely had something about him, a bored animal twitchiness that suggested chaos was his element, that intense violence meted out would be just the thing to make this tedious shift pass quickly. He smiled and waved back and the drunk guy scarpered, disappearing into the crowd.

The owners came in after hours during the week on their way to the casino and sat with Gavin, drinking whiskey, talking about takes and percentages and the tits on the new girl and what they'd done with those two Ukrainians. They were there tonight. As she was on her way out one called her over. She came and stood by their table.

'Who's this lovely girl?' the man asked Gavin, staring calmly into her eyes.

'This is Agnieszka.'

'What a beautiful name,' the owner said, a hard smile tickling the corners of his mouth. They all laughed, too loud. 'Jesus, darling, you must have been an ugly baby.'

'It was my grandmother's name,' Agnieszka said.

'My apologies,' the owner said. 'So, Agnieszka, would you like to join us for a drink?' He was drunk already. No different from the customers, apart from his money and confidence and the cut of him. He might even be good-looking, if the shadow of cruelty in his demeanour was just the drink.

'I can't. I'm sorry. I have a night bus.'

'Sure we'll drop you home later. We're out for the night. Come on. It'll be fun.'

'Thank you. But I can't.'

'Do something, Gavin. Make her stay.'

Agnieszka saw the panic that flitted across Gavin's eyes. He wasn't smart enough for this. He would sacrifice her. He would fire her if she didn't do as she was asked. He put his hands up. 'Hey, her shift's over. If she wants to go she can go. I can't make her do anything.' She didn't look at him but for the first time she felt there might be some trace of humanity at his core.

'Next time,' the owner said.

'Maybe. Yes. Okay. Good night.'

'Promise me.'

She laughed and walked off.

'Agnieszka. Promise me,' he called after her.

'No,' she called back, as she walked out of the door, and this gave her more comfort than she would have thought as she walked along the slick, steamy streets to her bus stop.

3

The air in the car-park was thick with diesel fumes and the smell of sewers undercut by hay from somewhere unseen. It had been a hot day, mid-thirties, and even now in the late evening Marcin's shirt stuck to him as he tried to drag his rucksack out of the boot of his father's car. When it finally came loose he turned and smiled at his parents with no conviction. They stood in silence beside the car, waiting, loath to move, as if they were condemned but could stay the execution by remaining still.

'Got to go,' he said. It would be short, he told himself. If nothing else, it had to be short.

They went inside the grim grey station and checked to see where his bus was leaving from, then walked in silence to the platform. A small crowd was already there, quiet and low-key in the middle of the night, as if the usual backslapping and cheerful hollered goodbyes would have to be forgone because it might wake the people sleeping in the town two kilometres to the east. It was how Marcin had known it would be. 'So,' he said. 'You go on. There's no point in waiting.'

'Okay,' his father said. 'Let us know when you get there.'

'I will.' They hugged briefly. Marcin was aware that he was damp and sticky. Before his father could speak again, warnings, admonishments, declarations of love, disappointment or envy, he turned to his mother. 'I'll be back soon anyway. One way or another.'

'I know,' she said. 'Still, I'm allowed to feel like this.' She smiled, trying her best but inescapably tragic.

'You are,' he said, 'but it doesn't make it right.' Another damp hug. He squeezed her hard and long enough to leave her with a warm impression of himself that might provide her with comfort later.

'If there's any problem, come back,' his father said. 'Anything at all. Don't try to be brave or independent or proud. Just come back. We won't even ask.'

'I know. I won't. Or I will.' He wasn't sure what he was saying but the tone seemed right. The bus drove up, braked sharply, then honked as it began to back in. For his last trip in Poland he would be in the care of some macho idiot speeding through the night. It would be a frustrating way to die, so close to escape.

'I'll ring you when I get there,' he said, thinking it was something he should say.

'Goodbye,' his father said. 'Good luck with everything.' A tidy, cursory little wave and he left. His mother walked backwards for a moment, waved, blew a kiss and then she, too, was gone. Watching them as they went, his father ten feet ahead of his mother, both slouched and visibly unhappy from behind, he knew that, if he let himself, he could cry right now to think of them. If he pictured them making their way home in the car in silence, waiting for his call in the morning, after which their relationship would be defined by phone calls and the space between phone calls, it would make him cry. They were good. They had given him a lot. And now he was leaving them.

But he wasn't inclined to think this way. He shivered, gave a shake and let out a little grunt. In four hours he would be in Warsaw and in another five he would be on a plane. He would arrive in Ireland and get a job, maybe share a flat with Artur, and then he would just live for a while. Do his own thing. Not think too much or worry about the future or where things were going. He thought he would find he liked buying things. Clothes and shoes and books and televisions. A laptop. A stereo. He would dress better. Go out drinking and meet girls, bring them back to his place and listen to music with them, then take them to his own large bed. There was nothing wrong with these aspirations. He was allowed to have them. They weren't the reasons he'd given his parents for leaving but they were as important. He had talked about Ireland and archaeology, its ancient Celtic culture and the importance of its sites. How the booming economy meant there were huge resources for digs, research, college departments. It all seemed plausible.

'And if it takes me a while to find something I'll get a job doing something else.' Clouds had rolled across his father's face. 'To keep me going, that's all.'

'Like what?' his father had asked.

'I don't know. Anything. Working on a building site or in a bar or a shop.'

'You don't have to go to Ireland to do those things. You can do them here. Why would you waste your time? You have the degree. Get the job you're qualified for. I don't know why you went to college if you wanted to work on a building site. You could have saved us all a lot of time and effort if you'd let us know.'

He was a good son. He'd never given them cause for concern. He'd done plenty of things but nothing that had caught up with him, very little that they knew about. He was bright but a shade lazy in school, had done what he wanted in college, which had caused some arguments at home but nothing serious. He had delivered on what was expected of him and now, at twenty-four, he was surely entitled to go his own way. Not to keep living at home, continuing with his studies, until a job came up.

He was getting on a plane and going to a place where he could shake off all the pathologies that had afflicted his parents' generation. He reserved the right to develop his own. Drunkenness, vapidity, laziness, chronic fatigue, rampant, proselytizing capitalistic urges. He might end up a heroin addict or a gigolo or homeless, coughing and puking on the street. None of these was his intended path, the future he would choose, but it was now, as the bus pulled away from the station, within his own hands.

4

He walked along the corridor in silence. Heavy carpet, a quiet suit, breathing through his nose. Without the sounds coming from the bedrooms, the television conversations that were too even in their give and take to be real life, it would be easy to think that this was a dream. There was a tightness in his stomach, a sick unease that was balanced by a tickling sense of urgency, a twitch that made him feel awake, drove him forward, one foot in front of the other. When he came to the room, he expected, as always, to find someone on the other side of the door. The end of it all could be waiting for him. The thought of this scenario slowed his heart and stilled his breath as he put the card into the slot. The click of the door, the green light and the moment of fear as he walked in. Empty. It had always been empty.

He walked across and turned on the light in the bathroom,

picking up the remote control for the television as he passed. He flicked it on over his shoulder while pissing some of the tension away, then came back into the room. He flipped through the channels until he found a film, something dark and serious that he had watched at home some time. Or was it in a hotel abroad? He tried to remember had Helen been with him and found something, a flash of her saying she'd heard this was supposed to be good but it was getting very stupid. The pair of them laughing. Was it real, this memory?

He stood up and quietened his mind with action. Took off his jacket and draped it across the back of a chair. Undid his tie, folded it and put it in the inside pocket of the jacket. Opened his top button and rubbed the back of his neck. It was sticky. The end of a hot day. He went into the bathroom and splashed water on his face, wiped his neck with a cold damp cloth and felt better. Woke up a bit and looked at himself. He went back and lay on the bed, his head propped on a pillow folded in half. When the knock came he checked through the spyhole and saw the girl standing, smiling vaguely. He opened the door. 'Hi,' he said, and stood back to let her in.

'Hi. I guess I'm in the right place?'

'I guess you are. So, you'd no problem finding it?' he said. Same line every time. It set the tone.

'No,' she said, smiling still, curious. 'No problem. It's a big hotel. The taxi driver knew it.'

'Just a joke,' he said.

'Ah,' she said. 'That's funny.'

She was no first-timer. He could see that straight away. It had an effect on him. 'Where are you from?' he asked her. It sounded like he was making conversation but he always wanted to know.

'I'm from Russia. Originally. Moscow.'

'I know Moscow,' he said. She looked at him for a second before she spoke again. He thought she was lying but wished he could let her know that it didn't matter.

'I live now in England,' she said. 'Four years.'

'London?'

She hesitated. 'Near to London, yes.'

'And you just come here to work?'

'Yeah. To work.'

Why was he here? Why would he risk everything? He thought of the words 'compulsion' and 'addiction' and 'perversion' and none of them seemed to fit. This was just a thing he did. Natural, ancient, understandable. A necessary urge defined by physical realities. Look at this girl. How could you not? Standing here before him doing exactly what he wanted without being told. He reached out and gently pulled her a step closer to him. He was here and this girl was moving towards him and he could do what he wanted. Nothing strange. Just to be active and enthusiastic and uninhibited. In the nowhere space of this room, which officially was empty, he was a man with no history or name meeting a girl whose name would be Natasha or Olga or whatever she had said it was.

She was dark-haired, this one, pale-skinned, with the pointy, girlish features that Eastern European women often had. Young, but then they were all young. It wasn't his thing, just the way the business seemed to work. What he was interested in were the more womanly features. Curviness. Tits. Arse. She had all of that. You wouldn't know it when she'd walked in the door, she didn't dress to flaunt her attributes, but with every item of clothing that dropped he saw she was just the kind of girl he liked. It was all arranged for him; he was told who was available, an inventory of measurements and body sizes was quoted to him, a list of overblown brochure descriptions phrased in a way that tried to make everything sound filthy and classy.

As she undressed in front of him he lay back on the bed and watched through half-closed eyes, his heart pounding in his throat. Always the same feeling, the same urge to get up and run away while he still could and never do this again, but knowing that he wouldn't, that he would stay there and that things would proceed in a way that was predetermined, that had nothing to do with him. He watched her now. Her paleness. The weight of her breasts, which came together as she bent forward to take off her pants. Sometimes the girls carried evidence of their lives beyond this world – scars from operations, appendectomies and Caesareans, stretchmarks from pregnancies, an assortment of tiny lines, cuts and etchings that told stories he couldn't always translate. He hated seeing them, not because they were imperfections or brought reality into this neutral space but out of a sense of propriety, as if he was trespassing into territory that the money he paid gave him no right to access. This girl, though, was a blank slate. Close to perfect. He would remember her later. She came to him across the bed and he abandoned any notion that this was something that would not happen for the second-by-second pleasure of what she would do to him and then what he would do to her.

'So what do you want to do first?' he asked her.

'It's your money,' she said, and together they laughed.

'Come over here,' he said, 'and I'll sort you out.'

5

There were three of them.

'See these?' Gareth said.

'I see them,' Victor said.

The attitude was wrong as they walked in silence with purpose to the door, already tensed, and then the first words that one of them spoke – 'What now?' – as if there was a long history of grievance between them. They were never going to get in. Don't be drunk. Don't dress wrong. Don't come to the door like you're spoiling for it. Just don't be the way you are in every facet of your being. Maybe they wanted the fight. Maybe that's what they were there for. Hard for Victor to imagine. Why would they all not just get in a taxi and go back to somebody's house and drink themselves into the ground the way they wanted to? Maybe tell each other that they were loved and cared for or whatever it was that they needed to stop them doing things like this. Did the thought that things might go badly even occur to them before it started? Or was there no thought involved? Was it just three drunk men moving through their future one second at a time? This cunt's not letting us in. Something has to be done.

Victor saw it happen. Gareth was halfway through a sentence, 'There's no way, lads . . .' and there was a flash in the corner of his eye. Not long to react, less than a second maybe, but for Victor it was enough. The second punch would come and he would be ready by then, in the way, ready to grab the wrist of whoever had decided to hit his colleague. He would hold on like a pit-bull and, whatever else might happen, the evening for the owner of the fist that had thrown that punch would end unhappily. He would do no more than he had to. There was a certain pleasure in knowing he was in control. What to others was a chaotic, scary, violent mess was to him something clear, predictable, choreographed. When he saw the hand advancing for the second time, he grabbed it and spun out of the doorway, moving the arm at speed through an angle that meant a sudden end was coming. When the arm tightened and the guy screamed and bent at the same time, Victor pushed him to the ground and knelt on his back, knocking the wind out of him. He smacked him on the head once, hard enough to make him think, then looked up to check. He saw that the doormen from the club across the road had come over and everything was just about under control. The three were all on the ground.

Gareth called over to him: 'Get that fellow down the lane.'

Victor lifted his man, the one who had thrown the first punch. He was cursing at him in a whining, crying voice that Victor couldn't really understand. His face was a mess. Only fucking this and didn't have to fucking that. 'Okay,' Victor said. 'Good man. You just relax now.' One of the bouncers from across the street came over to give him a hand and the two of them lifted the guy, feet dragging, away from the light and the main thoroughfare down a side lane of dirty puddles and wheelie-bins, fire-exit doors and smoking chefs, who stood up to watch as Victor and the other doorman pushed the guy against a wall and held him there. Gareth came down after them, his nose bloody and lip already fattening, still panting.

'The little prick,' he said to Victor.

'Oh, no,' the guy said.

'Are you all right?' Victor asked Gareth.

'I'm fine. Thanks for that. This little bollocks, though. Out of nowhere. How are things?' he said to the other bouncer, whose name, Victor thought, was Ben.

'Not so bad. Hit you, did he?'

'He did.'

'Getting slow in your old age, what?'

'A momentary lapse of concentration,' Gareth said, and Victor and this Ben fellow laughed a little harder than they needed to.

'And you, you piece of shit,' Gareth said to the guy, 'what do you say now? What now, big man?'

'Please don't fucking hit me again. Please. I've had enough. My head's fucking busted.'

Gareth punched him hard in the ribcage twice, then stood back and kicked him once between the legs. An 'Ooh' sound rose from the chefs at the kick. The guy dropped in a heap. Gareth and Ben walked back in the direction of the bar. The chefs dispersed. Victor crouched down and spoke close to the fellow's face. He was holding himself, his face a mess of blood, and moaning quietly in pain, barely conscious.

'You'll be all right,' Victor said. 'In a few days you'll be okay again. Just stay away from bouncers, yeah?' The man curled up into a ball. 'Good man,' Victor said. He patted him on the shoulder and went back to the bar, to get a pint of Coke. Sugar. That's what he always needed after these things.

6

His phone rang: six o'clock in the morning. He reached into the darkness and his hand closed around its pulsing body first time. He pushed a button and spoke. It could only be Sylvester. 'Good morning.'

'Are you up?'

'Almost. Yeah.'

'Everything all right?'

'I think so.'

'You won't be late?'

Dessie yawned and stretched. 'Are you trying to annoy me?' he said.

A familiar laugh. 'I'll see you in a while.'

'Right so.' He dropped the phone on the floor and waited. His body felt too heavy, sunk too far into the mattress. He couldn't prise himself out. Too much to expect. A small man trapped in someone else's bulk. If he could just sleep until he woke. If he could just sleep.

'Are you getting up or what?' she said, bringing him back with a jolt. He pushed away the covers and sat on the edge of the bed, holding his head in his hands.

'Every day,' she said. 'Would you not say something to him?'

'You're as bad,' he said, as he stood and made his way, slow and rickety, into the bathroom.

A beautiful morning: the sun rising in front of him, low in the sky, the world orange in the rear-view mirror. He drove with the visor down, sunglasses on, through the trees and greenery of the riverbank before the city claimed it. The same traffic report at this time every day, the girl with her husky voice still drawling happily before the calls came in notifying, alerting, complaining. His body relaxed into the seat and he knew that, whatever the day might hold, for this trip he would have comfort. He would feel better than the others around him. Better car. Better suit. Better life.

He pulled into a garage and bought cigarettes and tea. He stirred in five sugars on the counter beside the till as a new Indian boy watched him with an expression between wonder and distaste.

'What?' Dessie said to him, looking up.

'You are very sweet.'

'Thanks, but I'm married,' Dessie said, and went outside.

He stood there, smoking and drinking, watching the traffic pass and feeling his body begin to right itself. 'I need my drugs,' he would say, too loud, to Sylvester first thing in the morning in hotel lobbies when they were away on a job, just to watch the flash of panic. 'I can't do a thing without my drugs.'

'Some day somebody's going to hear that,' Sylvester would say, half warning, half joking, 'and then . . .'

'Sure nobody knows you here,' Dessie would reply, for the luxury of hearing himself say it, the thorn not even hidden within the joke. 'Nobody's interested in you here.'

He checked the time and got back into the car, waited too long for the traffic to break. Smoke from the cigarette in his mouth burned his eyes. He pulled out, checked for cops, then accelerated into the bus lane to make up time. He left the window open to clear the smell, but when he hit traffic on the quays the air disappeared and in the heat he felt a tickle of sweat on his collar. He sealed himself in, turned on the air-conditioning and the temperature fell as he rolled along at walking pace.

Through town and out again on the far side, against the rush now. Past the sleekness of the money and the new city through the old collapsed grandeur, the streets clean and empty first thing in the morning, up and down over the river and canal to the curve of a park, past the village and on to a road by water. Flashes of it at first among the cranes and the containers. Then where the river became sea, the buildings thinned out, the city eventually let go and the sky took over. Blue above, sparkling water below, the grey-green steadiness of Howth in the background. He speeded up, the engine roared briefly, then kicked into the lower gear, past the stationary traffic heading inch by inch in the opposite direction towards town. The wheels made a comfortable high drone on the rippled concrete, the sound of his day going to plan.

A mile on he stopped at lights and watched cyclists drifting along on the bike paths, safe and smooth and alive. If he wasn't doing this, he might be there, on the other side of the street, slowly pedalling on the flat, smooth pathway that would take him out as far as the wooden bridge. Rumble across it, down to the end of the road, cycle on to the beach, then run into the water. To swim in the sun, the warm morning air, while the road here was clogged with people contained in their drudgery – that was something he might have done once.

He turned when the light changed and the car purred up a slope, away from the water into the stillness of the suburb on an early-summer morning. Tree-lined on both sides. Enough space for two cars to pass, just, but around here the locals were too uncertain of other people's driving even to try. As he turned into Sylvester's road, Dessie tucked in beside a parked car and flashed his lights at an old fellow in a Micra coming the other way. No rush anyway. The two of them sat and looked at each other across twenty yards. Dessie beckoned him forward and flashed again. 'Come on to fuck,' he said, through smiling teeth, 'like a good boy.' The other car crawled towards him and passed, the driver waving vaguely in his direction. Dessie waved back, a picture of relaxed politeness. The car was too well known around here for him to do anything else.

He pulled up in front of the house. When he saw a face in the living-room window he cut the engine and waited. The news at seven had just started when the door opened.

The wife came out in a dressing-gown and wandered across the garden towards the car. Dessie rolled down the window.

'Listen to me,' she was saying. 'I don't want him staying out half the night. I want him back here by nine at the latest. I've family coming over for dinner and it would be nice if they believed my husband still lives here.'

'I'll do what I can,' Dessie said.

'That's not much, I suppose,' she said. She stood watching the house.

'Not a lot. You know yourself.'

'I do. Here's Sylvester now.' She turned back to him. 'Anne well?'

'She is. She's fine. Same complaints as yourself but however. What can we do?'

'What indeed? It's when she stops complaining you should worry. Good luck, Dessie.'

'Good luck,' he said. Then called after her, 'I'll do my best for you.' She smiled back at him.

'What was that about?' Sylvester said, as he got into the back.

'She wants you back by nine.'

'Well now, Madam. I don't think that's going to happen.'

Dessie started the car and pulled off. 'Where are we going?'

'Do you not have your schedule?' Sylvester asked.

'Don't annoy me. I have it here somewhere. The airport hotel, right?'

'I'm meeting that guy Campbell at the Hilton at eight.'

'See? I did know that.'

'You're a real pro.' He sniffed the air, a short act of theatre. 'Have you been smoking in here?'

'No,' Dessie said.

'I could get done for it, you know. People watch me. This

car counts as a place of work. Some clown makes a call to the papers . . .'

'The papers. Jesus, what are you like? Nobody cares. Nobody's watching.'

'Still, it's my car.'

'I didn't even have one in it. I got in after.'

'After, my arse. I wish you'd quit.'

'I'm touched that my health is of concern to you.'

'Your health? What health is that? You should have gone years ago. You're on borrowed time. It's my reputation I'm worried about.'

'And what reputation is that?' Sylvester fixed him in the mirror for a moment. Maybe a step too far. He let it go.

'Enough,' Sylvester said. 'No smoking in the car.' He looked at his watch. 'Here, I want to get breakfast before meeting this fellow.'

'Did you not eat before you left?'

'I had something she made. I walked it off on the way to the car. Long day ahead.'

'Isn't it always?'

They were at lights now, about to turn back on to the main road.

'Are you all right for tomorrow night?' Sylvester said, down at his paper.

'Tomorrow night?'

'My visit.'

'Oh, yeah,' Dessie said. 'I'm about.'

'Then don't be long coming around.'

Dessie flashed a glance at him in the mirror. He sat with his eyes down, reading. Tidy haircut, good skin, white shirt, steady blue tie. A respectable man. No sign of anything else. There never was, but still, from time to time, Dessie looked.

7

It would be better if he wasn't so tired. This traffic, the endless roadworks, the shabby greyness that was too familiar – all of it wouldn't be getting to him so much if he had slept at some point on the trip. He rested his head on the window, the glass cold on the side of his face, and watched commuters standing in loose groups at a stop. Unfamiliar tired, angry faces with red puffy eyes that surely mirrored his own. I don't know who you are, he thought, but I don't think I like you. He caught himself and pulled back. Too tired. Issued a general apology to the world and then, without thinking, said out loud, 'This is taking too long.' The girl sitting in the seat across the aisle from him looked over and, not understanding what he'd said or why he was speaking, kept looking to the point where he felt he should say something else. If he'd slept it might have been different.

On the plane he'd missed the explanation, if that was what it was, for the delay in take-off because the crew spoke too quickly and didn't translate it for the benefit of the Polish passengers. The plane was full of people like him, all doing the same thing. None of them seemed excited or interested or even happy about it, they just sat in silence with fixed expressions that he felt must be affected. He had nothing to eat or drink, nothing to read, and what was available to buy he didn't want to pay for. He sat wedged into a seat that was too narrow and too upright to allow even the thought of sleep.

The first person he spoke to at Dublin airport, a security official, yawned in his face when he held out his passport before waving him on wordlessly. He walked past partition walls, following temporary signs through the sound of hammering, as if the set for the film of his arrival wasn't quite ready. He went out through sliding doors into the public area, keeping an eye out for Artur. Maybe he would have felt that his arrival was a significant enough event to come out. They could go to a bar and have one to celebrate, then a taxi back to Artur's and spend the day drinking before collapsing into twenty-four hours of sleep. That would be a good introduction. He was outside before he understood that no one was there for him.

When the bus arrived at the terminus he collected his bag and walked into a dirty grim station of sick greens and yellows and unhappy-looking people. He turned on his phone and dialled Artur's number. It went straight to message. He checked the time. It was almost nine. Artur had said he would have his phone on from eight but it would be like him to forget, to have stayed out last night and be asleep on a floor or in a park somewhere, his phone left in the back of a taxi. He carried his bags downstairs and put them in Left Luggage. On the street outside he walked towards where looked busiest. In a café he ordered toast and coffee and took out his cigarettes. The woman shook her head at him and pointed at a sign – not for the first time, he felt. The food helped; the coffee lifted the muggy bleakness that had been sitting on him.

He ordered another coffee to take away and walked out on to the street. He had a map in his bag but he didn't bother going back for it. Just wanted to get a feel for the place. He wandered along a pedestrianized street of grubby shops and badly dressed people in the direction of what looked like something happening. Every couple of steps he heard Polish being spoken. He saw the faces of people he felt he should know. A rough crowd. Hard language. He walked up one side of the main street, a wide boulevard of takeaways and sports shops, then at the river turned back in the direction he'd come and found the bus station again. He rang the number but Artur's phone was still off. He had his address, forty-five minutes from the centre. He could take a taxi out and sit in a café or bar until Artur got in touch. But he needed to sleep now. The bench he was on was too narrow and he worried about being robbed or moved on. He stood up and retraced his steps, turning this time into a road of high, terraced houses facing each other with grim determination, signs on the steps outside to lure the undiscerning and the desperate. He wandered along until he found one that seemed better maintained than the rest and went inside. The girl behind the counter looked at him with suspicion.

'Do you have a room now?' he asked.

'What? For tonight?' She spoke in English but he knew just to look at her.

'Are you from Poland?' he said then.

'Is it for tonight?' She answered him in Polish, but that was her only acknowledgement of his question.

'It's for now. But I'll stay tonight.'

'We have a room.'

'How much?'

She gave a price that seemed too high.

'That's the best price?' he asked.

'Yeah.' He waited for a moment, looking at her to see if she was holding out. Whether she might suddenly melt into friendliness and reveal that this harshness was just a game she was playing.

She half smiled at him. 'Do you want it or not?'

'I'll take it,' he said, without hesitation.

'We need a deposit. Or credit card.'

He took out the card and in silence dropped it in front of her outstretched hand. She picked it up and disappeared into a back office.

He thought of sleep and how he could be in darkness and bed within fifteen minutes. She came back, gave him a form to fill in and returned his card. He took the key and climbed a thinly carpeted creaking stairway to a room at the top of the building, what must have been servants' quarters when the house was built. The room was small and low-ceilinged, with a mean window that barely let in light and the lingering sense of a thousand compromised nights. But it was clean and it had a bed. He went back to the bus station and got his stuff, dragged it past Reception, past the girl, up the stairs and dumped it all on the floor. Took off his shoes and got into bed. I should pull the curtain, he thought, and closed his eyes.

8

In the middle of the morning the gym was quiet. Victor spent five minutes warming up, then got going, working his arms and neck and back. There was a tightness there from the night before. The burst of adrenalin and the brief exertion of getting that guy on the ground had left a reminder in his muscles. He would work it out now in the routine. Count his way through the repetitions, move from the weights to the machines and back again, over and over like a religious rite. Clearing his mind. Fixing his body. Improving his spirit. Finish with a run, a nice cardio burn. It calmed him to be here. People got gyms wrong, he thought. There should be no judgement of others or any vanity. No talking or staring or flirting. To come here was to explore your relationship with yourself, turning your gaze inward, seeing who you wanted to be and then working until the external matched the internal and you achieved a state of equilibrium. Your own straining face in the mirror, like an icon, would bring you what you prayed for. He was close to his ideal but wasn't worried enough to make the kind of sacrifices that would get him there. When he finished he would sit outside the Turkish café down the street and have cappuccino and cake.

The work took its toll. Staying up all night waiting for something to go wrong, hoping it wouldn't. He enjoyed being on the doors, meeting people, flirting with girls, but he'd enjoy it more if he knew that nobody was going to hit him with a bottle. Here, all was knowable, calm, relaxed.

He had a nice smile, or so people said. It seemed gormless to him when he looked at himself in the mirror, like a child's, his face splitting, little dimples, tidy white teeth showing. But people responded and found themselves smiling back. It came as a surprise when the bouncer held the door for them and beamed, throwing out encouraging messages to send them in upbeat. Have a good night. Enjoy yourselves, lads. Be good girls.

There were other bouncers who didn't get it. Not just the psychos drawn to a job where they could kick heads, break noses or stamp on necks. But the guys who saw themselves as gatekeepers, suspicious of every group that wandered up to the door. The ones who let that suspicion show in their faces, enjoying the moment when they put up their hand blocking the way. Hold on there a moment. Where do you think you're going? What was the point? Talk to people, check them out, but hope for the best and it would happen most of the time.

The punters you had to worry about didn't just explode into violence from nowhere. You could feel it coming. Hear the change in the voices, see the body language. Victor could tell when it was going to happen. When his smiles and his gentle, mildly lisping voice didn't do the trick, when everything he said seemed to aggravate the situation, when they talked themselves into a rage – 'Who the fuck are you? Who are you to tell me where I can go? In my own fucking country! What are you smiling at? You've a face like a prick' – Victor would tense and prepare himself.

'That's a nice trick,' Gareth had said to him, one time early on, after he'd stared down two guys who had seemed ready to start something but instead walked off in silence. 'How do you do it?'

'I think about bad things,' Victor said.

There was a toughness in him and he could access it. When he'd been in school it had been a wave of rage that would overwhelm him and carry him places he didn't expect. But when he got bigger he'd hurt a fellow one time and scared himself. He learned to control it, talking himself down when the adrenalin kicked in. Steadying himself. Breathing slowly. Now he could turn it on and off, letting out just enough for the situation. It took a lot for him to lose his cool and it was something he was always aware of. Without self-control he could kill someone. The gym helped to keep him focused with its order and counting and routine, and the promise, posted on the walls, that you could become the person you wanted to be.

9

Dessie looked up from the paper and saw them coming. The two men walked slowly, leaning in slightly towards each other as they came. Campbell, a Northern businessman, taller and bulkier than Sylvester and wearing a suit that might have appeared expensive on someone else, was talking, emphasizing his point with a finger he wagged close to Sylvester's chest. It seemed that he was cautioning him, warning him off. His words were slow, clear, deliberate. If he had wanted, Dessie could have read his lips. But he didn't want to know. At the point where Dessie thought Sylvester was going to have to do something, to stand his ground or put him back in his place, the two men suddenly laughed. Heads turned around in the lobby at the sudden explosive sound. Har har har. Dessie relaxed. A big joke. Some of these men were just clowns. They came to do business and acted like it was all a game to them, spending other people's money. Sylvester could buy or sell these guys. Dessie knew that. People underestimated him, with his clean, obvious good looks, his accent that could have been from anywhere, his bland generalizations that people took to be schoolboy philosophy rather than appropriate careful sounds. They dropped their guard. Said too much and thought too little around him. This big dope looked to have done the same. Dessie smiled as they approached. Sylvester nodded at him.

'All done?' Dessie asked.

'Yes, indeed.'

'So, that was very useful,' Campbell said, as they walked out on to the steps in front of the hotel. 'We'll be in touch with you. I think we've made some good progress.'

'I'll talk to Marek and get him to send that information on to you.'

'Absolutely, yes. Excellent. Excellent.' They shook hands.

'Are you going into town?' Sylvester asked him. 'Can my driver bring you anywhere?'

'No, I've a car here. I'm heading on to a meeting in Waterford. Bit of a drive ahead of me. Thanks anyway.'

'No problem. Good to see you. Take care of yourself.'

'And you. Good luck. Goodbye to you.' They walked off in different directions, Sylvester lifting a hand in a salute as they went.

'Our car's that way,' Dessie said to him.

'We'll let him go.' They walked together loosely across the car-park.

Dessie took out a cigarette and lit it. He inhaled deeply, blew out and spoke: 'Your driver?' he said. 'Is that what it is now?'

'They love that kind of thing,' Sylvester said.

'I don't,' Dessie said. 'I've told you before.'

'What would you prefer? Secretary?'

Dessie smiled. 'Associate.'

'I'll talk to Helen. Get some cards made up. "Dessie. Associate." '

'You do that.' The two smirked at each other, then turned it into a smile to wave again as Campbell drove by.

10

If she hadn't forgotten to turn off her phone and his call had gone straight to message, what would he have done then? She wondered about this later on when she was in the shower. On her day off she normally slept until the afternoon but his call woke her at ten and she answered before she was awake enough to check who it was.

'Is that Agnieszka?' A male voice, very clear and clean. A low conversational hum in the background.

'Yeah. Who's this?'

'Agnieszka, it's Luke White.'

'Who? Sorry?'

'This is Luke White. I'm one of the owners of Symposium. I spoke to you last night.'

'Oh, okay.' Her stomach gurgled lightly. It distracted her for a moment from whatever he was saying. 'Sorry. I didn't hear you.'

'I'm sorry. I was just saying, the reason I was calling was to apologize for my behaviour towards you last night.'

Was he still out? Was the hangover beginning to kick in? Was he atoning for the sins of his night before it ended? He didn't sound drunk. His voice was lower and more measured than before.

'That's okay,' she said.

'No, really, I'm sorry. I was out of line and I shouldn't have put you in that position.'

'It's no problem.'

'Well, you're very kind,' he said. 'It won't happen again. It was inappropriate.'

'All right.' There was a moment of silence. The noise in the background rose for a second, a heightened murmur and then what sounded like quiet applause. 'Okay, so thanks for calling,' she said, thinking that when she woke again later, this would seem very much like a dream.

'I'd like to put it right,' he said.

'Don't worry about it. It's fine.'

'Maybe you'd join us next week for a drink? We want you to understand that you're a very valued part of the operation.'

Who was 'we'? What operation? She worked in a bar. 'Thank you,' she said. 'But you don't have to do that.'

'There'll be a few of us going. We're taking the managers and a couple of the supervisors out. As a thank-you for their work since we reopened. We'd like you to come along too.'

'Right.'

'That's great. Gavin will tell you about it anyway. I hope you can make it. And I'm sorry again for last night.'

'It's okay.'

'Goodbye,' he said, and was gone.

There would be no sleep now. She lay in the bed for a couple of minutes trying to think of a way out that she had missed. Her stupid sleeping brain.

II

It was dark when he woke again. He lay there blinking, trying to remember where he was, and when it came to him he felt a surge of happiness. He sat up and fumbled for the light. He found his phone and saw he had no missed calls. He dialled Artur's number and this time it rang, but there was no answer.

Outside, he passed along a dark street, apartments facing open ground across which wild-looking children called and whistled. He turned into another street and saw a pub ahead of him, lit up. It was glass-fronted, old wood, painted lettering, the kind of place he'd seen in pictures. He went into a room with a line of old men drinking on their own at the bar. He sat on a stool and ordered a beer. When he turned he saw that everyone was staring straight ahead, each maintaining the sovereignty of his own territory. He was glad. He wanted to be alone. He wanted to sit at the counter in an Irish bar and have a drink and know for sure that he was away. His clothes still smelled of home, and the half-remembered flight of this morning felt like a dream, as if he'd experienced some sort of flashback or mild epileptic event. When he nodded to get the barman's attention, the barman nodded back. 'Same again?'

'Same again.'

'Good man.'

He was a good man. It was true. A glow of happiness washed over him, one drink in and another on the way. He need not have worried. There was no problem. He could handle this.

That night when he got back to the guesthouse he tried Artur's number one more time. It rang and then, finally, he heard Artur's voice on the other end.

'Where are you?' he asked Marcin straight away, as if that was the issue.

'Where am I? Where am I? I'm in a hotel in Dublin, that's where I am.'

'That's strange. So am I.'

'What hotel?'

'The one I'm working in. It's a five-star.'

'Yeah, well, mine's not. What happened? Why didn't you answer your phone?'

'I know, I'm sorry, but I'm working nights. I tried to get in touch . . .'

'How?'

'I rang you.'

'When?'

'I don't know. A couple of days ago. Anyway, I'm sorry. Are you all right?'

'I'm fine. But this room cost me sixty euro and it stinks.'

'You should have haggled.'

'I did.'

'Well, come and meet me in the morning at my work and we'll head out to the house together.'

'What time?'

'I finish at eight. I'll give you the address. You can get a train.'

After five minutes on the train the city thinned out into back gardens and apartment blocks, trees and grass. The walk from the station to the hotel was through a suburb of red-brick houses, most of which had been turned into offices that had plaques with words he thought he should remember but didn't. He came to a corner and saw the sign first, just the two words spelled out in green plastic letters that might have signified quality when they were put up thirty years before but to Marcin just looked cheap. Trees and hedging hid the building from the road, but as he got closer he could see parts of it through breaks in the shrubbery: odd unexpected wings that jutted out, stuck on as afterthoughts. Then, through a gap cleared for some sort of pipe main-tenance, he saw the main building, modern and enormous with no obvious shape, like a child's vision conceived and executed in Lego, then blown up on the whim of an architect, a bizarre mix of brown and red and cream bricks, spectacular in its loose awfulness.

He came to the gate and looked past an empty security hut up a driveway that led to the entrance and saw that from here, at ground level and hemmed in by willows and landscap-ing, the view was quite different. The canopied arrival area, revolving doors and liveried porters waiting, the bell trolleys and Mercedes that were dropping off and collecting and the tinkle of a water-feature from somewhere unseen suggested some sort of luxury. This was the first impression he would have had if he'd arrived in a taxi or a limo or by horse and carriage. Not many guests, he supposed, arrived on foot.

It was ten to eight. Artur hadn't said where they should meet. Marcin stood at the gate for a moment, cars passing him on the way in and out, and he began to feel like a beggar watching the rich folks, hoping that one might throw him a handful of change or a sandwich. It was a hotel, he thought, open to the public, and he was a member of the public, even if he was Artur's friend. He walked up the drive, the air smelling of flowers from the beds beside him and a distant gassiness from a hole in the ground a little way off. He had thought he would ask the porters where he'd find Artur but as he got closer they watched him arrive with a low-grade, curious hostility that they didn't let interrupt their chat. He kept going, through a revolving door that seemed to take twice as long as it should have to deliver him into the lobby.

And then he knew he was in a five-star hotel. There was a tiny but perceptible hiccup in the background hum as he came in, a moment when the population of this vast open space saw the same thing and shared a thought. Something unexpected had happened that seemed unpleasant but would surely be resolved quickly. Nobody looked at him, not the businessmen standing in a group drinking coffee around a trestle-table, or the German tourists checking out *en masse*. Not the three perky waitresses who crossed Reception with trays of pastries for a meeting somewhere else, or the manager type in a grey morning suit standing alone at a small mahogany table in the middle of the floor talking into a phone. And yet he had been seen and noticed, and when he caught his reflection in a mirrored pillar he realized that the only thing to do was to leave. Turn right around and get out before they could put him out. Already somebody was walking towards him with purpose, a scowling, aggressive-looking uniformed man, whose face suddenly broke into a smile.

'The international traveller has arrived. Can I take your bag? Are you checking in?'

'Yeah. The penthouse.'

'You don't look great.'

'Well, if you'd slept where I slept . . .'

'I can show you where I slept. Right over there,' Artur said, pointing to a couch where two women in suits were hunched over a laptop. 'Oh, look. They've got dressed.'

'When do you get out?'

'I have to herd these Germans on to buses. That should be it. We'll go to the house and have a drink.'

'A drink?'

'It's my evening.'

'Yeah, well, it's definitely my morning.'

'You can sleep all day. We're celebrating.'

'I had a premonition that this was going to happen.'

'You must be psychic.'

Standing behind Artur now was the manager Marcin had seen talking on the phone. Thin, balding, a fun-looking half smile on his face as he spoke. 'Good morning, Artur,' he said.

'Good morning, Mr Doyle.'

'Have you finished?'

'No, I do that and finish now.'

'And who is this?'

'He is my friend. He is just arrived.'

'And are you another of our Polish brethren?' Mr Doyle said to Marcin.

The word 'brethren' meant nothing to him. 'I am Polish, yes.'

'And are you staying with us? Are you checking in?'

'No, I'm not.'

'Well, in that case would you mind letting Artur get on with his work? You can continue your reunion when he's finished. Somewhere else, I would suggest. Thank you.' He smiled, nodded at them both and waited as they said goodbye.

'I'll see you outside,' Artur said. 'Five minutes.' The manager took him by the arm as they walked back across the lobby and spoke close to his ear.

When Artur emerged from the hotel half an hour later, Marcin thought of a day maybe ten years before, coming out of school at the start of the summer holidays. Now he was underslept and hung-over but these waves came to him when he needed them. 'What did the manager say to you?'

'He said that my homeless friends should keep their begging off the premises,' Artur said, taking a bottle of beer from his backpack and handing it to Marcin.

'It wasn't really a problem, was it?'

'No. He's a daytime manager. Nothing to do with me.' He produced another bottle, took a key-ring from his pocket and opened both. 'Cheers,' he said. 'Good to see you.'

'*Slàinte*,' Marcin said. 'Is that how you say it?'

'Probably. You're welcome anyway.'

'Thanks.'

They sat on the upstairs deck of a bus that took them back through the centre, along the river into a valley filled with trees and new apartment blocks, then into a rougher place. Artur kept falling asleep and Marcin kept waking him again to be sure they wouldn't miss their stop. He would lift his head and look out across a landscape of garages and bus-stops and scruffy bursts of shops at traffic-lights, rows of the same houses over and over, off into the distance.

They got out at the entrance to an estate of solid-looking semi-detached red-brick family homes, with small patches of grass in front, each of which, he thought, had no greater ambition than to look exactly like the one next door.

'Stepford,' Marcin said. 'You live in Stepford.'

'It's left, then right, then left, then right from the bus-stop,' Artur told him. 'That's the easiest way to remember. The opposite for getting out.'

'That's the easiest way to remember?'

'It works for me. Until I learned that, I spent days just walking around this stupid estate trying to figure out how the numbers went.'

'And how do they go?'

'Not the way you'd think.'

They arrived into the house, dropped their bags in a bare, tiled hall, then turned into an empty living room that smelled of stale smoke, damp clothes and maybe feet. There was a plasma TV, two couches in some kind of black vinyl and a coffee-table covered with cans and an overflowing ashtray.

'Drink?' Artur said.

'Do you not need to sleep?'

'I'll sleep in a while.'

'Okay, then. Great.'

'Have you thought about what you're going to do for work?' Artur called from the kitchen.

'I'm going to get my CV into a few places to see if I can get on a dig or something for starters.'

Artur came and handed him a beer. He looked at him, smiling. 'Right.'

'What?'

'Why would you do that?'

'Because I may as well try to get a job doing what I want to do.'

'Okay.' He was still smiling.

'If you don't either tell me what your point is or take that look off your face, I'm going to have to hit you.'

'I can ask if there's anything going in the hotel, if you want. They're always looking for people.'

'How do you know? I thought you'd only just started.'

'Because apparently they're always looking for people,' Artur said. 'That's what I'm told. It's the word on the street.

They were looking for a recent graduate with a degree in archaeology last week.'

Marcin laughed. 'Really?'

'Yeah, they're going to get him to dig through the foundations of the place, right down to the core of the Earth to see if he can find his balls.'

There was a banging noise and the house shook as somebody came downstairs. One guy appeared in the kitchen, then another came into the living room. Monsters, both of them. 'This is Marcin,' Artur said. 'He's just arrived.'

'Andrzej,' the first one said, standing above Marcin and holding out his hand. He looked about seven feet tall from where Marcin was sitting. Shaved head, wide shoulders, ex-army vibe. Marcin shook his big, leathery paw. The other guy stood behind him. Marcin stood to shake his hand.

'Basil,' the guy said. Only slightly smaller, cropped dark hair, wearing a sleeveless T-shirt that showed off his arms. He had a scar that ran from his hairline down his temple and finished under his left ear, some of which was missing. Marcin stared a second too long.

'What's the problem?' Basil asked, staring back.

Get this wrong, Marcin thought, and Artur will be giving those ridiculous directions to an ambulance crew in about twenty seconds. 'What happened?' he said, honesty seeming like some sort of policy.

Basil grinned. 'My parachute didn't open.'

'Right,' Marcin said. 'Okay.'

'You should see the other guy,' Andrzej said, and they all laughed together – Artur, Basil, Andrzej and Marcin – as if it was the cleverest joke in the world.

'Drink?' Artur said.

'Nah,' Basil said. 'You night-shift boys have it handy. Drinking all day. Some of us have to go to work.'

'Yeah, but I work when you're drinking.'

'Work, my hole,' Andrzej said.

'What do you do?' Marcin asked.

'Sites. Labouring.'

'Do you like it?'

'It's a pure cunt,' Andrzej said, and Marcin laughed for a second, then stopped. His laugh had sounded very loud.

'Got to go,' Basil said. 'See you later. Are you staying here?' he asked Marcin, who looked at Artur.

Artur nodded. 'For a while, yeah,' he said.

'Tell him about the bog,' Basil said. 'Good luck.'

'Take care,' Marcin called.

The door slammed and then slammed again. There were ten seconds of silence.

'Okay,' Marcin said.

'What?'

'Who are those guys?'

'They live here.'

'Yeah, but where did you get them?'

'They're friends of Zak's.'

'Who's Zak?'

'A fellow I used to work with. He's at home at the moment. He'll be back next week. He's a great guy.'

'Is he like them?'

'What's wrong with them?'

'I don't know. They might kill us.'

'Just because they didn't do degrees in Sanskrit or whatever doesn't make them criminals.'

'What happened to that guy's face?'

'I don't know.'

'What were we laughing at?'

'I don't know.' He smiled. 'Seemed like the better option.'

'I'll give you that.'

Marcin sat back down and drank from his bottle. He discovered he was panting slightly, as if he'd just run upstairs. Artur yawned and stretched, then went into the kitchen and started looking through a drawer. 'Why don't we have a little spliff to relax ourselves?'

'Okay.' It would be a long time before Marcin could relax. 'What's wrong with the toilet?' he asked then.

'Oh, yeah,' Artur said, coming back in with a lump of hash the size of a golf ball and a pack of jumbo papers. 'That's complicated.'

12

Sylvester sat in the back. His mouth was dry with a dusty stickiness that made him lust for something. Beer. Gin and tonic. White wine. The cut and then the glow of it. He pined for drink. 'Do you know what I'd like?' he said into the mirror.

'I do,' Dessie said. 'I really do.' They travelled on in silence, lost in the same thought.

Sylvester sighed. Rolled his shoulders. As they pulled up in front of the house he sat forward to look out of the window. 'How long have they been waiting? What time is it now?'

'Half six.'

'Oh, Jesus.'

'Relax. He's still here. See him?'

'She's going to go ballistic. After this is done.'

'She'll be all right. She looks okay.'

'Yeah, but she's not.'

Helen was standing in front of the house, talking to a man with a camera. As Dessie and Sylvester watched, she looked over and saw the car. Sylvester raised a hand and she turned back to continue with her smiling, light conversation. The dutiful wife for everybody but him. 'I'll see you in the morning,' he said to Dessie.

'I suppose so.'

'Thanks for today.'

Dessie shifted around and eyeballed him over his shoulder. 'Sorry?'

'Thanks. For your work today.'

'I never knew you noticed.'

'You know I appreciate you.'

'I most certainly do not.'

'Well, you can't take offence at me thanking you.'

'It just brings into relief all those other times,' Dessie said. 'The long, lonely drives home without a kind word . . .'

'Oh, to hell with you, then.'

If he could have delayed any longer, if there was anything else he could have said to Dessie, he would have. Another jokey little circuit to hold himself until he was ready. But there was nothing. Empty head. The knowledge that Helen would be unhappy with him. That was all.

He walked across the lawn towards Helen and the photographer. A steamy, still evening, a light hint of barbecue in the air, the suggestion of other people's evenings being enjoyed. Daniel and Jessica were sitting together on the porch, he saw now. He smiled first at the photographer.

'I'm sorry,' he said. 'Michael, isn't it?' He came to him with his hand outstretched.

'Hello,' the photographer said. A brief, weak, damp handshake. He flashed an unsmiling glance at Sylvester's face before turning away.

'I couldn't get out of a meeting. I'm very sorry. Has Helen been looking after you?'

'Oh, yeah, she's been very good to me.'

'Michael's been here almost an hour,' Helen said. 'He's got to get out to Bray after this.'

'I'm sorry to have kept you. What's in Bray?'

'My house.' He shrugged. 'This is my last job. Not a problem. Can't be helped. Where do you want to do this, anyway?'

'Maybe in front of the house. What do you think?' He turned to Helen.

'Whatever you want. It's your thing.'

'I'll get myself set up and you can decide between yourselves how you do it.'

'Thank you, Michael,' Sylvester said. 'Are the kids ready?' he asked Helen then.

'Why don't you find out for yourself?' It was too sharp. She had walked away before he could say anything else. He went over to the children. 'Will you go up and put on a shirt, Daniel?'

'A shirt?'

'What's the problem?' Sylvester asked. These muttered half-statements of rebellion would some day, he thought, lead to the death of one of them.

'It's, like, thirty degrees. I'm sweating already.'

'Just do it. Go on. Like a good lad.' Sylvester had come to recognize the inability of a privileged child to visualize the reality of other people's existence. The fear and boredom and compromise of a poorer life. If he understood how close they all were to it, Daniel would see that it was worth putting on a shirt to stand in front of this house, smile and not flinch or squirm when his father's arm came around him. Most people didn't go to fee-paying schools, didn't speak with the bored American accent and cadences that Daniel and his friends had picked up from somewhere. Who knew? Maybe all of this would signify enough in the future to ease his passage through life. Maybe not understanding what it was like for everyone else was a part of privilege. Better not knowing, Sylvester thought then. He'd surely find out in time.

'How are you?' he asked, looking down at Jessica.

'I'm okay.'

'Had a good day?'

'All right.'

'What did you do?'

'Nothing. Went to the beach for a while with Jenny.'

'Busy?'

'A bit, yeah.'

Sylvester sat beside her on the porch step. Helen was talking to the photographer about his lens, a short, fat, pug-nosed thing that, from here, didn't look as impressive as Sylvester would have expected.

'How was your day?' Jessica asked him.

'It was fine.' Silence for a moment. 'It's nice to be asked,' he said.

'And what did you do?'

'I met a man who maybe wants to do something in Croatia.'

'I thought it was the Czech Republic.'

'Well, it is normally. But Marek might be able to set something up. Between us we should be able to do it. Anyway. If it works it will be good.'

'Is it going to take long?'

'I don't know. It might. A couple of months, maybe.'

'No. This. This now.'

'Oh, sorry. No. It shouldn't. Why? Do you have something to do?'

'Not really,' she said. She yawned and stretched, then stood and walked slowly towards the photographer and Helen. Sylvester saw now that Michael was young, early twenties maybe, and good-looking in a pretty way. Jessica stood beside Helen and listened to them talk.

'Daniel.' Sylvester shouted it and his voice echoed across the houses down towards the sea.

'God almighty,' Helen said. 'What's wrong with you?'

'It doesn't take five minutes to put on a bloody shirt.' He stood and walked into the hall. He called Daniel again, and when no answer came he went upstairs to his son's room. 'What are you doing?' he said on the landing.

'I'm putting on the shirt like you told me.'

'What's the delay?'

'I had to go to the bathroom.'

'Come on now. This photographer guy has to go.' Daniel emerged from his room, wearing a yellow striped T-shirt.

'Are you joking me?' Sylvester said.

'What?'

'This is important. Put a proper shirt on.'

Daniel walked back into his room. 'It's not important to me,' he said from there.

'If you want me to hear these things, say them to me. If you don't then keep them to yourself,' Sylvester said. 'We'll be outside waiting for you. Hurry up.'

Outside in the heat Helen and Jessica were standing with the photographer. They watched Sylvester in silence as he came to them.

'He's on his way. So, how's this going to work, Michael?'

'I don't know,' the photographer said. 'You said it's for a website, is it? What kind of thing did you have in mind?'

'A family shot. Something that makes me look like a happy, trustworthy person.'

'Right.'

'That's why I called in the professionals.' Sylvester laughed, nervous and high-pitched. He regretted it. 'Come on,' he said then. 'You're the photographer. How do you do this sort of thing? What's your style?'

'Okay. Well, I'd be inclined to take shots of the four of you together. Like, if you wanted to sit on the steps there in a line and chat away, just be normal and relaxed, I can move around you and hopefully you'll forget about me. That's the way I'd do it. Doesn't suit everyone.'

'Sounds fine,' Sylvester said. Daniel was down now in an unironed white shirt buttoned up to his neck. 'We can be normal, can't we?'

'Together?' Daniel asked.

The four of them sat on the step. Daniel, Sylvester, Helen, Jessica.

'What now?' Daniel asked.

'Just relax. Talk to each other,' the photographer said.

'What about?'

'I don't know. Whatever you think.'

'This is stupid,' Daniel said to Sylvester.

'I know, but go with it,' Sylvester said, leaning in to him, pushing him with his shoulder until the boy had to put his hand on the ground to stop himself falling.

'You've got heavier,' Daniel said.

'Better to push you around.' Sylvester could forget everything in one moment of happiness. Believe in its power to transform. He turned to Helen. 'Are you all right?'

'I'm fine.'

'Sorry I was late.'

'And last night as well.' Her face was in a loose smile; she was always aware that the camera was there. The photographer was off on the grass, shooting from mid-range. 'Where were you?' she asked. 'It was after three.'

'It was dinner with O'Donnell. There were a couple of English guys over. They were drinking until then.'

'Were you drinking?'

He turned briefly to her, his face six inches from hers. 'Of course not. Why would you even ask me that?'

'It's just these nights are getting a bit frequent.'

A little exasperated puff. 'This is my business. I have to do these things. You know that. Do you think I want to be out until three, getting up at half six?'

In the still solidity of the evening they could hear the shutter closing and opening over and over. 'Okay,' the photographer said at last. 'That should do.'

Sylvester stood and walked over to him. 'How was it?' he asked.

'Grand, I think. Do you want to have a look?'

Sylvester leaned over his shoulder as the photographer scrolled through the shots. There they were. The four of them. His family. Jerky movement from shot to shot, like an old film. Smiles rising and fading away. Looks into distance and at the ground and occasionally at each other. The final photos, the ones where they were all looking at the camera, were no good. The children appeared unhappy, and Sylvester and Helen were tense beside each other, the angle wrong between them.

'Right,' Sylvester said. 'Do you know what?'

'Will we just do a posed one in front of the house?' the photographer said.

'Yeah. Is that okay?'

'Fine, yeah.'

'Folks,' Sylvester said to the others, 'just one more.'

They stood in a row, arms around each other, Daniel's shirt open now at the neck. They smiled and smiled and smiled again, and finally, after one last shot, it was done. The children were in the house by the time Sylvester was able to check the shots.

'So thanks for that,' Sylvester said, as he walked with the photographer across the garden to his car.

'No problem. I'll send the contact sheets on to you and you can decide which one you want to use.'

'And sorry again for keeping you.' He shook the man's hand, then held out a fifty, rolled up like a cigarette. 'That's for you.'

'Ah, no,' the photographer said, taken aback. 'There's no need.'

'I know, but I delayed you. Buy yourself a bottle of wine or something.'

'Really. Thanks, but it's okay. I get paid well enough.'

'I know that,' Sylvester said. 'I'm paying your company. But this is for you.' The tone was harder now. No messing. Two men doing business. 'Come on.'

The photographer laughed. 'Okay,' he said. 'Okay. Thanks.'

'Good man.' He stood back as the photographer got into the car. Rapped on the roof before walking up towards the house. Michael watched him as he went, moving slowly, hands in his pockets. Sylvester turned as if he knew he was being observed and gave one tidy, professional wave before heading back inside to whatever was waiting for him there.

13

Victor knew them as they arrived, this crowd from a place on South William Street who came in after work mid-week, still in the black uniform with all the tightness. He would smile and nod and say encouraging things as they passed to let them know they were welcome. It meant that when the time came for them to leave they didn't mess around. They were easy anyway. Maybe just the one or two drinks. Maybe the start of an all-nighter that would end in someone's apartment later. For Victor and the others it was a chance to pick up on any parties that might be happening.

She must have walked by him on the way in but he didn't see her until the end. He was clearing the punters from downstairs. She was standing in a group, looking across the room, and for a moment their eyes met. She turned away immediately but he noticed her. She was tall. Dark hair. A face that was beautiful, yes, but that wasn't it. She was apart from the others. They were all talking and laughing and she was there but she wasn't. She wasn't interested in anything that was going on around her or anything that was being said. He saw her and he felt he could understand this. The feeling that she was always being watched. The sense that this was where she had to be but that something else was going on. He thought he could see this in her. He thought he recognized it.

He saw her when she was leaving with her crew and smiled as she passed him.

'Good night?'

'Goodnight.'

'No. I was asking you. Did you have a good night?'

'It was all right.'

'Just all right?'

'It was fine.' She kept walking for a second, then stopped when she saw him still watching her. She nodded at her friends, who walked on and lit cigarettes outside.

'Are you all right?' she asked him.

'Next time you come here I'll take you to a place you'll like.'

'Next time?' She laughed. 'What makes you think there'll be a next time?'

'Because I'm inviting you now. If you come here again I'll take you somewhere you'll like afterwards. When I finish. I'm serious. Believe me.'

'Why would I want to go anywhere with you?'

He smiled at her, baby-faced and innocent. 'Because I'm a great guy.'

'Who says?'

'You can ask anyone. Here. This man here.' He stopped a customer who was leaving. 'You know me, don't you? Tell her.'

'This guy is a gentleman in his heart,' the man said, putting his arm around Victor. A messy hug, then he wobbled off.

'You see?' Victor said.

She laughed. 'That was just lucky.'

'No. They all know me here. You're safe with me.'

'Where are you from?' she asked him.

'I'm Italian,' he said.

'You're not Italian. From where in Italy?'

'From Torino.' He smiled as he said it.

'And what's your name?'

'Di Paolo.'

'That's your first name?'

'Salvatore di Paolo.'

'You don't look like a Salvatore to me.'

'Why not?'

'You're too blond.'

'There are people with my hair colour in Italy.'

'Not many,' she said.

'People call me Victor.'

'Why?'

'Because that's my other name.' He left the statement hanging. 'What's your name?'

'Agnieszka.'

He looked at her in silence. Cocked his head like a dog. 'Yes,' he said.

'What's "yes"?'

'That's a good name for you.'

'People here think it's ugly.'

'It's beautiful,' he said. The word didn't sound tired to her.

'What's your real name?' she asked.

'Victor,' he said.

'And where are you from?'

'Italy,' he said. Then, with a smile, 'But my mother was Romanian. And I lived there before.'

'Ah,' she said.

'Ah. Is that a problem?'

'Why would it be a problem? I don't care. I just wanted to know. Now I do.'

'Next time you come here,' he said, 'I will show you a very nice place. You will like it.'

'Do you think I'll come back?'

'I hope so,' he said. He looked at her and she stared back. 'Yes,' he said then. 'I think you will.' There was no arrogance in it. Nothing she might have expected from a stocky bouncer in a black T-shirt. Just a calmness, a hope that she would understand what it was he was saying.

'We'll see,' she said. 'I'd better go on.' She nodded at the three guys who were still waiting for her.

'Who are those men?' Victor asked.

'They look after me. Keep me out of trouble.' She smiled at the expression on his face. 'They're friends. They do security for our bar.'

'Where are they from?'

'Albania.'

'They told you that?' he said.

'Some people aren't embarrassed about where they come from.'

'Well, maybe they should be.'

'They're lovely people,' she said.

'If they're friends of yours I'm sure they are.'

'Goodnight, Victor. Or whatever.'

'Goodnight, Agnieszka.'

Gareth walked up to him as she left and watched her go. 'Very nice,' he said to Victor.

'Yeah.'

'No luck?'

'I don't know,' Victor said. 'We'll see. I don't think she would be a girl to rush.'

'Right,' Gareth said. 'Well, you know, good things come to those who wait.'

'What?'

'It's an expression.'

Victor thought for a minute. 'So is she the good thing?'

'Yes,' Gareth said, 'and you're the one who's going to have to wait.'

14

They were stuck in traffic, heading home, when Sylvester's phone rang. It was a private number. 'Is that the councillor?' a man's voice asked.

Sylvester knew who it was immediately. 'Not any more, I'm afraid,' he said, then laughed gently. 'How are you, Mr O'Donnell?'

'I'm in good form. How are things with young Mr Kelly?'

'Things are excellent.'

'I'm delighted to hear that. Did Campbell get in touch with you?'

'He did.'

'And? Is that going to happen?'

'Looks like he's interested. I've met him twice now and it's gone well. Marek's going to send him some stuff over the next few days and hopefully then we'll get him over there.'

'Bratislava?'

'Prague.'

'There's nothing left in Prague,' O'Donnell said.

'Marek thinks there is.'

'How is old Marek? My Czech mate.'

'He's fine,' Sylvester said. 'He's himself.'

'Tell him I was asking for him.'

'I will. And thanks again for putting Campbell my way.'

'Glad to help. I hope it all works out.'

'I hope so too. But, you know, I really appreciate it. It makes a big difference.'

Dessie made eye contact with Sylvester in the mirror. 'What?' he mouthed at him. Sylvester shrugged.

'Listen,' O'Donnell said. 'I've got a job for you.'

'Oh, yeah?'

'Just the thing for a well-connected ex-councillor. Put your legendary charm to work.'

'Well, I don't know about "legendary",' Sylvester said. 'What's the story?'

'The story is you won't even have to get in your car for this one.'

For the next ten minutes, Dessie watched as Sylvester listened and nodded pointlessly while O'Donnell spoke.

15

Where was the city? Everything was too small, like the back-streets of a country town struggling to cope. Narrow lanes where the map showed thoroughfares. The mad push and rush of the people, like spawning fish. The traffic that crawled along streets that couldn't take it, as if God had shrunk the city and left the people and the cars and the buses and the lorries the same size. Watch this, he told the angels. They won't see the joke. Everything and everybody on top of each other. Paths and shops and bars and cafés and supermarkets, all too small. No room to breathe. Too many people.

That morning Marcin stepped off the bus into the pedestrian flow and let himself go with it until he was carried to a place he recognized from the night he'd arrived. The pavement beneath his feet was sticky and diseased, the air like that of a sick person's room. The river smelled like a drain, slow and murky and green. There were tourists moving slowly, oblivious as the crowd parted around them, around him as he checked his map. And then, as he walked through a door into the college, the world opened up into green and architecture and cobblestones, but even here there were too many people. He walked by playing-fields, saw a tractor cutting grass, and he remembered the last time he had smelled that smell, the same way in warm air before he had ever been here. He came out the other side. There was money around. He could feel it now. The cars parked outside offices in old creeper-covered buildings with luxurious colours and doors and couriers. A better class of air. There was business going on in these houses, and the steps up to the door let you know where you stood in relation to it. Low-pressure jobs too, it seemed, for the girls who stood outside smoking on breaks, the middle-aged men in suits.

The day was his. He could sit outside one of the cafés he had passed and read the guidebook. Try to find a way to spend a day in this new city while Artur slept at home. He was off tonight and they would drink, maybe go out, maybe do something. Artur had said his housemates were going to a party somewhere. Marcin saw it already – meatheads, vodka, war stories, techno. All fired up and on edge, just fucking waiting for him to say the wrong thing. The thought sent him in the wrong direction.

Later on, back at the house, Marcin sat on the doorstep with a can in his hand. Artur was lying spread across the grass in underwear that had seen better days.

'You'd want to get started. They'll make you work a back week so it could be close to a month before you get paid.'

'Just give me a while. I want to see what's out there.'

'Come and work with me. You won't get better than this. I'm telling you. I get paid to sleep. The quiet nights, I go in, do a bit of hoovering, have a meal and go to bed for a couple of hours. Come home. Back to bed. Cheque every two weeks, and the money's good enough to live well. I'm going to get in on the tips soon and then it'll be really good. I'll be living like this and saving money.' Marcin said nothing. Artur sat up and leaned on an elbow to look at him. 'I know what I'm talking about. There's loads of work and most of it is just shit. Get serious here. You're going to need to start earning soon. You can't be hanging around waiting for the right thing to come along. You'll be on the street by then.'

'You wouldn't put me on the street.'

'Maybe not. But these guys would. Gladly. Come on. We'd be working together. It'd be fun. I can ask them.'

'I have a CV.'

'Give it to me now and I'll put it in my work jacket.'

Marcin went inside and took the piece of paper out of a folder in his bag. He brought it out to Artur and handed it to him. 'Why are you so sure they'll give me the job?' he asked.

'Because they're desperate. And you're not a criminal. You speak English. You're educated. You have some experience.'

'Not much.'

'You have some experience,' Artur said again. 'And you'll tell them what they want to hear.'

'Which is?'

'That you won't get drunk and that you won't steal. You like people. You like working. You hate sleeping and drinking and drugs. They won't care. They just need someone. If it's not you it'll be someone else.' Marcin looked at him. 'It's very simple. They won't hang around. You'll be fine. Just don't mess about and they'll hire you. If you turn up on time and don't get caught doing anything stupid they'll never fire you. That's it. You can quit when you've had enough.'

'And when will you have had enough?'

'Another three months. I'm not doing this through the winter. No light? I'd disappear. I feel like I'm hung-over all the time as it is.'

'That's because you drink all the time.'

Artur smiled. The day was beginning to get hot. He looked at Marcin and saw into his future. 'When I'm in charge, you'll do what you're told. I'll have you cleaning shitty toilets by the end of the week.'

'We'll see,' Marcin said.

In the end it wasn't exactly as he'd pictured it. The party was in the garden of some friend of somebody. There were about twenty people, some girls from home, bottles of beer, two guys cooking at a barbecue. It felt comfortable. The music was loud and most of the guys, though they came from shit parts of shit cities that Marcin had passed through, were fine. They weren't interested enough in him to start a fight, preferring to stand three guys to a girl and see who could shout the loudest. The sun was going down and the conversation flowed around him as Artur and one of the guys from the house slagged each other about whose job was harder. Who was the real man.

He looked up at the house they were standing outside, its rough pebbledash back painted yellow, and the plastic gutter that was starting to sag although the house could only have been a couple of years old. A movement caught his eye from an upstairs window of the house next door. A girl of maybe ten was peering down at them from underneath a net curtain, just her head visible. Long brown hair. Sharp little features. When she saw Marcin looking back at her she held his gaze, expression set, not hostile or scared but not friendly either. For five seconds they stared at each other. Who did she think he was? He raised a hand and gave one slow wave. Half smiled. Nothing too showy. The guy talking to Artur turned around and looked up at the window.

'Bit young,' he said. 'Still, I'd say you're in. You've more of a chance with her than with any of these.' He laughed and Artur threw back his head as if this was the wittiest thing he'd ever heard.

'Right,' Marcin said, staring at Artur, waiting to let him know with a look that he understood what was going on, but he just kept on laughing away with his new-found best friend. For a moment he thought they might high-five each other. When he glanced back up at the window the girl was gone.

16

They came out along the strand road. A mile beyond the turn-off for Sylvester's house Dessie pulled into the car-park of a hotel. It was a Victorian seaside place, one of a type that cropped up all around the bay. They were remnants of a time when days spent in the near suburbs beside the Irish Sea counted as a holiday, when the stony beaches and freezing water and unreliable weather were good enough for anyone. There were a few of these places left, good venues for lunch with an elderly relative – half grapefruits, small glasses of orange juice, egg mayonnaise, followed by roast meat, wet vegetables, four styles of potato. A bar with wood panelling and ship's paraphernalia, where there were delicate bottles of beers and ciders branded for women. A place that young couples living locally would try once out of interest, or a sense of irony, but never come back to.

This place had been shut for three years. The caretaker was waiting for them at the front. Sylvester walked up to him, hand outstretched.

'Sorry we're late.'

'You're not. I was early.'

'This is my associate, Dessie.' Dessie smiled.

'Jim.'

He shook their hands.

'Will we get started so?'

'Lead on.'

The caretaker unlocked the front door and they walked into the settled damp smell of it, old-fashioned but not yet unpleasant. As he guided them through, he told them about the need for fire escapes and safety doors, how the whole place would have to be rewired, the kitchen taken out and put in again. They went up one set of stairs and along the corridors, Jim opening occasional doors to different bedrooms, singles and doubles and suites. A bit stale but nothing to worry about. They came down another set of stairs and walked through the bar. Sylvester stopped and stood at the counter. He turned and looked out of the window, across the main road and on out to the sea and the bay beyond. 'Oh, yeah,' he said, into the room. 'It was some place.'

'You were here before?' Jim asked.

'Often. When I was a kid. Confirmations and christenings and that.'

'Used to get them, all right. Not that long ago. Twenty years back it was still thriving.'

'It's no time,' Sylvester said, shaking his head at the thought.

'Still. It's long enough,' said Dessie.

Outside, they stood while Sylvester asked a couple of questions. The tarmac of the car-park was breaking up and weeds were beginning to rise to a height. There was graffiti on the gable wall, loops and whirls and the names of couples written in black marker, and in the middle 'Tammy Byrne is a fat bitch' was sprayed in green paint. Dessie lit a cigarette and walked around a bit further towards the back. There were still a few empty kegs piled at the rear entrance of the bar, a couple of crates of empty bottles.

'What do you think?' Sylvester asked, as he walked towards him.

'Lovely,' Dessie said. 'Just needs a bulldozer to sort it out.'

'It could be done, you know. There's enough space.'

'They'll never let it happen.'

'They might.'

'I can't see it.'

'But I can,' Sylvester said. 'I can see it very clearly.'

17

In a room in a prefab building in the staff car-park at the back of the hotel, the night manager, the front-of-house manager and Ray sat together in a row. It was nine o'clock in the morning and the two night workers were anxious to go. That meant nothing to the front-of-house guy, who was happy to sit and discuss the candidate they'd just interviewed. Better than being on the desk at check-out time, arguing about breaks with the four girls.

'What did you think?' he asked Ray.

'All right. Better than the last fellow.'

'And you?'

'Fine. Yeah. Seems okay.'

'Do we take him?'

'Give him a shot. If he's any good we may as well.'

'If he's really good we can get rid of the other one,' Ray said.

'Is he that bad?'

'Too smart,' said Ray. 'He'll get into trouble.'

'And isn't this guy some friend of his?' the front-of-house manager asked.

'He said he'd heard about the job from him. He didn't say they were friends.'

They looked at each other.

'He was solid enough, I thought,' the manager said.

'Are you happy, Ray?'

'I liked him.'

'So we'll give him a trial of a week, say, then all going well take him on and look at letting the other fellow go. What's his name?'

'Who? This one or the last one?'

'The last one.'

'Artur.'

'Right,' he said, standing. 'I'll sort that out with Lisa. You boys can head off to the pub or whatever it is you do now. I've got to get back to work.'

'I'm going to bed,' the night manager said.

Ray said nothing, just stood and stretched.

'Ray?'

'I might go for one,' he said, a low, happy chuckle ready to roll in his throat.

'I wish I was going.'

'You wouldn't like it. Dirty place. Full of dirty drunks. Not for the likes of you.'

'In my day,' the night manager said, 'I, too, was a dirty drunk.'

18

They'd sat beside each other at a meeting. That was how they'd met. Dessie had seen him on the street afterwards trying to get a taxi and stopped.

'Which way are you going?'

'Into town.'

'Hop in so.'

There was comfort there from the start. Sylvester was smart enough to keep quiet because Dessie was not someone who said more than he needed to.

'You don't drive,' Dessie said.

'I can't. I can but I can't, if you know what I mean.'

'I know what you mean,' Dessie said.

'They took it from me,' Sylvester said.

'I understand,' Dessie said, smiling now.

'That's why I'm out at these meetings,' Sylvester said.

'We've all got our reasons.'

'Are you off it?'

'Three years,' Dessie said. 'You?'

'Nearly six months.'

Silence. They flashed through the streets.

'Where will I drop you?' Dessie asked.

'Anywhere near the river.'

'And where are you going after?'

'Home,' Sylvester said.

'Where's that?'

Sylvester told him. Dessie had no desire to head home himself. The days were long enough. Anything to stay out. He could say the meeting ran on. Half an hour extra out to the north-side would be nothing.

When they arrived Sylvester made a move to his wallet. 'Can I give you something?'

'Not at all.'

'Thanks for your time.'

'My time is my own. Time I have plenty of.'

'What do you do?'

'Not much. I was in hospitality before. As they call it. I got out of it. Just couldn't handle it.'

'I'll tell you something,' Sylvester said. 'I'm spending five hundred quid a month on taxis and couriers. Is your licence all right?'

'It is, yeah.'

'Would you be interested in doing a bit of driving here and there? A few nixers?'

'I might be.'

'Have you got five minutes?' They walked across the lawn to a garage door. 'Wait until you see this.'

The door lifted up automatically, slowly shaking as it went.

'That's it,' Sylvester said. It was a maroon Mercedes, some mid-eighties model, sleek and wide and shining.

'Very nice.'

'Would you be interested?'

'No,' Dessie said. 'I can't afford that.'

'I mean would you drive it for me? Just the odd meeting and that?'

'I could,' he said. 'What would we be talking?'

'We should be able to work that out so we're both happy.'

'All right,' Dessie said. 'We can give it a shot.'

'And if it works, great,' Sylvester said. 'If not, you're up a few quid.'

That had been three years ago. Dessie was still being paid by the hour. There were extras: the tips, the cash given and the change not looked for. For a businessman Sylvester was easy with money. Generosity, Dessie thought at first, but then, as the years passed, he saw that it was something else.

Anne had never liked any of it. The days and nights that he was gone, trips abroad. The unpredictable income that made it impossible to plan. Dessie calmed her, assured her, promised her. This was better for him. Always moving, always busy, no time to think about what was lost, what had been done. No time sitting around waiting for the boredom to drive him out the door and down the street to Walshe's. His drinking was an affliction that had got him into trouble. His face would for ever bear the marks of his love for it. But one day, he thought, he might go back. If Anne couldn't handle him any more and Yvonne finished college and got a job, then maybe there would be the space to go back and do it right. Sink back into the life he'd had before that seemed to fit him better than this one. Some day, he thought, he would sit again in an armchair on his own and stick at it until he could feel nothing again.

In the early days he had thought it would be better once Anne had met Sylvester. Once she saw the cut of him, heard the smooth voice. He would be charming and funny and would try to establish a bond with her, an alliance to rib Dessie.

It hadn't worked out like that. They'd met at a christening. Sylvester arrived over, friendly but presuming nothing. She was polite at first, but the more Sylvester tried to find a way in, the higher the barrier went. After a minute Sylvester said it was very nice to have met her and off he went.

'What's wrong with you?' Dessie asked her.

'Empty,' she said.

'What's empty?'

'He is,' she said. 'There's nothing there. He's just raw ambition in a suit with a handshake and a smile.'

'What else could he do?' Dessie said. 'He was just being polite. You could at least have been the same.'

'I was polite.'

'He looks after me. After us. Think back a year. Think where we were then. He's made a big difference.'

'We were okay.'

'I wasn't.'

'You were coming through.'

'He got me out of a hole.'

'There was never any charity with that fellow, I can tell you.'

'I didn't need charity. I needed work. And I'm still working. I'm working hard.'

'Too hard.'

'I don't hear you complain about the money.'

'Just don't believe anything he tells you,' she said. 'This guy is a messer. A man like that would drop you tomorrow and have forgotten your name by Monday.'

'Where are you getting this?' Dessie asked, laughing. 'He says hello and twenty seconds later you know him better than I do?'

She put a hand on his arm. 'I think you know him well enough.'

19

He had been sized for the uniform and it was waiting for him in the porters' office when he arrived. He shook hands with Ray and was taken across the expanse of the lobby, plinking Muzak audible on a slow night, through the doors into the kitchen. The sudden roar of extractors and the hot steam of the dishwashers, the smell of food on the turn and the sweet average sickness of the bins full of a day's scrapings. The threat of slip underfoot and the one-second future of landing on your arse if you were to forget.

They went down to the changing rooms, male side, which smelled of feet and sweat, and damp, blocked toilets. Finished paper rolls, bits of food and wet shoes lay in puddles of something on the floor.

'If you get yourself dressed there,' Ray said, 'and come back to me upstairs like a good lad.'

Marcin picked his way through the space in shock, touching nothing but feeling already that if he stayed in this job too long he would eventually get all it had to give him – athlete's foot, scabies, crabs, nits, food poisoning.

They had him stocking shelves, carrying trays of glasses

from the bar with its rat-faced manager across the floor to the porters' office, where Ray was in charge. Filling buckets with ice, checking that the kitchen fridges had food for sandwiches through the night. It was quiet, he was told. Ray introduced him to Tommy.

'There's nothing hard in this job,' Ray told him. 'It's just a lot of things to do. Tommy will keep you busy. He'll show you everything.'

'Okay,' Marcin said. 'No problem.'

Tommy took off through swinging doors into an empty dark ballroom. The two of them walked together across the dance-floor, Marcin keeping up because he could tell already that that would be important.

'What did Ray say your name was?'

'Marcin.'

'Mar– What?'

'Marcin. It's Polish for Martin. It's pronounced the same as Máirtín.'

'What?' Tommy said again. He had slowed down and was concentrating on Marcin's face.

'The Irish for Martin? A guy told me this in Poland.'

'I don't know what you heard. The Irish for Martin is Martin.'

'No, I mean the Gaelic. The Irish language.'

'Oh, that,' Tommy said. 'I don't care about that. I'll call you Bob. I can't spend my life arsing around trying to work out what your fucking name is.' They went through a set of doors into a long corridor of function rooms. Marcin fell behind. 'I'm only messing with you,' Tommy said, turning back to him.

'Oh, right,' Marcin said.

'I'll call you Marty. How's that?'

'Fine,' Marcin said.

Hoovering. Hours and hours of hoovering. Function rooms the size of football pitches that looked the same after as they had before. He was always too slow.

'Are you still at this?' Tommy said, every time he came back to check. It wasn't clear what Tommy was doing in between. Marcin moved from one function room to the next. Tiredness came in waves, sometimes just a heaviness in the eyes, sometimes enough to make him want to lie on the ground with the Hoover still running so that no one would hear a difference. At four o'clock they ate.

'How is he getting on?' Ray asked Tommy.

'He's been teaching me Irish. Do you know what the Irish for Martin is?'

'Máirtín,' the night manager said.

'A smart cunt like you would know that,' Tommy said.

'A fool like you wouldn't,' the manager said.

After they'd eaten, Tommy took Marcin in the lift to the top floor, a small space with steps up to an elaborate door.

'Penthouse,' Tommy said. 'Five grand a night. Usually empty but you have to check because if there's someone in here and they don't get their kippers or whatever, it'll probably be the President of Israel and he'll have a Mossad guy out looking for you with a gun by eight o'clock.'

Down one floor. Along the corridors taking the breakfast cards off the door handles. The two worked in silence along silent pathways, ghosts in a hundred guests' dreams. Then back to the lift and down one floor. This time Tommy stayed put.

'Now you do the same the whole way down. It's the same plan for every floor. Check every room and gather the cards. Okay? Think you can do that?'

'I think so.'

'No problem to you. Five minutes. I'll see you down there.'

With a swish and a faint ping, the doors closed and Marcin was alone.

20

Sylvester had never looked forward to the evenings going door to door. Even when he'd been a councillor and his visits were clearly meant to be helpful – seeing what people needed, listening to their problems, trying to resolve their issues – he'd always felt like an intruder, unwelcome, wasting people's time, getting attacked by dogs and, once, a cat.

Now, handing out leaflets and talking up this proposed development, it took an effort to steel himself for what the evening might hold. Doors that would open and close before he'd had a chance to speak. Old men who would tell Dessie that, no, they did not want to talk to that absolute bollocks, while Sylvester stood ten feet away, smiling stupidly, pretending not to have heard. Activists who had been waiting for the opportunity to vent their fury about land-grabbing oligarchs moving into their area. People with grievances, engaged in feuds, in dialogue with the voices in their heads. And some people who were just dying to talk to anybody. Yes. Yes. Indeed. Yes. Well, I'm not really a councillor any more but I can check that out for you. The evenings could be very long. If he'd had the option he would have moved into a castle with a moat long ago, pulled up the drawbridge and never talked to any of these people again. And yet.

The truth was that he was good at it. His manner was disarming, even for people who opposed this vision for the future that he was championing. Often he stood in front of some grim-faced local, wrong age, wrong class, and watched them thaw in front of him. Solidity, self-deprecation, serious-ness, gentle slagging. Asking the right questions. He had a feel for who he was talking to and what they wanted to hear. It might not make a huge difference but it would count for something, and that was why O'Donnell had asked for his help. 'He was around here last night,' they might say, in the canteen at work if his name came up. And? 'Not the worst,' they would say, 'a rogue, you know, but not the worst.'

When he was moving from estate to estate, changing the approach, the accent, the humour, to fit whoever he was talking to, he enjoyed all that. To be out on these streets that he knew so well gave him pleasure. To anybody from outside the area it would look like nothing at all, just another grimy, anonymous suburb, monochrome and traffic-infested. Lorries on the way to where the action was through tunnels and over bridges, throwing up dust and mud as they went. But he knew that you could find comfort behind the grey porridge of the pebbledash, in the shambles of the foot-paths, roused and put to sleep again. In the dirty patchwork of the road tattooed with the memories of significant events – the coming of gas, the improvement of the water, the life-expanding event that was cable television. The blackened green areas that were the site of the fun and fear of early Hallowe'ens. The rubbish on the street that meant kids were still around, infuriating and disobedient on a diet of Coke and multi-coloured corn snacks, but here still, another generation that would experience the same dysfunctional love for an unlovely place. Things could be improved, they always could. That was what he was trying to do. But see this place for what it was and what it meant and not just for how it looked. He was of it and he cared for it. He'd lived in the two ends of it. Whatever his failings, real, imagined or rumoured, nobody could ever say that he didn't understand what it was that made this place itself.

They had put it right. It could have been the end of everything but, between Helen and himself, it had been sorted out quietly and tidily. He'd never drunk around here, always in restaurants in town, hotel bars and pubs in the far suburbs. It hadn't affected his work as a councillor but his business had suffered. He could see now that it had been inevitable, that it was about pressure and tiredness and having to talk to people for twenty hours a day. That he used it as a way of bonding, doing deals, celebrating. Of relaxing and recovering. It had worked for a while. He was popular and successful but with everything going on, his phone ringing from six in the morning until midnight, he drank too much and stopped paying attention and things began to slide. He made a couple of bad choices and then, in trying to recover, made worse ones. He knew the drink had played a part but still, though he never expressed the opinion, he thought most of it had been down to bad luck and stress.

He could have been made bankrupt. It could all have been humiliating and public, but Helen sold a house she'd inherited from her aunt and paid off the debts. He retired from the council and gave up drinking and O'Donnell, who was the only one who stuck with him through it all, helped get him started again. A new beginning. It seemed to be clean. There were rumours among his fellow councillors, but his story of concentrating on a new business was plausible and, given the alternative, plausible was enough.

There were still times when Dessie found himself impressed by Sylvester. Out on the doorsteps standing three feet behind him, he would watch how naturally it all came to him. The right thing to say. The times when saying nothing was the better option. The way he could adapt himself, bend his personality to fit, sympathize, nod, listen, and all the time do it as if it was real. It was real. You could see that. There was no doubting that the impact he had on people was a solid, tangible thing, but whether or not Sylvester actually believed any of it was something that Dessie didn't know.

Most of the time, to anyone who would have noticed him, Dessie appeared to be tuned out. His undertaker's expression never varied in the face of all manner of poison, tedium and general buffoonery. Not getting involved was what he was good at. In this phase of his life, which had begun when his drinking had ended, judgement was not a part of the picture. It was why he and Sylvester got along so well. He saw everything but said nothing. Even if you were to do something in front of him, something awful and shameful that could haunt you for ever, to look at Dessie was to believe that maybe it had never happened, maybe it was all just a nightmare of your own imagination. If he was asked his opinion on any of the topics of the day Dessie would politely refuse to offer a view. But secretly, at his core, he would say that most people were driven by selfishness and greed, and that that knowledge could be used to predict their most likely behaviour in any given situation.

They stood on the doorstep of one of the semi-detached houses that sloped down both sides of a narrow, quiet street to the sea. Sylvester handed the brochure to a woman in her forties, blondish and mumsy. 'Hello. My name's Sylvester Kelly.'

'The councillor,' the woman said.

'Ex-councillor,' Sylvester said. 'I'm retired.'

'You look too young to be retired.'

Sylvester smiled. 'I mean from council work. I'm running my own business now.'

'I know your name all right.'

Sylvester nodded. 'Yeah, well, I was a councillor here for nearly ten years.'

The woman blushed and looked at the ground. 'We've only been living here a short time.'

'Oh, right. Where are you from?' Sylvester asked.

'From over there ...' she waved vaguely out across the water, towards the land in the distance '... on the other side.'

'A refugee,' Sylvester said. He smiled at her.

'Sort of,' she said.

'And do you like it out here?'

'Yes. Very much.'

'So do you know the hotel? You know where we're talking about? The old place on the coast road.'

'The eyesore,' Dessie said.

'I know it,' the woman said.

'We're giving out some information on the proposed plans for development on the site. Just there's been a bit of publicity about it and this is giving the other side.'

'I haven't been paying attention, really. Should I be for or against it?'

'Well, it's up to you to decide but I think it's a strong proposal. It would be good for the area. We're talking about a medium-size development of luxury apartments. There would be new retail space, a high-end supermarket, a couple of restaurants and a café, which would provide employment for up to a hundred people. The whole profile of the neighbourhood would improve and, putting it bluntly, it can only be positive for house prices up here. All of that has to be good for everyone surely.'

'It sounds good.'

'Have a look at the leaflet anyway.'

'Okay.' She turned the glossy little brochure over in her hand. 'Is there going to be a vote on this or something?'

'It'll be a City Council decision. We're just letting people know what would be involved. Some of the things that are being said are pretty wide of the mark so we're giving you the facts.'

'All right. Thanks.'

'Thanks for your time.'

As Sylvester and Dessie were walking down the path the woman called after them: 'Is it your company?'

'Sorry?' Sylvester said, turning.

'This development. These apartments. Is it your project?'

'No, it's not.'

There was a moment of silence.

'Right,' the woman said, sounding doubtful. 'Okay.'

'I just think it would be good for the area. Getting the information out there, you know. That's all.'

'Fair enough,' she said, and nodded.

Sylvester smiled. 'Thanks again,' he said.

21

She checked herself in the mirror of the cloakroom of a café around the corner from where she was meeting them. She looked well enough and she was satisfied with that, but her stomach was sick. Maybe they'll have gone, she thought, hoping. Maybe they'll have moved on to somewhere else and I can say I arrived late. Go home and take these clothes off and know where I am.

From the warmth of the summer evening, past the crowds sitting at outside tables and standing around under awnings smoking, through the heavy doors of the bar that were swung open before her by two suited bouncers, who looked like they were from back home, into the music and shouting and laughter of this place. Dark wood and low lighting and a well-dressed older crowd, women in pairs and threes, men in suits or shirts and jeans, all performing for each other. She walked the length of the bar watched by everyone because that was what this place was for. Watching. Where would she end up? To whom did she belong?

At the back, sitting in a large semi-circular booth, she found them. Luke White stood when he saw her. He took her hand and held it as he thanked her for coming. There were four men, including Gavin, and five girls. White introduced her to the ones she didn't know, name by name, none of which she remembered, too distracted and embarrassed at being the centre of their attention. She sat beside one of the managers, a girl she knew to say hello to but had never seen outside work.

'Hard to remember everything,' she said to Agnieszka. 'When you're standing there.'

Agnieszka laughed, soft and short.

'Agnieszka is one of the best bar staff we have in Symposium,' White said to the table. 'She could be a manager in six months.'

'If I don't take her from you,' one of the men said. Plenty of greying hair, one button too many open, nice jacket, an ease and strength in his voice that he'd been born with and not earned, it seemed to her. He smiled. 'I own a couple of casinos around town. I always need good people. I might abduct you.' The table laughed. 'Two minutes in and I'm scaring the girl,' he said.

Agnieszka smiled back. 'I'm not scared,' she said.

The champagne helped, two bottles in ice-buckets on the go all the time. She watched what she drank, sipped at the same rate as the others, but they kept topping everyone up and the bottles kept arriving until she noticed that three hours had passed and her nervousness was gone. Whatever it was White wanted didn't seem like anything to be worried about. Maybe he was checking her out to see if she could hold her own with these people. Suitable for promotion. Or maybe he was just interested in her. She watched him as he talked. All these men had the same absolute certainty in everything they said that made them seem more interesting than they were if you actually listened. He was good-looking in a clean way, dressed well in clothes that showed their money. The hardness she had seen in him before didn't seem to be there. The girls laughed and contributed occasional comments that were listened to and turned into jokes. Girl talks. Punch line. Laugh. It was comfortable in its pattern, nothing to be taken seriously. No topic was maintained for more than five minutes.

When two of the girls went outside to smoke, White shifted around and leaned in to her. 'Are you all right?'

'I'm fine, yes. Thanks. Very good.'

His hand was resting on the leather of the banquette close to her arse. Even in this noise there could be silence between them.

'I'd like to buy a drink,' she said. 'I can't just keep taking all this.'

'You can,' he said. 'I invited you and you're not allowed put your hand in your pocket.'

'Well, thank you. I appreciate it.'

'And I appreciate it. You have beautiful manners.'

She laughed. 'Really? You think so?'

'Yes,' he said, smiling. 'Is that a strange thing to say?'

'Nobody's said it to me before.'

'I think it's easy for you. You know – this. Talking to people. Being friendly. It comes naturally.'

'Yeah. Maybe. I don't know.'

'It's an important thing in our line of work. To be comfortable with people. To make them feel good. If you do that you can do anything. You can make a lot of money.'

'Yes,' she said. 'I suppose so.'

'I know so. I know how important it is and it's made me rich and happy. And I want the people who work with me to be happy.'

She didn't know what to say to that. 'That's a good philosophy,' she said finally.

'Yes, it is. I think you understand me. No point in bringing it to the grave, you know. You could die tomorrow.' He stood to let the girls back in. 'You know what I mean?' he said, as he stood above her. She nodded.

In the cloakroom later she was washing her hands when one of the girls whom she hadn't met before came out of a cubicle and stood beside her at the sink. 'These guys are fun, yeah?'

'Yeah, sure. I don't know.'

'Have you been out with Luke before?'

'No.'

'Lovely guy.'

'Yeah,' Agnieszka said. 'He seems to be.' It didn't seem to be enough. 'Is he?'

'Well, he's always been very nice to me. I've met him a few times. Paul and he have been friends for years.'

'And how did you meet Paul?' Agnieszka couldn't remember which one he was.

'I worked in the casino before. We went out for a bit. He's a great guy too. Still hang around with them. When they all go out it's . . .' She shook her head.

'What?'

'Big nights.'

'Right.'

'They like to spend their money. It's a lot of fun. They'll pay for everything. They get everything. Do you think he likes you?'

'I don't know.' Agnieszka watched her in the mirror. She realized now that this girl was drunk, maybe a bit wired. 'What do you think?'

'I think he does,' she said. 'Where are you from anyway?'

'Poland.'

The girl nodded. 'I think he does,' she said again, and smiled at her. 'You're really beautiful, you know. And much nicer than the others.'

'Thank you,' Agnieszka said.

Up in the bar the bottles were finished and the lights were on. The crowd was thinning out. The bouncers had opened the doors at the back and a breeze blew through the building as if to help them.

'There you are now,' White said, when he saw her. 'We're going to the club. Have a drink and relax a bit. You'll come.'

'Do I have to?'

'Yeah,' he said. They looked at each other for a moment. There was enough of a smile playing around the corners of his mouth to let her know that his words weren't really serious. 'Don't you want to?'

'Maybe another time,' she said. 'Not tonight, though. I'm tired now.'

'We'll talk properly then,' he said.

'Okay.' She laughed. 'Do we have something to talk about?'

'We do. But another time. You enjoyed yourself anyway? Are you okay to get home?'

'I'm fine. Yes, thank you.'

'All right, then.' He shook her hand, touched her arm and looked her in the eye as he did, but that was all. She said goodbye to the others, walked outside straight into a taxi and gave the driver her address. They drove for two minutes and then, with apologies, she changed her mind and got out.

22

In the orange light of the evening Marcin and Artur travelled to work together. Back then in the morning, the long bus ride against traffic to the estate, left, right, left, right until they arrived at the house. Cold beer in the fridge, a bit of an old smoke sitting on plastic chairs on the patio, kicking at the weeds growing between the slabs, lying on the sea of daisies that covered the patch of grass that did them for a garden. This could be the summer. Bed at noon. Up at eight. No need to eat because in work there would be fillet steak taken from the back of a padlocked fridge that someone had a key for. Dauphinoise potatoes. Bread rolls. Elaborate plated desserts taken from the pastry section. Could there be a better job than this for two young fellows out in the world, earning more in a week than they would in a month at home?

Ten feet through the door on the Tuesday night and Artur knew something was up. 'It's wrong for mid-week,' he told Marcin. 'People. And music. What's going on?' he asked Tommy, as they arrived at the desk.

'Fucking debs. We'll have fun tonight. Serve none of them. Do you hear me? Ray says it. Not one of them is staying here so come two o'clock they're out. I don't care who their daddies are.'

'What's debs?' Marcin asked Artur.

'I don't know. Some sort of conference?'

Two minutes later they stood in the door of the main ball-room looking across at the wonder of it all. Three hundred teenagers in black tie and ballgowns, flowers on dresses, bare feet on the dance-floor where ironic cheers came for the shit pop hits of three years earlier.

'These are rich kids,' Artur said. 'You can see it in their bones.'

'If I had a black suit I'd put it on right now and drink myself into the ground with them. Let one of these girls take me to her parents' big house. That one. Or that one. Any of them. Any of them.'

'We should turn off the air-conditioning,' Artur said. 'Raise the temperature. See what happens.'

Four hours later they were dispersing, a stream of them emerging, tottering like newborn calves on unsteady legs and high heels, makeup smudged, features blurry with drink. Girls crying, boys staggering, falling, too drunk to fight. But all moving in one direction, all heading out, away from there. The banqueting staff and the night crew together herding them, closing off the options, you'll get a taxi on the street, keep moving along. The noise of screams, laughter, occasional bursts of song choruses, the phone at Reception ringing with complaints but eventually, eventually, it was over. Every last young person gone.

'Now the fun starts,' Ray said. 'Two o'clock and we haven't even started. Fucking state of this place. No sleep tonight. Get hoovering, boys. Artur, you're doing the toilets tonight.'

'Again I do this?'

'Every night.'

'Me again?'

'You again.'

Marcin walked off, dragging the Hoover behind him, into the ballroom, into the lingering smell of perfume and deodorant, hair products and the sweetness of the drinks of the young. From the lobby he heard voices getting louder. He thought one of the kids had come back, causing hassle. He heard Artur shouting and started to move faster. When he came around to the corridor beside the cloakrooms and toilets, Tommy and Ray were standing watching Artur, who Marcin could see now was pissed off and ranting. He had a flashback to the last time he had seen this, in a bar in Warsaw on a weekend with friends.

'No,' he was saying. 'I won't do it and you know, you know. It's not right.' He stopped when he saw Marcin.

'What's going on?' Marcin asked.

'The toilets,' Artur said to him in Polish. 'Puke all over them. I'm not doing them. It's not fair. They get to do room service and bags and the bus tours, all the money jobs, all the tips, and we're fucking hoovering and cleaning up puke and shit. They're exploiting us.' Then in English, 'You do it, Tommy. Not me. Not tonight.'

'You'll do it,' Ray said, 'and that's all there is to it.'

'No,' Artur said. 'I won't.'

'It's up to you what happens,' Ray said, 'but I'm telling you to clean that cloakroom. If you don't you're going to be the one with the problem, not me. There'll always be somebody to do the work if you don't want to. I'm not going to force you.'

'No problem, Ray,' Artur said. 'You get someone else but I'm not doing it.'

He walked away from them back down the corridor towards the front desk.

'Are you coming?' he called back to Marcin.

'No, I'm going to stick around.'

Artur stopped. 'Oh, come on. We can get something else. Take a few days off and relax. Then start again. Is this what you want to do for the summer? Deal with drunks and clean up rich kids' puke?'

Marcin shrugged. 'I need the money. And I'm here now.'

'Okay. That's your problem.' He walked on and went out through the revolving doors.

'Where's he going?' Ray asked Marcin.

'Home. I think he is finished with this job.'

'I think so too. And are you staying or going?'

Ray and Tommy looked at him with considerably more interest than he'd felt from them before. Interest but not concern.

'I'm staying.'

'Okay so, you can clean that jacks when you're finished with the hoovering,' said Ray, as he walked off towards the kitchen.

Tommy shrugged at Marcin. 'If you hang around for long enough you'll be telling people what to do. We all started out doing what you're doing. If you don't like it there's plenty of others that will.'

'I'm still here,' Marcin said.

'Well, get on with it so.'

Two hours later a group of American software boys came in after a night out, drunk and hungry, and were told they could only be served in their rooms. Two sets of sandwiches to be made and delivered. Tommy called Marcin into the kitchen. The trays were waiting. 'You take that one,' he told him.

They went up in the lift and headed in opposite directions. The American handed Marcin a twenty. Back at the lift Tommy met him.

'What did you get?' Tommy asked.

'Twenty.'

'The other fellow gave nothing, the bastard. Give it here.' Marcin hesitated. 'I'm not trying to do you,' Tommy said. Marcin pulled out the note and Tommy plucked it from his hand. He rummaged in his own pocket, produced a ten-euro note and gave it to Marcin. The bell of the lift door pinged.

'There now. Fucking trouser that quick,' Tommy said.

'What?'

'Take that money. In your pocket. Now. For fuck's sake.'

'Why?'

'Because if you tell Ray he'll take your twenty and split it four ways – he'll take ten, give me and George five each and you'll get nothing.'

'Oh,' said Marcin.

'Yeah, "Oh",' said Tommy. ' "Oh" is about right.'

When Marcin got back to the house Artur was in bed. He woke up when Marcin came into the room.

'So?' he said.

'So what?'

'What did Ray say after I left?'

'He said nothing.'

Artur sat up. 'What do you mean nothing?'

'Nothing. I told him you were gone and he just didn't seem too bothered.'

'Fucking bastards. I'm finished with that place. It's no good. It's not what we're supposed to be doing. Dirty, servile work. We're better than that.'

'You may be,' Marcin said. 'But I'm down to my last two hundred and I've a back week to work. I can't afford to quit now.'

'Well, it's a shit job. There's no doubt about that. I feel better already to be out of the place.' Marcin said nothing.

'Stick it out if you want but it'll start to get to you. You'll see.'

'I've no choice,' Marcin said.

'There's always a choice.'

'No. There's not.'

'So who cleaned the toilets in the end?' Artur asked, in the semi-darkness of the room.

'I did.'

'You did?'

'Yeah.' There was silence for a moment, long enough for Marcin's mind to begin to drift.

'You're a fucking idiot,' Artur said. 'I'm telling you that for nothing.'

23

Just past two, and Victor was thinking of home. A fifteen-minute drive that at this hour seemed too far to go. The mid-week nothing nights that were just like any other for everybody involved, those were the ones that killed him. Time sticky on the quiet streets. His stomach jangling with endless cups of tea, his teeth sore from sugar. Jokes across the street with the guys from the sports bar, friendly slagging that had an undertone of something in it.

The last few stragglers were leaving now, being swept out by Gareth and the new guy. He would be in bed soon. Off tomorrow. Get up late. Go to the gym.

And then there she was, dressed up and looking like someone who had landed from another world into the damp grey of a Tuesday night in Dublin. It was like waking into a dream. 'Hey,' he said. 'You came.' There was nothing in him but delight.

'I was just passing,' she said, a contained smile that told him nothing.

'Were you out?'

'Yeah. I'm on my way home and I thought I'd see if you were here. To say hello.'

'Well, hello,' he said. 'I'm very happy to see you. You look nice.'

'Thank you. And hello to you.'

There was a moment of silence. Victor's mouth felt dry. He shook himself out of nervousness to say what he had to. 'I'm finished up now. Do you want to go for a coffee or something?'

'A coffee? At two in the morning?'

'Or a drink. Whatever you want.'

'It's just a drink. You understand?'

'Yeah, I know. I am a gentleman. You will see.'

'Okay,' she said. 'Where are we going?'

'Ah,' he said. 'I will take you somewhere that you have never been.'

They walked for less than five minutes, then turned into a narrow street that led to the south quays. Victor made a call. Just before the corner they stopped at an Italian restaurant with closed steel shutters.

'Is this it?' she asked. There was traffic on the quays, a post-club crowd around the place.

'Yeah.'

The shutter went up halfway from the inside. Victor bent and spoke to someone through the door. He waved his hand in front of Agnieszka.

'You'll have to bend over.'

She looked at him. 'What is this?' The sound of people talking came out, the smell of cigarette smoke, perfume.

'It's nice. You will like it. I promise you. If you don't we can go. I'll take you home.'

She hesitated. 'You can see,' he said, and he pointed. Agnieszka bent over and looked in. Then she passed through into the room and Victor followed. A young fellow, rosy-cheeked and wholesome, pushed down the shutters again when they were in. There were maybe twenty people in the room sitting around at tables, drinking wine and vodka and coffee. Everybody was smoking. There was dance music playing low in the background.

'This is Mircea,' Victor said to Agnieszka. The guy who'd opened the door shook her hand.

'What is this place?'

'It's my restaurant,' Mircea said. 'And a place for friends to go when everywhere else is closed.'

They sat at a table. Victor nodded at a couple of people in the room and laughed when a guy called something out to him.

'What did he say?' she asked him.

'Nothing.'

'Tell me.'

'He said that a guy like me has no business with a girl like you.'

'He doesn't know me.'

'But he knows me. And he can see you.'

'I knew you weren't Italian.'

He smiled. 'My ID card says I am.'

'But then it's not your ID card.'

'The guy looks like me,' he said, putting the card on the table in front of her.

'Nice picture,' she said.

'This was taken the day after I got out of the army. I drank too much the night before and this photo was in Bucharest station at seven in the morning. I don't drink, and if you look at this photo, you can see why.'

She drank water and he drank espresso, short bursts to keep him awake and alert, to hold him in the reality of where he was. The feeling of conspiracy in the room fed into the way that they talked to each other. The space in which they sat, the dark intimacy of it and the background noise, meant that they leaned in across the table to talk.

'So you're a bouncer?' she said.

'We don't like this word "bouncer".'

'I do. I think it's funny. You know what bouncing is?'

'Yes. Of course. Like a ball . . .' His hand mimed it in the air above him. 'Bouncing.'

'So?'

'We don't bounce.'

'What do you prefer?'

'Doorman. Security.'

'Do you think you're still a soldier? Is that it?'

'Not soldiers,' he said. 'We don't fight.'

'But you hit people.'

'Not normally.'

'Isn't hitting people your job?'

'No,' he said, sitting forward. 'No. It's the opposite. People don't understand this. When you do it right you never have to touch anyone. You talk to them. You use your head. It's not an easy thing. It's easier to just, you know . . .' He clenched his fist. 'But a good doorman doesn't need to do very much. You watch and you're good to people. That's the way to do it.'

'There must be times?'

'Yeah. Sure.'

'And?'

'And what?'

92

'Do you enjoy it?'

'That? No. I don't enjoy it. I can do it. I'm good at it, maybe, but I don't enjoy it. I prefer, you know, "Have a good evening", "See you again", this kind of thing. And I don't think . . .' he said, then paused for a moment. 'I don't think I've ever hit anyone who didn't deserve it.'

'You make it sound like you're a diplomat.'

'Yes,' he said, without hesitation. 'That's it.'

'You're the UN,' she said. 'Peacekeeping.'

'I know them. I've seen those guys. We're much better than them,' he said.

Victor didn't know what to make of her. Was she here because she liked him, because he'd been direct with her? If a girl comes back when you invite her out, it must mean something. She wasn't just passing. A girl like this, though. Her eyes, which were almost too bright for her face, too blue and clear against her tanned skin. Why would she come to a guy like him, working on a door?

'I want to ask you something,' he said.

She looked at him.

He waited for a moment. 'Were you just passing tonight?'

'Yes. More or less. Why?'

'I was wondering.'

'Were you hoping that I got all dressed up and came into town to see you because you'd asked me to?'

He couldn't tell if she was joking with him. It seemed likely. 'I hoped that, yes.'

'Not too disappointed now?'

'Not at all,' he said. 'Not one bit. Where were you before?'

'I was out with people from work. It was nothing. Boring. This is better.'

When the lights went on suddenly the two of them faced each other, blinking and embarrassed as if they'd been caught doing something inappropriate. They laughed the same laugh.

'Mircea has to go to bed,' Victor said.

'We all should,' she said.

'I'll drive you home.'

'I'll get a taxi.'

'It's no problem.'

'Thank you. But it's fine.' They ducked out on to the street, blue and cold and clear in the first light. He walked with her down to the quays. He stuck up his hand and a taxi stopped immediately.

'Thank you for that. It was fun.'

'Maybe again,' he said. 'Some time. Or something else?'

'Yes,' she said.

'Good.'

She leaned forward and kissed him quickly on the mouth, then got in the car.

'I don't have your number,' Victor said through the window.

'I'll come to you,' she said. 'I'll call in.'

'You'll have to,' he said. 'I can't do anything else.'

The taxi moved off. She waved at him once, and then was gone. Victor walked back towards the car-park, the taste of her lipstick on his mouth, a lingering smell of her perfume on his skin.

24

In the daytime Marcin moved like a ghost around the house, skin grey, eyes sunken, barely there, barely visible, while Basil and Andrzej and Artur were out at work. And while they drank in the living room together, like citizens of the real world, Artur with his newly shaved head bending to fit in, Marcin was brushing his teeth upstairs getting ready for work. The others all headed off every morning together in a car to build new estates in Kildare and Meath and west Wicklow while Marcin came home to sleep. On the weekends Artur went to two-day house parties with people he'd met through work. Marcin worked weekends, and when his days off came, all he wanted to do was sleep.

He got a couple of extra shifts and worked two weeks without a night off. When he got paid he bought himself a *Herald* and went looking for a place. He found one, a room at the top of an old house divided into flats, that was not far from his work and just about affordable. He told Artur when he got back that night.

'It makes sense,' Artur said. 'I mean, it's been good having you here but it's the wrong side of town for you. You'll be better off on your own.'

'I think so.'

'And we'll still meet up.'

'Of course. Maybe without the boys. I'm going to miss them.'

Artur smiled. 'They were beginning to come around to you, I think.'

'Oh, yeah?' Marcin said.

'Not really. I thought you'd know that was a joke.'

'I did,' Marcin said. 'But anyway. We'll go for drinks.'

'When you get off nights,' Artur said.

'Maybe, yeah. It's okay for now.'

'It'll kill you,' Artur said. 'Believe me, I know what I'm talking about.'

'I'll find something else. I just have to get a bit of money together.'

'I could see if we need anyone,' Artur said. 'If you wanted.'

'Maybe,' Marcin said. They smiled at each other, both aware of the reality that existed between them now but knowing it would be easier if they pretended not to be.

He had a single bed, a built-in wardrobe, cooker, counter and sink. The first day he came back to it after working he climbed the stairs, one floor too many, and at the top collapsed on to the bed. His dreams were guided by the things that happened in the house during the day, the comings and goings, the phone calls and the loud, African conversations in the hallway four floors below. The cooking smells that came up to him and the whirling, grinding flush of the communal shower and toilet not far from his head through plasterboard walls. He woke disoriented, exhausted from living the life of the house. The water in the shower was cold and he didn't have the right coin for the meter. When he turned on the light in his room to get dressed for work, the bulb flashed and squeaked and went out with a pop.

He got dressed in the dark, then went downstairs to go to work, every step bringing him lower. The handwritten signs in the hallway, telling him to close the door properly and not to put the bins out early and to leave messages attached to the cork-board, which was there for that specific purpose, did not improve his mood.

But walking home along the canal the following morning, after a quiet night, he felt there might be hope. That when he got a bit ahead of himself and had sent some money home, put aside a bit for comfort, he could start thinking about getting another job. Something maybe working among the people who marched in their droves north and south along the routes into town and out to offices while he walked steadily across their path heading west. Some day soon he would walk along this path, heading home after a long night but knowing he would not be going back to the hotel, and that thought was enough to sustain him. Behind him as he walked he heard a siren, faint but getting louder. When he turned he saw it was three swans flying above the water having just taken off, their wings wheezing as they strained to gain height. They flew over him in formation, necks straining forward like runners at the tape as he watched, mouth open, with the rising sun on his back.

25

Dessie walked into the kitchen just before seven.

'I wasn't expecting you,' Anne said.

'I wasn't expecting to get back myself.'

He sat at the table and lit a cigarette. She was slicing vegetables at the sink and putting them into a small pot.

'And where's Yvonne?' he asked.

'In town. Won't be back. She went out after college with a few of them.'

'Right.'

'Do you want some of this? I can put another one on for you.'

'What is it?'

'Pork.'

'Yeah. Please. Maybe two.'

She put food in front of him ten minutes later and sat across from him to eat.

'All right day?' he asked her.

'Not bad.'

'Did you go in to see your mother?'

'I did.'

'And how was she?'

'The same.'

Silence. If there was anything for him to say he would have said it, but he was frozen by the knowledge that the conversation would only go one way.

'How about you?' she asked him.

'Oh. Driving in traffic. Going places to pick up things that weren't where they were supposed to be. Phone ringing every five minutes.' He stopped. 'It wasn't so bad. He was in meetings most of the day.'

She looked at him. Say anything, he thought. Just not that, not now.

'Nice to have you here for dinner,' she said. 'I thought I'd be alone.'

'Yes. Makes a change. This is good,' he said, pointing at his plate.

'It's nothing much.'

'It's the best thing I've had today.'

'You can relax tonight, anyway.' She was smiling at him. He tried to smile back but couldn't.

'No,' he said. 'Not tonight.'

She sat still, stopped chewing for a moment. 'Out again? Again?'

He nodded.

'I'm not going to say it,' she said.

'Good,' he said, not sure if he meant it to hurt or to defuse the situation.

'Please,' she said then. 'Will you just look?'

'I thought you said you weren't going to start?'

'Anything will do. I don't care. We don't need that much.'

'This much. We need all of this. Yvonne needs everything she gets. She could use more.'

'For all that you do it's not enough,' she said. 'Without you, what do you think would happen to him? Do you know how much he'd have to pay to get what you give him?'

'Do you know what he gives me? By the time you add it all up?'

'Yes, I do, Dessie. But I'd rather have less for you to be doing a proper job. Not all envelopes, fifties here, hundreds there. Not to have you out working all the hours God sends and you never being here.'

'It's a mercy,' he said, standing up. The cruelty could come now for both of them if they let it. He would regret it soon, even two minutes later when he was getting into the car he would be sorry, but that knowledge wouldn't be enough to stop him now.

26

The girl was older this time. She'd told him she was twenty-five but she could have been ten years more than that. She was English, some accent that reminded him of a soap opera – grey light, tight rooms, conversation in pubs. Bleached blonde, solid, curvy. There was very little talk and very little hurry. He had two hours and she said she would make them the best of his life. Something he would always remember. It was sales patter but he liked the ambition of it. She stripped naked slowly in front of him, pressed her stomach against his face and placed his hands on her arse.

'Feel that,' she said.

'I feel it. Kneel down,' he told her. She knelt and rubbed her face against his crotch.

'Do it,' he said, and she undid his belt, unbuttoned his

trousers. He felt the cool of her hand, slightly rough, against his cock, and then the warmth of her mouth as he lay back and looked at the ceiling. He needed this one. It wasn't the weeks where he'd been busy or stressed that really built it up in him. It was the slower ones. When he was waiting for something to happen, when he had time to wonder about what was coming. Failure. Exposure. Mockery. These were the things that reared up in front of him when he had time. In the past he'd travelled out to hotels in Greystones or Navan for meetings that didn't exist just to fill in those days. Spend your life the way he did and anyone would need this. He sighed at the ceiling above him. A deep exhalation to clear his mind and get back to where he should be.

'All right?' she asked. 'Should I stop?'

'Keep going,' he said. 'I'll tell you when you can stop.'

His hands rested against the tiled wall of the shower. There was a numbness around his groin and a jittery thrill still pulsing in his stomach. A neutral emptiness – freedom from feeling, a new start, another day. The water battered against his head. If the time came that he wasn't able for this any more he would still like to come here just to take a shower, to be beaten and pummelled by endless jets of hot water with nobody banging on the door, nobody talking to him or asking him things. He checked himself in the mirror, turned around twice, looking for bruises, marks, swellings. There was nothing. He got dressed in the room, straightened the bed and put the pillows back in place. On his hands and knees he checked the floor, under the bed, the chairs, the desk. All clear. He would walk out, and by the time he got home there would be no trace that he had ever been here. He put his tie on and texted Dessie. When he got the reply he left the room, closing the door gently behind him.

27

Marcin had been told by Tommy that some of the porters wouldn't collect the breakfast cards or do room-service orders. There was something about those corridors at night, the sameness of every floor, the muffled sounds of conversations and televisions left on. Whimpers and cries and shouts. Doors that opened and closed and lifts that went up and down of their own accord. If someone ran up behind you suddenly, should you punch them or offer to make them a sandwich? It was all too much, he said. It freaked them out.

'You're telling me this so I have to do it all,' Marcin said to him.

'On my children's lives I'm not,' Tommy said. 'I swear to you. Ask George. He saw something on the fifth floor. Scared the fuck out of him. He'll go up during the day or with somebody else, but you will not get him up there alone at night.'

He still wasn't sure if they were messing with him. If Tommy had children he couldn't have seen much of them. One way or another it was Marcin's job to get the cards. He took the lift up to the penthouse and worked his way downwards. When he got to Reception he was ready for a cup of tea and a cigarette. It was half four now and the first alarm call wasn't until six. He was hoping to sleep until then. He dropped the cards with the night manager at Reception. As he was walking across the lobby, the manager called after him: 'Third floor.'

'What about it?'

'You didn't do it.'

Marcin walked back to him. 'What do you mean?'

'I mean you didn't collect the cards from the third floor. You must have missed it.'

'But how? I came down the stairs each time and out on to each floor.'

'I don't know,' the manager said. 'You're tired. We're all tired. But there's sixty people on that floor and not one card.'

'I'll go back,' Marcin said.

'You'll have to.'

When he pushed the button for the lift he saw that one was on the seventh floor and the other on the sixth.

'What's happening with this?' he called to the manager.

'I don't know. Ray's doing papers.'

Marcin cursed to himself. He went through the doors into the kitchen and took the stairs. Between the second and third floors he turned the corner and a man was standing in front of him, absolutely still. Tall, good-looking, well-dressed, watching him in silence with a fixed expression on his face.

'Christ,' Marcin said.

The man said nothing, then put a hand to his chest in shock and sighed. 'Woof,' he said.

'Can I help you?'

'I'm fine,' the man said. He started walking on, and as he passed Marcin he reached into his pocket and rummaged. Marcin stood, back pressed against the wall, trying to ready himself for whatever it would be. The man pulled out a fifty, looked at it, then gave it to Marcin. 'For your trouble,' he said, and before Marcin could say anything he kept on walking.

Marcin's heart was beating so hard he could feel it in his temples. He stayed where he was for a second. Then looked over the banister to see if the man was still there. He saw nothing, cocked his head to listen but heard nothing. He shrugged to make himself feel normal and went on up to the third floor to get the cards. His hands shook as he walked the corridors and he checked over his shoulder every couple of paces. When he got back to the landing he pressed the button for the lift. When it came Ray was in it.

'Ray,' Marcin said.

'What?'

'Just now. There was a guy on the stairs. It was weird.'

'What sort of guy?'

'I don't know. Forties. In a suit.'

'What did you get?' Ray said. 'What did he give you?'

Marcin said nothing. The crumpled breakfast orders were clenched in his right hand and the fifty was in his left. Before he knew what was going on Ray plucked the note out of his hand.

'Hey,' Marcin said.

'Now,' Ray said, 'don't worry. You'll get your cut. But I'm going to have to tell you something.'

'What?' Marcin asked, not at all sure that he was ready to hear it.

28

The bar Victor worked in was very different from Agnieszka's place. They packed them in to the chart dance music of the day. The air was sweet with the smell of Fat Frogs, tequila shots, Sambucas and beer. Agnieszka watched men in short-sleeved shirts and blonde girls in not very much bouncing around each other. Not her thing, but the people seemed to be enjoying themselves more than they did in her place.

It came to her suddenly, a sense that something was happening and that she was the last person to know. The sound of the pause that happens as everyone tries to figure out what's going on, heads rising like those of animals spooked at a waterhole. A crash of glasses breaking and then a couple of screams. Before she had time to think of him, Agnieszka saw Victor moving a guy towards the door. The man was older than most people in the place, late twenties maybe, and bigger than Victor. He was struggling as they moved, flapping ineffectually, trying to get hold of something that would stop their movement towards the door, the street, outside, where there would be nobody to see what happened next between him and this calm, set-faced block of a man who was removing him with the efficiency and emotion of a machine designed for the purpose.

Victor might have been getting a sheep ready for shearing, so relaxed and unthreatened did he seem. He didn't look in her direction as they went by. He held the guy in front of him as they passed through the swinging doors held open for him by another doorman and threw him out into the street where he landed, stumbling. Five seconds later another bouncer threw out a second man, evidently a friend of the first. The two of them stood in the street at a distance from the bouncers. Agnieszka looked out through the window as they shouted abuse. They kept their distance. One of them was bleeding from his head and as the adrenalin faded away he became more aware of the pain, touching his forehead as he gesticulated at the bouncers. Victor just stood still, hands together in front of him, feet spread slightly, solid and immovable. There was nothing in his face to convey that his heart was beating harder, that he was nervous or even exhilarated by the result of his effort. Behind her the noise in the bar was back at full volume. A Chinese lounge girl was in the middle of the dance-floor with a dustpan and brush, clearing up the broken glass as the throng bounced around her.

Agnieszka watched Victor and his colleague coming back in now. They were joking with the guy on the door, all laughing together. She saw his wide, childish grin, which made him look fifteen. It got wider when he saw her. 'I'll be ten minutes, is that okay? Just got to clear the downstairs and then we can go.'

'Are you all right?' she asked.

'Yeah. I'm fine.'

'What was that about?'

'Just idiots. Drunk. It was nothing at all.'

'But you're okay?'

'I'm perfect. Think about what you want to do later on. Where you want to go or whatever.'

'I will.'

She stood and looked out of the window, the crowds of mostly tourists who passed up and down the street, staggering boys and singing girls and a family, maybe Italian, going home after a dinner that had obviously dragged on and got them involved now in a world that wasn't hostile to them, but wasn't where they should have been.

When Victor came back they said goodbye to the barman and to the guys on the door and went out on to the street.

'So,' he said, 'what do you want to do?'

'I'm tired,' she said. She saw the look on his face and laughed at him. 'I just had a busy weekend. Do you have the car?'

'Yes.'

'Could we maybe go back to your house? I want to go to bed.' She watched him process this information.

'Sure,' he said. 'You won't have to ask me that twice.' She kissed him as they walked.

29

A public meeting to discuss the planning application for the hotel, organized by one of the local Labour councillors, was held in the community centre at eight o'clock on a Thursday evening. It was busy when they arrived, the car-park full. Hard white light spilled out from the hall into the low orange of the evening. Dessie parked at the side of the building across a painted yellow box that didn't seem to mean anything. A small group of people were standing around outside the door smoking cigarettes, waiting for things to get started. They watched Sylvester and Dessie as they went by, a moment of recognition marked by silence as they passed.

'Hello to you,' Sylvester said, and a couple of them nodded before returning to their cigarettes.

It was loud inside the hall, a full room of people who were anticipating something, ready to talk or to argue. A wave of nausea hit Sylvester but he held the feeling in check and fought it back, staring into the middle distance as he walked. There were councillors from all the parties ahead. As he passed Sylvester said hello to some, nodded at others and smiled at a few old enemies, who pretended not to see him. He walked with confidence through to the front of the hall and sat with Dessie in the third row, directly in line with the podium.

After a few minutes the chairman introduced a Labour councillor, a humourless plodder with whom Sylvester had battled often over the years. He gave a dreary PowerPoint presentation, outlining the reasons why locals should object to the development. He spoke of traffic flow and the effect on it of poorly planned high-density projects like this one. Of the replacement of a public amenity by a private, possibly gated, complex. Of overlooked gardens and his concern for the changing character of the area. When he finished there was a round of applause and the chairman called the next speaker up. Sylvester looked out across the room as people spoke. He recognized a lot of faces. Most of the crowd were from the bottom end of the ward, nearest the hotel. Older people. And there were the usual headcases who came to everything. He sat there in the smell of new paint, under the white fluorescent light, an expression of patient interest on his face as a different councillor explained in more detail than anyone needed what impact the potential building would have on local waste management, talking of sludge and grey water.

Sylvester had come here as a child with his aunts to bingo. Ten years old. Warm bottles of minerals. Bags of clove sweets. Occasional cigarettes that one aunt would let him have surreptitiously as the atmosphere grew tighter and heavier, the droning slang of the caller, the titters and drawn breath that greeted each new number until somebody shouted, 'Check!' and heads would turn and the noise would rise in a blend of disappointment and release that he always thought strange. He'd been bored in this hall many times.

The councillor finished speaking in a shriek of feedback and some half-hearted clapping. The chairman opened the meeting to questions from the floor. An old sacristan from the church wandered the room with a microphone, following the chairman's direction. The discussion went back and forth for fifteen minutes, at which point Sylvester raised his hand.

'Mr Kelly,' the chairman said, and when the microphone arrived Sylvester stood and began to speak.

'Good evening to you all. I'd like to say a few quick words. I have the greatest of respect for Councillor McDonald, as he knows, and he's done a good job of looking at this proposal and imagining the most negative possible scenario.

'But I think it's worth looking at the positive aspects that this development could bring to the area. Some of the things that have been said here tonight are just factually incorrect. There's no suggestion that this development would be gated. How could it be? Shops and restaurants behind iron gates? Let's keep things realistic.

'Councillor McDonald speaks of how a public amenity would be replaced. But what use is that hotel to anyone today? What amenity is it providing? What use will it be tomorrow or next year as it slides further into disrepair and ruin? What effect will that have on local property values? Surely restaurants and a supermarket and a café are useful public amenities. Surely the profile of the wider area would be improved by the building of these amenities and luxury apartments. Are house prices in the area realistically likely to rise or fall as a result of this development?

'And no mention has been made here tonight of the potential effect on employment that this development would have. There would be jobs in construction, in security and in the shops and restaurants that are part of this plan. One hundred full-time jobs at the end of the project. One hundred extra people working. At a time like this, do we just dismiss that prospect out of hand?

'I would appeal to people here tonight from the area – people actually from the area – to see for themselves what is in Mr O'Donnell's proposal and make their judgement based on a proper assessment, not just what you've heard here tonight. Thanks very much.'

There was more applause than he had anticipated. One of the Labour councillors on the stage stood up and was waiting at the podium when the room fell silent again. 'Mr Chairman, if I can just come back on that.'

'Go ahead.'

'For those of you who don't remember him, Mr Kelly used to be a councillor for this area before retiring ...' he paused after the word 'retiring', smiled to himself '... a couple of years ago to concentrate on his work in the area of property development.'

'No,' Sylvester said, the microphone still in his hand. 'That's not true.'

'A pretty clear case of gamekeeper turned poacher.'

'Now hold on,' Sylvester said to the chairman. 'Are you going to allow this?'

'Sorry,' the councillor said. 'I just don't think your speech was completely honest. You didn't mention that you work for the developer.'

'I'm speaking purely as a local resident. Everything that I said is true. I genuinely believe this project would be good for everyone in the area.'

'But you do work for David O'Donnell?'

'I'm not an employee of his, no. I've done some work for him over the years ...' There were jeers from further back in the hall. Sylvester held the microphone a little closer to his mouth. 'But let me repeat that I am speaking now solely as someone who lives in the area. And I would say again to people here tonight, look at what is actually being proposed, read what's in the document and make your mind up on that basis. Don't just take the word of a group of people for whom development is a dirty word, for whom property is theft and private enterprise a terrifying ideological notion. That's all.'

There was laughter and another round of applause. It was drowned by the booing of party activists at the end, but the room felt more evenly divided.

'We have your point,' the chairman said. Sylvester handed the microphone back to the sacristan and sat down.

'That's just ridiculous,' the councillor said from the stage. 'I don't know what to say to that.'

'Thanks very much,' Sylvester said, smiling up at him and holding his gaze.

30

There was too much to do. There was getting the bar set up for the evening, finding knives and lemons and limes in the kitchen, among the last of the chefs, sweaty and red-eyed, pissed off and looking at him as if he was a thief. There was organizing the glasses, bribing a kitchen porter to make sure a tray of highballs came out clean. There was tallying the bar, checking that the closing stock from last night matched the opening stock. Watching the day-shift boys and asking the right questions to make sure there weren't any hidden nasties that would crop up during the night. Lost luggage. Overbookings. Broken promises.

They had to establish who was staying and who wasn't. Differentiate between the non-residents who were not allowed to be there and those who spent enough or were regular enough or close enough to someone important to be allowed to hang around and drink. Everybody thought they were entitled to be there and claimed to be connected. Friends of the manager. The general manager. The manager's wife. The former manager. The owners. Old Mr Kennedy who used to run this place. Mr Bell. Mr Doherty.

These well-dressed, comfortable, middle-aged people would look Marcin in the face unblinking and lie to get themselves that last brandy and port to take the sting out of the trip home. When one of the other porters was around he could check and see if they were legitimate. Usually they weren't and he could say goodnight and walk away. But sometimes they were and because of that it was never safe to assume.

He got it wrong sometimes. Gave drink to the people he shouldn't and turned away entitled red-faced men who looked at this pup, the thin line between them and the last jar, and assumed that the way to deal with it was with outrage and threats. I'll have your job. Mr Doyle will hear about this. I'm going to see to it personally that you apologize to me.

When he arrived one evening to the duty manager asking why he'd refused some VIP a drink the night before, he asked how he was meant to know the difference.

'You could have asked one of the others.'

'There was no one around.'

'Well, you should have gone and got someone.'

'But I didn't know where they were. It's a big place. They could have been anywhere. Do you know how many times a night people tell me they're VIP? Every night there's someone and most of the time they're lying.'

'I know all that. I've been here a lot longer than you. Just be careful.'

He was turning to leave when Marcin spoke. 'Hold on.'

The manager stopped. Raised his eyebrows.

'Do you have a book maybe, with pictures of all the important people? That way I could learn who it's okay to serve. Do you have something like that?'

'Are you being smart?'

'No. Just when you tell me not to make mistakes, I don't see how I can avoid it. If I don't know who's in and who's out, how do you expect me to get it right? Should I serve everyone?'

'No.'

'Is it better that I serve someone who's not entitled?'

'No.'

'So what you're telling me to do is to know something I don't know. And that you can't help me with.'

The manager smiled. 'What I'm telling you is to do the job of night porter properly without fucking up. If you don't think you can do it, believe me, that's fine. Some people aren't cut out for this work. We can replace you by this time tomorrow. It might make both our lives easier.'

His face was close to Marcin's now, close enough for Marcin to smell his breath.

'I'm trying to resolve the problem,' Marcin said.

'Just do your job.' The manager walked away.

One more comment would have done it. He spent the rest of that evening thinking what his next sentence would have been, and no matter what he came up with, it always ended the same way.

But he got on with his work and began to get some understanding of how things worked. He saw the division between night and day. How during the day the place felt glitzy and busy and buzzing and the people were brighter and there were girls and the managers smiled and the guests smiled back and nobody was drunk. In the business centre biddable girls in nice suits looked after the needs of executives. Hairdressers and boutique workers were part of the scenery. Lounge girls in striped waistcoats and tight skirts brought coffee and cakes and treats to people indulging themselves. Smiling families together for lunch at weekends. Daytime charity functions with blonde women and shiny men, BMWs and sports cars set up on podiums for raffles.

At night it was all men. Sitting in the residents' lounge drinking until their shoes came off. Get me another fucking pint, you, and he'd do it because they tipped and were sloppy, forgetting cigarettes, losing handfuls of change down the back of the couch. People tried to sneak people in, tried to pay with stolen credit cards. People complained about the noise of the functions or the traffic on the road outside or the next guests' television or their sex noises or their rows or the air-conditioning or just some non-specific problem that was keeping them awake, which Marcin thought was probably their own fucking insomnia and which, although this was a five-star hotel, was not his responsibility.

There were the early risers, trying to get into the gym at four, ordering egg-white omelettes and toast, no butter. There was thievery and cheating among the staff. Up there, in the corridors and the rooms, there was a whole world of activity that Marcin didn't know about but began to sense. Conversations stopped when he arrived. That evening in the lift Ray had told him that what happened during the nights was their own business. He had been working in this place since it opened and he knew what it was about. Sort things out. Make the calls. Take your money. Keep your mouth shut. Marcin was a part of their crew now. He was a pretty good porter and if he kept it up he'd get in on everything that was happening.

'The most important thing to remember is that at night this is our place,' Ray told him. 'We do our own thing, but you have to understand, we don't push it. We take home maybe half as much again as the day shift and they don't know that. They have their own set-ups. The fucking business is walking in the door at them. Fish in a barrel. We've got to work for ours. Do the job right. I know what it's about and you'll be looked after. Understand? You just can't talk to anyone about this, right? I'm trusting you here.'

He did what he was told and did not ask questions. He ignored doors that opened and closed again as he walked along corridors and the lift that went up and down when no one was there. The porters' phone that would ring three times and stop, prompting Ray or Tommy or one of the others to head off. The cars that came and went in the middle of the night. The girls who arrived and left or disappeared. The room-service orders to rooms that were supposed to be vacant. The men who handed money to him, always way too much, that he would bring back down to Ray. His cut came at the end of the week, a change bag from the bank with a small roll of notes.

Marcin didn't know if the night manager was aware of what was going on, if he, too, got a packet at the end of the week. He thought not. Because for all the odd things that happened up on the floors above, down at the desk if someone wasn't paying attention there was no reason why they would ever notice anything out of the ordinary.

He got used to the work and to the gap between himself and the others. The gap between day and night, worker and client, regular cherished guest and faceless worthless nobody on a package tour. He saw the people checking in and out, their luggage and their clothes, their days spent going places, doing things, deadlines and arrangements or free time and leisure filled with long afternoons drinking tea or cocktails or beer. Yawning and stretching until the next thing that had to happen happened. He saw all this but wanted nothing of it. He didn't envy these people, didn't waste his time imagining himself in their shoes or dream that his life would be happier or better if he was doing what they were doing.

But he envied their beds. The heat of this summer made day sleeping difficult, and in the airless, half-dreamed concert of comings and goings in his bedsit it was even harder. To be in a dark room, temperature control on the wall and a phone you could turn on or off, a sign you could hang on the door to communicate to the world that your rest was important, something to be borne in mind by others. That was a luxury for which he lusted.

The route to work became familiar. He began to see the same faces of the office workers, girls who looked through him or didn't see him or did. He passed along a terrace of old houses, now all businesses. Then along the canal and its endless non-moving traffic where he was a distraction in other people's worlds, something grey-faced and feeble, going against the crowd. Why does he walk like that? State of his shoes. That suit.

It put him off. He looked at the map and saw that away from the main roads there were any number of quieter routes he could take. North and east would do it. A combination of right turns and straight ahead would deliver him to Pembroke Road and from there he knew how to find the hotel.

The streets were quiet at night. He walked a jagged route along tree-lined roads of big houses set back from the traffic, gravel drives and gardens maintained by crews of Chinese guys with strimmers and blowers and equipment. Porsches and Jaguars and old Mercedes and BMWs in the driveways – 7-series for the man and 3-series for the woman. To look at these houses from the front, with their red brick and granite steps, the subtle shades of door paint, the open windows with their curtains swept back and the view into their living rooms full of books and art and fabrics and furniture, was to feel that this world would be beyond him for ever. But from the lanes that ran along the backs of these houses it was different. Marcin could smell the gardens as he passed, climbing plants, roses and honeysuckle and privet. The neatly cut grass and clipped hedges of the front gave way to weeds, petals and leaves blown into piles in the corners, cigarette butts and packets. Floating bathrooms clung to the back of buildings with plumbing and pipework, places where these people washed and pissed and shat. Dodgy extensions, patched-up paint jobs in colours that belonged to a more garish age. Cracked windows, flaking paint, leaking roofs, crappy skylights and clothes-lines running across small yard spaces.

It was a territory for the feral cats who walked all over these carefully negotiated divisions of space and light, through the rusting iron gatework, sharpening their claws on the louvred wood panelling, scaling the crumbling stone walls that had been there from the beginning and shitting in the scrappy flowerbeds, as if this other world had been created for their amusement. It happened every so often that someone coming out would turn and see him and stop, as if they'd found him in their bedroom. Then a moment of shifting reality as they realized that, technically, this was a public street and that he, whoever he might be, wasn't necessarily doing anything wrong by being there. By walking quietly with a bag on his back. By looking like that. By smiling shyly as if something was funny. They watched him pass, just to be sure that he was going, blaming him for their own surprise, justifying it by hanging on for a moment to make sure he wasn't waiting for them to go before hopping the wall and . . . He wasn't going to do it. Anybody could see that. Just some night worker. Who puts on a uniform to rob houses?

31

Victor's job was to watch and pay attention to what was going on, inside and out. But the reality was that on the quiet evenings mid-week, with no one inside to worry about and no one on the street coming in, there was nothing to be done. The hours passed slowly and as they did, with a dreamy half-smile on his face, Victor planned his empire.

He wanted to go home after his time in Ireland, maybe a couple of years from now, and to open a gym. He knew where he wanted the first one to be. The right area of Bucharest, close to the centre where the foreigners working for international companies lived. There were more of them every year. These people would get posted to Bucharest and do a stint before going back to Chicago or Lyon or Singapore or wherever they had come from. They weren't interested in living there; they would go out to eat and drink and meet each other, try to meet girls. Victor had no interest in running restaurants or bars, too much work, too much uncertainty. But every one of these people would work out. It was what they did.

He would do it right. He would get enough equipment together, get the place fitted out so that it looked good, better than anywhere in Dublin, and he would charge a lot of money. Because if his was the best place in town, the foreigners would join, and as soon as some of them came, the others all would. They didn't want to hang around with local wrestlers and weight-lifters in the industrial-style facilities of Dinamo. They wanted to run five kilometres on a machine. Do a few curls, sweat in an attractive way that made them feel good, and flirt with each other. Didn't bother Victor. He had no doubt that if it was built it would work. And after the foreigners there were the rich Romanians.

He could see the place. He knew the corner he would put it on. He had pictured it so often that it had become real to him. The place would come free for him when the time was right. He knew it made no sense. But he believed, and that belief was what would make it happen. He had got away from home, had made it through Italy and had spent some time in Germany. He had struggled. He'd thought at various stages that life might turn out to be a disappointment, all effort, no reward. And yet here he was. Working, living in a Western country, making good money. Liked and respected by his colleagues. Plenty of friends. A nice car. A beautiful girlfriend. When he thought about how he had got here, it seemed to him that he had never stopped hoping. Always doing the right thing. Working hard. Being as honest as he could be. Things just came right.

And so the fact that he knew nothing about running a business or the legal issues involved in importing a load of gym equipment, or the health and safety implications, the cost of insurance, local rates or a hundred other things didn't matter. It was simple. Someone would open a high-end gym in Bucharest. If it wasn't him, it would be someone else. But he had a vision and he believed in it.

He'd need money. He lived a quiet life and saved most of his pay. He could do the odd nixer here and there, bring in a bit more. Some of the boys here might be interested in getting involved. With a few people throwing in twenty-five, thirty, forty thousand, suddenly you had a bit of money. When everything was in place he would go to the banks and see what he could get. Because a local man coming back with a lot of money and an idea for something new was the kind of project banks were there for. He would show them an artist's impression, brochures, presentations of walk-throughs. The number of machines. The music system. The marble and chandeliers of the lobby. The juice bar. How could they say no? They wouldn't. It would happen.

And so he read the newspapers from home online, trying to keep an eye on commercial property. He sent his mother to pick up brochures of sites that were about the right size. He looked on the Internet at the gyms in the five-star hotels of Bucharest. The Marriott. The Sofitel. The Hyatt.

32

Agnieszka walked into one of the booths in a call shop and closed the door behind her. The room outside was full of people using the Internet. The door was flimsy. When the phone answered she spoke as quietly as she could. 'It's me.'

'Where were you?'

'I was working last night. It was late when I finished.'

'You could have called.'

'In the middle of the night?'

'Yeah. Better than leaving me waiting. I didn't know what to do.'

'Where is he?'

'He's here. He's with me. But how was I supposed to know what you wanted?'

'Because I told you already. It's not complicated. Nothing's changed.'

'Maybe not for you. Over there. You're not the one looking after him every day.'

She said nothing for a moment. 'What can I do?' Agnieszka said then.

'Ring him. Talk to him. See what he wants.'

'I know what he wants and so do you.'

'It might not be that bad an idea.'

'No,' Agnieszka said. 'Just no.'

'Even for a few months. Until you get yourself together. Because I can't go on like this.' Her voice was thick and Agnieszka couldn't tell if she was drunk or just emotional.

'Why? Is he being difficult?'

'No. Not that. But it's all the time. I have no life any more and everything costs money, you know. And I don't have it. The washing-machine. Again.'

'There's more coming,' Agnieszka said.

'How much?'

'Two thousand.'

'When?'

'Next Friday.'

'It's tight.'

'How is it tight? What does the money go on? It can't cost much to feed him, and what clothes does he need? How can you be spending so much?'

'I have to live. I have to look after everything for him. Not just food and clothes. Bills. Medicines.'

'Why? Is he sick?'

'Not sick. He had a cold but I got him everything he needed. I looked after it.'

'I know,' Agnieszka said, because it was easier, and if she hung up, she'd be left wondering.

'And it's not just the money. You know well what the problem is. How much time it takes to mind him. Do you know how my days are spent now? I only get out to see people at weekends.'

'I never get out. I understand all that you do, and I appreciate it, but all I'm doing here is working.'

'So let Lukasz take him. Come back at Christmas and look after him then.'

'No. Do you remember nothing? He's not going there. I'll send you the money as soon as I have it and I'll get home in a few weeks.'

'What am I to say to Lukasz?'

'Ignore him.'

'How am I supposed to ignore him when he's standing on my doorstep? What do I do if he kicks in the door?'

'He won't.'

'How do you know?'

'Because he won't. He's only doing this to get at us. At me. That's all. He'd get bored in a week and lose him in the mountains in Slovakia.'

'He says he'd be staying with his parents. They're okay, aren't they?'

'No,' Agnieszka said. 'And you can't think of it like that. Just don't believe anything he says to you. He'll go away in a couple of days and that will be it.'

'So Friday, is it?'

'Yes. Two thousand.'

'Okay then. I'll talk to you again.'

'Hang on. Don't go.'

'What?'

'Is he awake?'

'Yeah. Wait a minute.' Agnieszka heard her mother call the boy's name and then his feet in the echo of the hallway.

'Hello, Jakub,' she said. 'Do you know who this is?'

33

Sylvester had been waiting for the phone call, expecting the announcement some time around five o'clock, and he was getting tense. When at last it came they were heading back into town from Wicklow. He saw Dessie watching him in the mirror as he began to speak. 'So?' Sylvester said.

O'Donnell laughed at the other end of the line. 'Guess.'

'Can you just tell me?'

'Go on.'

'Well, I'd say because you're playing games that it's a yes.'

'It's a yes.'

Sylvester smiled at Dessie in the mirror. 'All right. That is good news.'

'It certainly is,' O'Donnell said.

'Congratulations.'

'I couldn't have done it without you. I mean that. I'll remember you for this. You'll be looked after.'

'That's even better news,' Sylvester said. 'Was it close?'

'Not in the end, no. Where are you now?'

'Near Bray. Driving back into town.'

'Well, I'm heading over there now.'

'Where?'

'To the hotel. Do you want to meet me? Have a look at it while it's still standing? Think about your lost youth? We'll go for a pint after. I'll buy you a Shirley Temple or whatever it is you lot drink to celebrate.'

'All right. We'll be there in about half an hour.'

Sylvester put his phone back into his jacket pocket. He rolled the window down and for a second Dessie thought he was going to start singing. Instead, having looked behind, he hawked and spat out on to the grass verge. 'Excuse me,' he said. 'I had to get that out.'

'So what happens now?' Dessie asked.

'Nothing. There might be an appeal but it's not likely.'

'So, congratulations, I suppose. Is it?'

'Nothing to do with me.'

'Ah, now. You made the speech. You delivered the brochures.'

'Wouldn't have made much difference.' The wind was blowing into his face and his eyes were closed. Dessie thought of a dog they had had when Yvonne was younger.

'It's a relief,' Sylvester said. 'I wasn't sure it would get through.'

'What does O'Donnell think about it?' Dessie asked.

'He's happy, which can only be good for us. He might start putting a bit more work our way. We could certainly use it.'

When they arrived at the hotel O'Donnell was standing in the car-park, pointing up at the fire escape. He was with his PA and two young guys who were nodding at what he was saying. When he saw Sylvester he walked towards him, hand outstretched. 'The man of the moment,' O'Donnell said. He shook his hand and whacked him on the shoulder.

'Isn't that you?' Sylvester asked.

'Congratulations, Dessie. You did your bit too.'

'Ah,' Dessie said. 'Sylvester helped.'

'So we're just waiting for television news to come along and do an interview and then we'll get going.'

'Whose idea was this?' Sylvester asked.

'Theirs.'

'Slow day for news?' Dessie said.

'Must be,' O'Donnell said.

The crew arrived a few minutes later.

'Thanks for doing this,' the reporter said, as she walked up to them. 'I'm sure you're very busy.'

'Always busy,' O'Donnell said.

'I'm just going to ask you what your reaction is to the decision and what you would say to the people who were opposed to the plan.'

'Sounds fine. Where do you want to do it?'

'Just there, on the steps.'

'Can these people be in the background?'

'Why?'

'It'll look better if I've a few friends around me. Not the big bad developer.'

'If that's what you want.'

So as O'Donnell was interviewed Sylvester stood in the background, smiling mildly and trying not to think about how he looked.

They did it in one take. The reporter stared at notes on a clipboard while O'Donnell answered. He knew what he wanted to say and he said it. At the end the cameraman nodded at him. 'That was fine. Thanks very much.'

'Okay,' the reporter said, raising her head now. 'So that'll go out at half eleven tonight and probably tomorrow morning as well.'

'That's it? Nothing else?'

'Nope.' She smiled briskly. 'Thank you. I've got a bit more to do but you can go,' she said, and wandered away in the direction of their van.

'Right,' O'Donnell said after her. 'What did you think?' he asked Sylvester.

'I think you got your message delivered. Job done.'

'She wasn't the friendliest,' O'Donnell said.

Dessie took two pulls from his cigarette and flicked the butt in an arc in the direction of the reporters' van. 'She could have been pissing on your feet and it wouldn't matter. You were the one on camera.'

O'Donnell smiled at him. 'Ah, Dessie. You always know the right thing to say.'

It was close to ten o'clock as Sylvester wandered up the hill towards his house along the tree-lined street, a light warm breeze rustling above him in the direction of the sea. There was a two-litre plastic container of milk tucked under his arm, bought on the way back. When his phone rang he jumped. It sounded wrong, a note of panic in this settled environment. He didn't know the number.

'Is that Mr Kelly?' a man's voice asked.

'Yes, it is,' Sylvester said. 'Who's this?'

'My name is Declan Hennessy. I'm a journalist.'

'Oh, right. What can I do for you?'

'I just wondered would you have five minutes to talk to me.'

'Well, it's kind of late,' Sylvester said. 'And I'm not at home at the moment.'

'I know, yeah. I rang your house and got your mobile from your wife, I think it was.'

'Did you? The number is on the website. Could have saved yourself the trouble.'

'Oh, it wasn't a problem.' Disingenuous? Stupid? 'It'll only take a few minutes.'

Sylvester was ten minutes from home. There was no one around.

'Okay,' he said. 'What do you want to talk about?'

'Thanks very much. I wanted to ask you about David O'Donnell's planning application for the hotel site that was accepted earlier today.'

'Yes,' Sylvester said.

'You must be happy with that result.'

'I am, yeah. It's good news for everybody, I think. Good news for the area.'

'You were involved in the campaign to get the project approved. Is that right?'

'I don't think I'd call it a campaign but I did provide information about the development locally, yes.'

'You went door-to-door.'

'Yeah, well, there were people, members of a certain political party, who were against the idea before they knew what was actually involved. And they started giving out leaflets that were very one-sided, full of inaccuracies. I just thought in the interests of fairness that, before people started objecting, the other side of the argument should be heard.'

'That would be the Labour Party, would it?'

'Yes.'

'Were you asked to do this by David O'Donnell?'

'I was happy to do it because I genuinely believe that this plan is a good one.'

'But did he ask you to do it? And did he ask you to lobby councillors on the issue?'

'Yes,' Sylvester said. 'He did. I've known David for a long time. I have the utmost of respect for him and I think that this project will be enormously beneficial for the people of this area.'

'And you presumably still know a lot of the councillors personally?'

'I know a few people, but I have to say I don't think my involvement would have made a huge difference to the vote in the end. I'm a long time out of politics and I'm just one person. They approved the plan because it was the right thing to do.'

'Mr O'Donnell obviously thought you had some influence when he asked you to get involved.'

'I don't think that's how it was at all. He's a friend. I live in the area. He asked for my help. That's all there is to it, really.'

'And you're retired from the council, what is it, three years now?'

'That's right.'

'And why did you retire?'

'Look, Declan, I did enough interviews about it back then. I don't feel the need to be talking about it now.'

'It's just for background.'

'I'd been at it long enough. I was starting a new business and I wanted to concentrate on getting that going.'

'This is the foreign property company?'

'That's right.'

'And how is it going?'

'Very well. It was tough at the start but the past eighteen months or so have been extremely good.'

'And is Mr O'Donnell involved in that business?'

A tightness spread across Sylvester's chest. A feeling of uncertainty that made him think back to what he had already said. 'No, he's not.'

'But he's bought property through your company? Is that right? Twenty apartments in the Vienna Park complex in Prague?'

'Listen, Declan, I can't discuss this with you. It's not fair for me to say things in the public domain about a third party. I know Mr O'Donnell. I admire him and respect him greatly . . .'

'But he did travel with you to the Czech Republic two years ago?'

'I'm not going to talk to you about it any more. I thought we were going to discuss the hotel.'

'I believe you got him a very good deal.'

Sylvester went to speak, then found there was nothing he could say. He took the phone away from his ear for a second. Then breathed out. 'Unless there's anything more you want to ask me about the planning approval I'm going to go.'

'Can you tell me, where did you meet Dessie Considine?'

'I'm hanging up now,' he said, after a moment. 'And I don't really want to talk to you again.'

He was around the corner from his house, just a few minutes away, but he stopped. Turned around and started walking in the opposite direction. He had no idea what he should do now. What would be waiting for him at home? Had this man been talking to Helen and, if so, what had she told him? Was there anything he could do to make him go away?

He dialled O'Donnell's number. The background roar of the pub could be heard when he answered.

'Hello again,' O'Donnell said. If he wasn't drunk he was close to it.

'Go outside,' Sylvester said.

'What?'

'Go outside away from everybody.' The clamour faded and he heard O'Donnell's footsteps as he crossed the road.

'What's going on?'

'Listen, I just had some journalist on the phone asking questions about you.'

'Yeah? So?'

'He was asking about Vienna Park. He knew you'd bought twenty of them and he knew you'd underpaid.'

'He said that?'

'No. But he said you'd got a good deal or something like that.'

'Well, I did. That's not a crime. Who is this guy?'

'Declan Hennessy,' Sylvester said.

'Who does he work for?'

'I don't know. He didn't say.'

'Can you Google him?'

'I'm not at home.'

'And what did you tell him?'

'Nothing. Not one word. He started out talking about the hotel and that was all fine, and then he blindsided me with this. I told him politely to piss off and that's when I rang you.'

'I'll check it out,' O'Donnell said. 'Thanks for letting me know.'

'Should we be worried?' Sylvester asked.

'No. I told plenty of people I invested in that project. He's just sniffing around, chancing his arm. If he knew enough to hammer us, he'd have done it by now. We'll find out who he is and see if we need to do anything.'

'Okay,' Sylvester said. 'That's grand.'

'Don't let it ruin your evening. This is a happy day for us all.'

'All right. I'll talk to you tomorrow.'

Sylvester thought about ringing Dessie but he'd see him in the morning. Dessie wouldn't tell him what he wanted to hear tonight either. That everything would be fine. That there was nothing to worry about. That just because this guy was asking questions didn't mean he knew anything.

34

Beneath the flowers and polish, the heavy perfume of the Sunday women with their red-faced, blazered husbands, the coffee from the espresso machine and the ozone freshness from the water-feature, there was something else. Marcin met Tommy coming towards him across the lobby. 'What is that?' Marcin asked.

'What's what?'

'That smell.'

'What smell?'

At three o'clock that morning a woman from some film company came in. Marcin nodded at her as she passed the desk.

'Was there a fire or something?' she asked him.

'I don't know,' he said. 'Why?'

'When you come in. The air. You know?'

She was French. A little old, maybe, but still, if she asked him up he'd go. He smiled. 'Yes. Yes. Maybe,' he said. Vagueness seemed like the best approach. The woman paused for a second, then went on.

At six in the morning, the first puffy-faced suited men and women began to check out. Marcin watched them as they walked out of the lift into the lobby, their faces puzzled at first, a half-second before they realized it was bad.

'What is that?' the first guy asked the night manager.

'It's the sea, I think. When it's hot it gets quite strong.'

'I'll say. It's awful. I don't know how you can work in it.'

The manager shrugged. 'You get used to it, I suppose.'

'I don't think I would.' After he'd signed, he went outside to wait for a taxi. He came back in a moment later.

'It's not the sea. It's this place.'

'Really?' the manager said. 'Are you sure?'

'Well, if it was the sea, the smell would be worse outside. But it's not. The air outside is beautiful. It's just this place that stinks.'

'Oh,' the manager said. A flicker of sadness crossed his face.

'Sorry,' the guy said. 'It's nothing personal. I just thought you should know.'

'Yes, indeed. Thank you.' The man walked back out and got into his taxi.

'Nothing personal,' the manager said, watching him go. 'You wanker.'

The operations manager came on at half six. His face crumpled as he walked through the doors. He went straight to the night manager. 'Where is it coming from?' he said first, no greeting, nothing.

'I don't know. I didn't realize it was a problem.'

'How could you not realize it was a problem? The place reeks.'

'I can't smell anything.'

'Then there's something wrong with you.'

'I can't smell it either,' said Ray. 'In fairness.'

'What about you?' the operations manager said to Marcin. 'No.'

'Well, go outside for a minute and come back in.'

The three of them stood under the canopy. The air was warm and still.

'Another beautiful day,' Ray said. 'For us to sleep through.' He lit a cigarette and offered one to Marcin.

'That's not what you're out here for,' the operations manager said, through the door. 'Come on.'

It was obvious when they walked back in. A dirty tang that they had spent the night breathing. They followed the operations manager, who was already striding towards the function rooms.

'It's everywhere, this stink, being pumped through the whole place.'

'It's just the public areas,' Ray said.

'That's no consolation. We've got two hundred delegates at a conference in this room in five hours and the place smells of . . . What is it?'

'It's death,' Marcin said.

'For Christ's sake. The Pole speaks.'

'I'm serious. It's like something dead.'

'That's what it is,' Ray said. 'In the air-conditioning. The duct.'

'Fucking Alex,' the operations manager said, walking off.

'Who's Alex?' Marcin asked.

'Maintenance man.'

They walked together in silence after the manager.

'Is he dead in the pipe?' Marcin asked, hoping it was a joke.

Down in the basement, in the steam and the damp, the operations manager opened the padlock on the steel cage that held the air-conditioning unit. The three porters stood watching him as he tried to get the cover off the access point above their heads. He had taken off his jacket and was cursing and sweating in the heat. The plate eventually fell to the ground with a clatter.

'Now what?' Tommy said.

'Have a look and see what the story is,' the manager said. 'See if that's where the smell is coming from.' None of them moved.

'Who? Us?' Ray asked. 'Are you joking?'

'Not me anyway,' Tommy said. 'Sorry, but I have a thing about pipes.'

'A thing about pipes?'

'Yeah. I'm claustrophobic or whatever. Tunnels and every-thing.' The manager said nothing. 'You can stare at me all you like. I can't go in there.'

He looked at the others. Ray seemed older and frailer than he had in the light of the lobby. Then at Marcin. He was thin and agile. Light.

'Will you go up?'

'In there?' Marcin said, pointing. 'For what?'

'For what? To have a look. See what the story is.'

Marcin shrugged. 'Yeah, I can have a look. A look is fine.' He dragged over a chair and stood on it. He put his hands on the edges of the hole and pulled himself up.

'Oh, Jesus.' The voices of the others were muffled beneath him. The smell was stronger in here, but not impossible. Beyond the first couple of feet in either direction there was blackness. He reached down and the manager put a torch into his hand. He lifted it up and shone it. Five metres away there was a furry clump. 'I see it,' he shouted.

'What is it?'

'I don't know. Some sort of animal. A cat, maybe. Or a big rat.'

'Fucking Alex,' the manager said again. Marcin dropped the torch and lowered himself back to the floor.

'Why?' Marcin said. 'What's it to do with him?'

'Because he poisons the cats hanging around the back of the hotel,' the manager said, 'and then burns them.'

'Jesus,' Marcin said.

'And obviously one of them has got in here and died.'

'Why does he poison cats?' Marcin asked Tommy.

'Because he's a miserable cunt,' Tommy said.

'How do we get rid of it?' the manager said.

'Get Alex to come in and sort it out,' Ray said. 'It's his problem. Or your problem. It's nothing to do with us.'

'We don't have time,' the manager said. 'We need to get this fixed now.'

'So get the company,' Tommy said.

'What company?'

'The maintenance company. Duct cleaners. I don't know.'

'In an hour a hundred people are going to start checking out and they're going to notice that they've paid three hundred euro to spend the night in a place that smells like a fucking rendering plant.'

'So what do you want to do?'

The manager looked at Marcin.

'What?' Marcin said.

'You can't make him do that,' Ray said. 'He's a night porter. The union will go ballistic.'

'Union, my hole. He's not in the union,' the manager said.

'That's not the point. This is your problem, not ours. Get yourself a pair of rubber gloves and go to work. It's nothing to do with us.' The three porters began to walk off.

'Will you do it? Marcin?' the manager called after them. It was the first time he'd used his name.

'Do fucking not,' Ray said.

'Sorry,' Marcin called back. 'I don't think so.'

'I'll give you a hundred euro,' the manager called after him.

Marcin stopped. 'No. Sorry. I can't.' The two of them faced each other across the damp floor.

'Two hundred. Cash.'

Marcin hesitated. 'Into my hand? Today?'

'Yeah. Okay, come on. Let's get this thing sorted out.'

He wore an apron tied around his face and a pair of rubber gloves. He had a bin liner in his hand as he worked his way along the duct on his stomach, clanging and booming as he went. The pipe swayed from side to side. He did not feel safe.

'Is this thing going to fall?' he shouted, but he couldn't have heard any answer. It was hot and airless when the machine was switched off and the smell was intense. Sweat began to run on his face. When he got closer he saw the cat, a little stripy thing, grey and brown, not much more than a kitten, lying on its side and faced away from him. It was a very small animal to be causing all these problems, Marcin thought. He got the torch into a position where he could see what he was doing.

'Got to move you now, fellow,' he said.

He lay on his side and opened the bag, held it in one hand as he reached out to lift the cat's body by the tail. It came away in his hand and the air clouded with little black flies. The smell got much worse.

'Oh, fuck,' he shouted, his voice too big in the tight space. He gagged and thought he could hear Tommy laughing below him. He threw the tail into the bag and grabbed at the body trying to get it all over with in one go. But his hand passed through the animal's fur as if there was nothing there. He looked at the glove and saw a brown slime that was all that was left of its body. He tried to wipe his hand on the side of the duct and knocked the torch so that it skittered away and landed out of reach beyond the cat. Marcin lay still for a moment in the darkness trying to keep himself calm. He breathed in slowly but the smell was too bad now. It was a horror film. He took off the dirty glove first, then the other, threw them as far away as the limited space allowed. He turned back on to his stomach and began to wriggle towards where he'd come from as fast as he could, panic rising in him as he went.

Marcin sat in the canteen drinking tea and eating toast. He needed something to put himself right. The day shift were starting and the place cleared out after eight. Tommy came in.

'Are you not gone?' Marcin asked.

'Not yet. Is there tea in that?'

'Yeah.' He poured a cup and sat back.

'Will you come for one after?'

'Okay,' Marcin said.

'I thought you might need one.'

'I do. Thanks.'

They sat not speaking, the television booming out the news above their heads. The remote control was somewhere around the place. Marcin finished eating. He was going to ask Tommy for a cigarette when he saw someone he recognized on the screen. It took him a moment to place the face. 'It's him,' Marcin said.

'Who?'

'Our friend.'

'What friend?' Tommy said.

Marcin looked over his shoulder. They were alone.

'From upstairs. In the room. Five three eight. Every week.'

Tommy shook his head. 'I don't know him,' he said.

A man was being interviewed on the steps of a building. He spoke in a strong, confident voice, welcoming this decision and expressing his pleasure at what it would mean for the residents of the local area. His full head of white hair was ruffled every so often by a breeze coming in from the sea, visible in the background. He was surrounded by a small group of smiling supporters.

'This guy behind.' Marcin got up, stood underneath the screen and pointed.

'I don't know what you're talking about,' Tommy said.

'What?'

'I've never seen him before in my life. And neither have you.'

'Oh,' Marcin said. 'I understand.'

An hour later they sat together at a counter drinking in silence. The change from one of the fifties that the manager had given Marcin was on the counter in front of them and he knew they would sit there until it was gone. Outside on the street it was the middle of the morning rush-hour, a great common enterprise. To be doing the same thing as everyone else, that was worth something in itself. To be participating in the real world. There could be comfort in routine, no pain in boredom.

'None of them will have to clean up a cat today. Not one person.'

'Will you stop?' Tommy said. 'You got paid. Three hundred quid for five minutes' work. You should be happy.'

He had done it. He had gone back in. He hadn't wanted to but he couldn't say no to the better offer. He'd spent twenty minutes in the shower afterwards. But if he thought about it, the smell was still there, as if it was in his clothes or in his skin or in him. He tried to think of something else but after a minute spoke again. 'It was like a paste, Tommy.' He rubbed his fingers together. 'Sticky, you know.'

Tommy put a hand to his mouth and hiccuped. 'Enough,' he said. 'Just forget about it. Have a drink. Shut up.'

35

At half six Dessie pulled into a garage on his way into town. He bought tea, twenty cigarettes and two sausage rolls, which the deli girl heated for him in a little toaster oven that did the job almost as quickly as a microwave and kept the pastry flaky. He gathered his things and went outside where he sat on a low wall facing out across the traffic. He was just finishing his breakfast when a man got out of a parked car and walked towards him. Dessie looked around to see if there was anything near him that the man might be heading for – a water can or a bin or something that would bring this guy in his direction. He might have said something, but his mouth was full. The man came closer, then stopped a couple of feet away and Dessie looked up at him. 'What's the story?' he said, as soon as he'd swallowed.

'Dessie, yeah?'

'Who?'

'You're Dessie Considine, right? You're Sylvester Kelly's driver.'

Dessie stood up. He was much shorter than this man. 'Hang on. Who the fuck are you?'

'My name is Declan Hennessy. I'm a journalist with –'

'Are you the fellow was talking to Sylvester before? Annoying him with phone calls and ringing his wife and all?'

'I spoke to him. I tried to ring you as well but you never answered.'

'I don't answer my phone to cunts I don't know.'

'I was just asking him questions about his relationship with David O'Donnell.'

'Ah, here. You can stop with this now.' Dessie started walking back towards the car. 'I've nothing to say to you.'

'Do you know anything about the Vienna Park apartment complex in Prague?'

'I don't know anything about anything.' He opened the car door.

'Come on, Dessie,' Declan Hennessy said. 'You were there too.'

Dessie took two steps towards him and held his finger pointing at his face. 'Don't you talk to me like that, you prick. You don't know me. Who are you to come up to me out of the blue when I'm having my breakfast, asking me questions and calling me by my first name? You need to get some fucking manners. Or have them put on you.' Declan Hennessy stood at a safe distance watching him impassively, as if his words meant nothing to him. Dessie made a move as if he was about to rush him and Hennessy flinched and took a step back. Dessie laughed. 'You arsehole,' he said, and got into the car.

When he was closer to town and had calmed down he rang Sylvester.

'Early for a call, Dessie.'

Dessie laughed. 'You're saying this to me? You? The scourge of my wife's mornings?'

'What's the problem?'

'I just got doorstepped by some little pup of a journalist.'

'Where?'

'Eating a fucking sausage roll at the side of the road near Chapelizod. Walks up to me and says, "You're Sylvester Kelly's driver." Starts asking me about David O'Donnell and Prague.'

'Jesus Christ.'

'I know.'

'What did you say?'

'Nothing. Not a thing. I told him to piss off.'

'How did he know who you were?'

'I don't know. I don't know if he knew I'd be there or if he was following me or what.'

'Hennessy. Was that the name?'

'Yeah. Where is he getting this stuff?'

'I have no idea.'

'Well, you should put a call in to his editor and tell him that it's not on. He can't be doing this kind of thing. He just walked up to me. How are you, Dessie? I thought he was going to fucking shoot me.'

'Why would anyone shoot you, Dessie?'

'I had a life before I met you.'

'I know that. But I thought you'd buried all those skeletons.'

'I did. But still. Sometimes they come back from the grave. What will I do if this guy comes near me again? Will I batter him?'

'No,' Sylvester said. 'Jesus, are you mad?'

'I wasn't serious,' Dessie said. 'I just thought I'd check.'

'Ignore him and he'll get bored.'

'You ring his editor and say you'll get an injunction.'

'What kind of injunction?'

'I don't know. A barring order or whatever.'

'He's a freelance. There's nothing I can do about it. Just say nothing and don't hit him.'

'Cheeky little cunt, isn't he?'

'He is,' Sylvester said. 'But it goes with the territory. I think it's O'Donnell he's after, not me.'

'I've had enough of it already.'

'I'll have to get you media-trained.'

'The only media training I want to do is with an iron bar.'

'Oh, Dessie. Bad press. There is such a thing.'

36

After a couple of drinks one morning on his way home Marcin wandered into Rathmines, the smell of fast food in the air and the ground sticky under his feet. In a Spar he bought a card with the red and white colours of the Polish flag on it. He held it in his hand like an ID as he crossed the road to a payphone, calculating that he had enough credit to talk to his parents for ten hours, more than he'd need in a year. He dialled, the familiar last seven digits beeping a melody he knew. The background noise of the street at least would convey to them that he was somewhere else. Maybe the sound of people passing would be foreign enough, the gull-like voices of the swaggering kids in tracksuits could transform into something exotic if you didn't understand them. The different tone of the police sirens might distract them from the implausibility of what he was saying. But it wasn't that implausible. It could have happened.

'Hello,' his father's voice said, and Marcin waited a second before speaking.

'Hello,' he said. 'It's me.'

'Ah.'

They talked about phoning. About how long it had been. How their Internet had been down or broken or had some minor technical problem that probably meant something needed to be turned on.

Marcin told his father he was working on a dig. That he was excavating a site in the centre of Dublin, possibly Viking, and that it was going well. He said that the money was just about enough but he thought he might be able to get something related to supplement it. That the people he was working with were from all over the world, that he had seen

Artur a few times and that he was doing okay. He asked for their news and his father told him, you know, nothing really. Everything was fine. The weather was a bit hot but not too bad. The cat had been at the vet because the fur on her back had got very thin, but she was home now. Taking the tablets.

'That was before I left.'

'Was it? Yeah, not much has been happening, really. Do you want to talk to your mother?'

'Is she there?'

'She's here. She wants to talk to you. Fighting to take the phone out of my hand.'

'Hello,' came her voice.

'Hello.'

'How are you?'

'I'm fine. How are you? Any news?'

'No. Tell me what you've been doing.'

The same conversation over again. 'Yes,' she said, every so often. 'Right.' He stopped speaking. He could picture her where she was, sitting in a wicker chair facing down the hallway, staring blindly into the distance as she always did when she was on the phone, always lost in some sort of vision of whoever she was talking to, her memory of them, that distracted her from whatever they might be saying. He could walk through the door of their apartment now and she wouldn't even notice. Go to the kitchen and find whatever leftovers were in the fridge and head out on to the balcony and drink juice and look across the playing-fields and the school building to the town beyond.

'Are you even listening to me?' he said then.

'Of course I am. What else would I be doing?'

'I'm going to go,' he said, and put the phone down. He went into McDonald's and bought a milkshake. On his way home he dropped the phone card into a bin, then a minute later thought better of it, went back and fished it out.

37

She saw Luke White walking through the place looking straight ahead but aware of the people around him. He came up to the bar, and when he saw her he nodded her over. 'Are you finishing now?'

'Ten minutes.' She had arranged to get out as soon as the bar stopped serving.

'That's fine. Have you got half an hour?'

'For what?'

'It's work-related.' He smiled.

'Half an hour is okay,' she said, 'but then I have to go. I'm meeting someone.'

'That's fine. No problem. Will we go?'

'Should I not . . .?' She pointed down the bar at her manager.

'I'm borrowing Agnes,' White shouted over.

She got her jacket and bag and they walked out on to the street. It was throbbing and messy, a blur of colour and noise, shouting and lurching.

'It's different when you're sober,' White said, over his shoulder at her as he walked along quickly, then turned down towards the quays. 'How was tonight?'

'Okay,' she said. 'Where are we going?'

'Just to meet someone down here.' He waved his arm vaguely towards the river. Her pace slowed and she walked behind him slightly at a distance. He turned and saw this. 'It's fine. Don't worry. I'm not taking you anywhere dodgy. Just here. Do you know this place?'

It was some sort of club. Three big, suited bouncers, red carpet at the door, velvet rope and a few people standing around outside. The bouncers stood back when White approached and smiled at him. 'Luke,' one said.

'How are you?'

'Upstairs, is it?' The bouncer held a door open. White waited for Agnieszka to go through. She walked up the stairs ahead of him, aware that the music she could hear was coming from the ground floor. Above, it seemed quiet. She turned into a room that was dark, lit by candles, spacious with more people than it seemed at first, sitting on couches and armchairs.

'You haven't been here before,' White said to her.

'No.'

'It's nice, isn't it? A good place to talk and there aren't many of them in town at this time of the night. I just want to see . . .'

He wandered away from her, looking for someone, then smiled and waved at a woman in a dark business suit who stood when she saw him. Agnieszka followed behind him.

'This is Julia.' She held out her hand to Agnieszka. She smelled nice, of something dark and spicy and warm. She looked in her late thirties but might have been older. When she smiled she was pretty but her teeth were crooked. 'It's nice to meet you,' she said. 'Luke's told me about you.'

'Yes?'

They sat. A waiter came over and White ordered a bottle of wine. Agnieszka didn't want to drink. She needed to get going soon. If Victor rang her she wouldn't be able to answer.

'They're savvy, these guys. They know what they're at. You should see this place over the weekend. You can't move for people paying fifteen euro a cocktail. And for the nights like these the club subscriptions cover it. Tell them it's exclusive and everybody wants to join . . .' He tailed off.

Agnieszka nodded and looked at the woman, who smiled back at her.

'So, anyway,' White said, 'what we wanted to talk to you about is your future. You're a bright girl and a good worker and we really appreciate that. But being behind the bar, it's a hard slog for not great money.'

Agnieszka shrugged. 'It's okay.'

'And a girl like you, with your intelligence and your looks, should be making a lot more money than you do. I mean, I assume that's why you're here? For the money? It's hardly the weather, right?'

'Yes. And the experience.'

'Yes. Absolutely, of course. But you know that working in a club is never going to make you rich. We could make you a manager but, first of all, I would have to get rid of somebody to promote you, then find someone else as good as you behind the bar. And, anyway, for you it would mean a lot more work for not much more money and I'm not sure if that's what you want.'

Agnieszka didn't know herself. It felt to her that just about now she was getting late. Victor might come down to the bar to see if everything was okay, and if they told him she'd left with White, what would he think? It was nothing. The boss wanted to talk about work. She shouldn't feel guilty but she did. This place and this guy, who put too much voice into everything he said and looked at her with a directness that was presumptuous.

'You're good with people. You're bright. You can talk and have opinions. And you're very good-looking. I can say that, I think.'

'Yes,' the woman said now. 'Very beautiful.' Agnieszka turned to her. The woman smiled again, her face encouraging and open. There was an interruption while the waiter brought the wine and glasses, set an ice-bucket on the table and poured. Agnieszka held up her hand when he came to her. White asked was she sure, and she shook her head.

When the waiter left it was Julia who spoke. 'A girl with the skills you have, the type of girl you are, you could make a very good living for yourself while you're here. The reason that Luke asked me to come in and meet you is that he thought I might be able to put some work your way.'

'Right,' Agnieszka said. She didn't say anything else. From her bag she thought she could hear her phone ringing but it was hard to tell.

'I run an agency and we're always looking for bright, well-educated, presentable women.'

Agnieszka felt her stomach contracting. She didn't say anything.

'The work would be something that might be of interest to you, given your personality. It involves meeting people and going out with them. Talking to them. Most of our clients are professionals looking for a bit of company.'

Agnieszka watched her as she spoke. There was nothing to indicate that she felt uncomfortable or uncertain as she said these words.

'It's a very upmarket operation, very well organized, and we look after our girls. There are some fellows, but it's mostly girls. We take good care of them. You'll always feel safe and you will never feel any pressure to do anything that makes you uncomfortable. And the money is really excellent. In one night you could easily make what you're earning in a week. If it suited you. It's not for everyone. But a girl like you I think would be very popular and would do very well.'

'There's no pressure here,' White said. 'Just I thought you seemed like someone who would be very good if you were interested. And I could cut back your shifts at the bar. If things worked out well for you, you could give it up altogether. It would be a much easier life, choosing when you want to work and not having to answer to anyone.'

'Might it be something you'd be interested in?' the woman asked.

The sickness Agnieszka had been feeling had faded. She'd known already from weeks ago. The first time she'd seen him. She shook her head. Get on with it now. Be done with it. 'Maybe,' she said.

'You know what we're talking about here?' White asked, his voice sharp, perhaps to punish her for the delay.

'Yes,' she said, without looking at him.

'Would I be right in saying that you've done this sort of thing before?' he said then.

She wondered if he cared what her answer would be, and realized it was of no importance to him at all. 'No,' she said.

'No,' Julia said, benign and relaxed, almost motherly. 'No. But that's not a problem at all. We can talk to you about everything. Let you know how it works, and if you're still keen we can get you started.'

'And I'll sort it out that your shifts in the bar get covered if you're busy,' White said. 'Assuming you want to hold on to the job.'

'Yes,' Agnieszka said.

'That's wonderful,' Julia said. 'I'll give you a call over the next few days to talk to you properly. I'm so happy you came here tonight to meet me. Thank you very much.'

Out on the street Agnieszka took out her phone. There was no missed call. As she passed the bar it rang in her hand and she saw that it was Victor.

'Are you finished?' he asked.

'Yes. Just now.'

38

The phone call was from a country man, bright-sounding. He told Sylvester he'd got his name from David O'Donnell. He and his colleagues had a bit of money to invest and wanted to talk to Sylvester about maybe putting it in property somewhere in Eastern Europe.

They arranged to meet in a hotel on the outskirts, close to the motorways heading south and west. The man was going home afterwards, he said, and he didn't want to spend half the night in Dublin traffic.

It was a hot afternoon. In the lobby of the hotel it was all business, twos and threes sitting close to each other at low tables, and groups gathering for sales meetings and seminars to be held in function rooms with antiquated English names listed on an electronic display board in red lights. The smell of a thousand carvery lunches, stale beer and burned coffee trapped in the soft furnishings, strangely comforting in its familiarity.

Sylvester looked around the lobby for his man, then turned to find someone coming towards him, smiling broadly, hand outstretched. 'Mr Kelly?'

'Mr Breen.'

'I recognized you from your picture on the Internet.'

'You're not a detective, are you? Am I in trouble?'

'Far from it. You're safe enough.' They chuckled at each other. Big open face and a firm, manly handshake. Good cut to the suit, a modern style that made more of a statement than he might have intended.

'It's good of you to come out and meet me,' Breen said to him. 'I'm sure you've a lot going on.'

'Happy to do it,' Sylvester said. 'Will we sit?' They found

a table and sat at right angles to each other. Breen waved a waitress over and they ordered tea.

'Something to eat?' he asked Sylvester. 'Would you have a sandwich? I'm going to.'

'I would,' Sylvester said. The girl took the order and left.

'So, David O'Donnell speaks highly of you,' Breen said, when she was gone.

'That's good to hear. We've known each other a long time. He was one of my first clients when I was setting the business up a couple of years ago. I recommended a couple of places that have done very well for him. I think he was happy with how things worked out.'

'I wouldn't be here if he wasn't,' Breen said. 'Dave's a super guy. A super guy.' Sylvester nodded. 'A great fellow,' Breen said then, a little sadly. In the moment of silence the conversations around them seemed easier and more interesting.

Sylvester tried to sound breezy. 'So, what can I do for you?'

'Basically, what it is, a few years ago myself and six friends got together and bought a horse. It wasn't a money thing, more for the fun of it. We'd all be betting men and a few of them would be more into it than I would. They'd have known what they were doing. A couple of us had sold houses around that time and paid off mortgages with a bit of cash left knocking around. We put a few quid together, a few grand each, and bought this horse. Do you know anything about horses?'

'Not a lot.'

'Meaning?'

Sylvester smiled. 'Nothing, really.'

'Doesn't matter. So we got him into a good yard and he did well for us. Ran all over Ireland and then we got invited to England and Europe as well. Flat racing. Five wins and a few places. That's a good horse. We made a bit out of him. By the time we'd paid everything and divided it up it wasn't a lot, but it was something and we were hooked. We did it again, bought two more. They weren't so good but they did all right for us. And there's money to be made in this. If you're on the scene and talking to people you get a good insight. It doesn't always work out but even with the bad days it's still an enjoyable thing to be doing.

'So we had a fund and wanted to put it into something a bit more secure. We took some of the money and put it into apartments on the dock in Athlone a few years ago and that worked out well. Sold them on. We were involved in building a hotel up near Carrick and in a golf course in Portugal. But we were interested in doing something in Eastern Europe, and I met Dave not long ago and he said you'd be a good man to talk to.'

'Right.'

'Because I was saying, you know, I thought we might have missed the boat there.'

'A lot of people think that. It's far from the reality.'

'That's what he was saying. I was talking about China or Vietnam, maybe, but we'd prefer to be a bit closer to home. Somewhere in Europe, within the EU even. If it's not too late.'

'No. Believe me. There are a lot of cities that haven't even come close to where they're going over the next five years. And even the more mature places are hitting a second boom now. If you're realistic and patient, these markets make for very good investments.'

'We're not interested in a quick buck. When you're used to winning and losing over the course of three minutes, a long-term investment has a lot of appeal. Security is important to us.'

'That's good. I think what we have would suit you.'

'So, what do you have?'

'Well, I'm sure you have your own financial people to advise you on anything you might be interested in, and in most areas they will serve you well, but when it comes to an area like this you do need to get someone more specialized. Because there are, frankly speaking, thousands of crooks and fly-by-night merchants willing to tell people what they want to hear.'

'I know all this,' Breen said. 'I'm aware of the world and how it operates.'

'So I've known David O'Donnell for a long time, from when I was working as a city councillor. As I'm sure you understand, he is a man who would expect the highest standards in everything he gets involved in. The fact that he would recommend me to you is greatly appreciated, particularly in that light. If things had not worked out as he wanted he would not have been shy about making his feelings known.'

'He might have thrown you off a building.'

Sylvester smiled politely. 'He wouldn't have been happy. But he was. And here's why. We have very good on-the-ground local knowledge that is totally independent. That's all. Most of the companies involved in this business claim to be independent but aren't. They're on kickbacks from developers, or are actually fronts for the builders themselves. People buy into a development being told that the price they're paying is typical and that their rent is guaranteed for the first year, but don't realize that they're the ones paying their own rent. My Czech partner, Marek Soldán, is an extremely good lawyer and an investor himself in property all across Central and Eastern Europe for the past fifteen years. We don't deal in the kind of new, low-quality apartment blocks that most of the others are interested in. Why are they getting involved in that end of things? Because it's easy. They bring people over and show them beautiful apartments that seem to be in an okay part of town and tell them that a thousand-square-metre two-bedroom place in an up-and-coming area in Brno is good value at a hundred and fifty thousand euro. But is it? Is it?'

'I don't know,' Breen said. 'How would I?'

'Exactly. You understand that even if it sounds good it doesn't mean anything. But for others, for people with just a bit to invest, they believe because they want to believe. They want to invest in anything and that kind of environment brings sharks. There's been nothing in Dublin for so long. There have been no hidden gems, nothing undervalued, nothing sneaking through under the radar. Everything here is known and it's over now. So these people who have a bit of money have to go further afield. And what they really want to hear is that they're getting in early, ahead of the crowd, and that they can double their money in five years. And there are plenty of people willing to take their money and tell them everything they want to hear.

'But it's basically all lies. Some people may do well. I can accept that. And the intentions of many of the people involved may be straight enough. I'm sure they hope that everybody does well. But by the time it all becomes clear they'll have moved on.'

He looked up. The waitress was standing above them with the tray, waiting for a break in his speech. 'Hello,' Sylvester said.

'Sorry,' she said.

'You put the man off his stride,' Breen said, and laughed.

'I am sorry,' the girl said, as she unloaded cups and saucers and plates on to the table in front of them.

'It's no problem,' Sylvester said, lifting the bill and handing her a note. 'That's fine, thank you.'

'You don't need change?'

'I don't.'

'Thank you,' the girl said. 'I won't interrupt you again.'

'You were saying,' Breen said, sandwich in hand, smiling at him.

'I hope you're impressed by this,' Sylvester said. 'I was saying that while others deal in cheap apartments sold at a premium we only deal in high-value spaces. Offices and luxury apartments in good areas. Places with proper transport links, areas that have actual proper plans for development. There are places that suit speculators and places that suit investors. Our places are for investors. You will make money with us over ten years. Maybe earlier than that. But you will spend more up front. If you want to buy a one-bed apartment in Bucharest for fifty thousand I can't help you. But if you're looking for something more solid and long-term we can help you. Marek has a small team of people with whom he consults and he personally checks out every place we recommend. The quality of the information we provide about our properties is of a totally different quality from anyone else's. It's a small business and you will get a more personal service that will suit your needs better than any of the bigger operators. I would absolutely understand if a syndicate like yourselves, people who are looking to build up a portfolio of investments, decided to go with one of the big companies. There is a security in that and they won't lead you too far wrong if you don't let them. I'm sure you wouldn't.

'But I can tell you that if you decide to go with us, you will not regret it. This is a good company. We have had excellent results and I can provide you with any documentation you might need and testimonials from every customer we have ever dealt with. Every customer has something positive to say. We keep the number of clients small and the level of attention high.

'That's what we're about. If you decided that you were interested in investing with us, I can show you some brochures for properties that we have at the moment. We would talk about how much you were looking to invest, the kind of timescale you would be thinking of and which countries you might prefer. Whether or not you want to take out mortgages or to invest fully. We generally recommend that clients travel and view the various properties in a given area before making any decisions.'

'Right,' Breen said. 'I get the idea. Thank you for that. Let me tell you something more specific about what we're looking to do. A few facts and figures and see how they sit with you.'

He spoke for only a few minutes. He talked about numbers, amounts of money to be invested. How if things went well initially there would be more to follow, and then more after that. He said he would need to discuss it with his partners but he thought it would probably be useful to make a trip and to meet Marek. To see what was available.

Nothing had been decided yet: this was only a first meeting and nothing would be agreed until names were on contracts, but Sylvester thanked God that this man had been brought to him. It could be the beginning of something new and bright. As all this was going on inside him, he kept eye contact with Paddy Breen and from time to time nodded as if everything he was saying would be possible.

39

Dessie started the car when he saw Sylvester coming. 'You were a while,' he said to him, as he got in.

'Start moving,' Sylvester said. 'I want to get as far away from that fellow as quickly as possible.'

'What happened?'

'Nothing. Just before he changes his mind.' Dessie put the car in gear and they took off out of the car-park and zipped through the roundabout, then down the ramp into an unmoving block of traffic that snaked off, red lights blinking, into the distance ahead.

'We'll be here a while,' Dessie said.

'That's okay. He's going the other way. Gives me time to think about this.'

'About what?'

Sylvester told him. He talked about horses and syndicates and country people with more money than they could spend. He gave him numbers and percentages and plans over five-year periods and ten-year periods. Seven people ready to go and look at what Sylvester would show them.

'So what happens now?' Dessie asked.

'We get on the phone to Marek and we set up the trip. We're going to hit these guys with everything. Put them up in the Four Seasons. Show them every building Marek knows about. Take them out, get them drunk and anything else they want.'

'Very good.'

Dessie watched him in the mirror as he stared out the side window at a girl in the car beside him. 'Oh, dear Jesus, do not let me mess this one up,' Sylvester said, as if to her.

'You won't mess it up,' Dessie said.

'I hope not.' He was fiddling with the window, putting it up and down a couple of inches. The car beside moved ahead.

'The air-conditioning is on. Will you close that?'

'It's my car,' Sylvester said.

'Not when I'm driving.'

'So this will probably be in the next week or two. We need to start thinking about flights.'

Dessie nodded. 'I'm not sure,' he said then.

'Sure of what?'

'I can't be going off to Prague next week.'

'Why?'

'Her mother's sick.'

Sylvester laughed at first. 'What? Just now?'

It didn't annoy Dessie: he understood that it was a mistake. But he didn't smile or say anything to lessen Sylvester's discomfort. 'No. She's been bad for a while. In hospital.'

'I didn't know. How sick is she?'

'Not good.'

'Why didn't you tell me before?'

'You've enough to be thinking about.'

'I should know these things, though, Dessie.'

'You know now. So I don't want to leave Anne at the moment. She doesn't like being on her own.'

Sylvester nodded. 'But she's got Yvonne, hasn't she?' he said.

'She's in college now.' Neither of them said anything for a moment. Finding their positions, Dessie thought.

'Believe me,' Sylvester said, 'I understand your reluctance and I wouldn't ask normally but this one is important. I don't know if you realize how tight things have been.'

'I do,' Dessie said.

'And, I swear, if anything happens while we're away I'll

have you on the first plane back. But for all of our sakes it would be best to have you there.'

'What benefit will I ever see from this?'

He saw the surprise on Sylvester's face in the mirror.

'You'll be taken care of.'

'What does that mean?'

'I don't understand what you're saying.'

'I do this job for you at an hourly rate and that's fine. But it's bits and pieces, lumps of money here and there, and I never know when they're going to come.' It gave him no pleasure to say this. He didn't look but he was aware that Sylvester was sitting forward closer to him now, very still.

'Is there a problem, Dessie? Me paying you by the hour – it works out better for both of us.'

'I know that. It has. But just now, getting older and thinking of winding down and that ... something a bit more official might be better.'

'This is all out of the blue.'

'It's really not. I've said this to you before. Just ...'

'What?'

'You could turn around tomorrow and say, "That's it, thanks for everything but good luck now." Where would that leave me?'

'I'm not going to do that. We've got this thing and the driving, all the admin stuff you do. There may be more work from O'Donnell. Why would I let you go? Do you think I don't value everything that you do? I thought you were happy with the pay.'

'I am. But I think we need to make it more formal. Draw up contracts. If you decide you don't need me any more tomorrow, what protection do I have?'

'We'll have to sit down and talk about it, but it can be done.

We can sort it out. I just need you to come to Prague next week. There'll be a lot of stuff to set up.'

'What do you need me for?'

'Driving. Talking to people. Entertaining.'

'You don't need me for that. You can use taxis. Hire cars and drivers. Marek can talk enough for anyone.'

'But it's better having you there. The clients love you. They always ask after you.'

'These people won't miss what they don't know.'

'Oh, come on, Dessie. It'll do you good to get away. You like these trips. I'll buy Anne a present. Give you a bonus.'

Nothing had changed. She would tell him that. The conversation about a contract would be postponed and might never happen. She would tell him this over and over as if he didn't know it, as if he was a fool.

'I can't,' Dessie said. 'That's the end of it.'

'Don't decide now,' Sylvester told him. 'Wait until it's set up. See how you're fixed then.'

'I can't do it,' Dessie said, and for a long while after that neither of them spoke.

'Are we all right for tonight?' Sylvester said, his voice quieter and higher-pitched, as it always was when he was annoyed.

'No problem,' Dessie said. As soon as Sylvester was out of the car, he would have to make the call to set it up.

40

He'd worked for ten nights straight and had managed to get four consecutive days off. He thought he would sleep for the first day, get up, eat something, go back to bed and sleep through the night, and when he woke again on the second day he would buy a paper, look at other jobs. Begin to see what he could do when he wasn't tired. But instead he slept for the first twenty hours straight and woke at four o'clock in the morning, head pounding as if he was hung-over. He went out to a twenty-four-hour shop and bought something to eat, took it back and watched television. The day had not quite started yet; the news stories from yesterday were still being repeated on a loop. American detective programmes and ads for mops and kitchen knives. Maybe he could keep going, get up now and live today like a normal person. But by eight o'clock he was exhausted and lay down.

He woke again at five o'clock in the afternoon. It was his normal rising time. He lay for ten minutes, trying to calculate how many of his four days off were left, but every time he did it he kept coming up with two and that just couldn't be right. Had he really worked all those shifts for this? Two days in bed and still he woke up feeling tired? He sat up and saw that it was bright and sunny again, traffic heavy on the road outside with people going to work. Or coming home. Which was it?

It was early evening and he didn't need to go to work the next day. That should be enough. He could ring Artur to see if he was free. It had been a while. He'd been happy enough to leave it, at least until he got himself set up doing something else. But now, five o'clock in the evening, his headache beginning to fade, the sun shining and a hundred euro of tips in his pocket, he thought it might be time to put whatever it was behind them and have a drink. He made the call.

'Who's this?' Artur answered in English.

'It's me.'

'Who?

'Me. Marcin.'

'You.' The line went silent for a second before he spoke again. 'I thought you were dead.'

'No. Still struggling along.'

'Was your phone broken or something?'

'No. Why? Were you trying to get in touch?'

'No. No. Just wondering. When I didn't hear from you . . .'

'It hasn't been that long.'

'Long enough.'

'How are you anyway?' Marcin asked.

'I'm okay. Working like a dog, but still . . . Making money, you know.'

'Are you free tonight?'

'I am. Sort of. What for?'

'Just to meet up. A drink.'

'Yeah. I've to be up early but, yeah, I'd be on for that. Do you want to come to the house?'

'Let's go to a bar.'

'I'm not going into town.'

'Why?'

'There's no point, buses and all that shit. Will you come out here? There's a local place in Lucan is pretty good.' Marcin was going to have to work for this.

'You're a pain,' Marcin said.

'Good man,' Artur said.

Marcin fell asleep on the way out and was woken by the driver in the middle of an industrial estate. He was twenty minutes late already. Then when he got back to the village he was coming at it the wrong way and couldn't see any of the landmarks Artur had been talking about. He hadn't called because he thought Artur might be late himself and because he felt foolish. But when he arrived Artur was there, sitting at the counter, drinking a pint that was probably his third.

'Ha,' he said, when he saw Marcin. 'Problems.'

'Listen . . .' Marcin said. Artur stood and they hugged briefly.

'You're like a ghost,' Artur said, looking at him.

'Yeah. And you're like . . . I don't know what you're like.'

'I look tough.' Marcin laughed. His hair was shaved tight, he was tanned and his T-shirt showed arms that were much bigger than Marcin had ever seen on him before. He was solid and he looked strong. He was wearing camouflage trousers.

'Are you expecting trouble?' Marcin asked. 'Snipers?'

'Don't be such a snob.'

'Yeah, right. Would you wear them at home?'

'We're not at home. We're here.'

'But would you?'

'What happened to you, anyway? It's like some curse. I've got fit and healthy and strong and you look like you've been eating ashes and sleeping in a river.'

'I'm tired,' Marcin said. 'It's the nights.'

'You're still doing that?'

'Yeah.'

'Fuck's sake.'

'What?'

'Well, it's not really sociable, is it? And the money's not great.'

'It's improved. I'm in on tips now.'

'Yeah, but still. You could be doing better.'

'I'm not sure that I could.'

'Well, wouldn't you rather be working with normal people? Out in the world? Sleeping in the evenings? Or fucking or drinking or at least doing something better than working?'

Marcin smiled. 'Have you found yourself a girl?' he asked.

'I have,' Artur said. 'A total slut.'

'When did you start calling girls sluts?'

'When I met one.'

'Lovely.'

'She'll be in later. Hold on, though. I had a point.'

'I know. I'm going to try and get something else.'

'Don't just try. You have to. Because this night thing is not good for you.' He wagged a finger in Marcin's face.

The way they had reverted to their roles was comforting. He nodded. 'Okay.'

'I'm just saying, is all.'

They talked for a while. Artur was a supervisor now, in charge of a crew of ten. He was the only one who spoke English and had organized it so that he told the others what to do. The bosses didn't much care how the work got done as long as it got done.

'Could you get me a job?' Marcin said it so quickly that it might have been a joke.

Artur looked him over as if he was buying a donkey. 'I don't think they'd go for you.'

'Why? What do I look like? An intellectual?'

'I don't mean it badly. I just know that if you turned up, they'd take one look at you and that'd be it. It's different now. They've got choosy. Do you know how many people we get wanting work? And if you turned up they'd laugh at you.'

'I'm stronger than I look.'

'No, you're weaker than you think.'

'You're wrong.'

'Want to prove it? I'll arm-wrestle you now.'

Marcin looked at him. There was no way he could do it. 'Arm-wrestle? I mean, what are you? Twelve?'

'That's a no, then, is it?'

'Yes, you complete moron. My skills lie in other areas.'

'Nobody gives a fuck about your poxy archaeology degree.'

Marcin laughed. 'That's not what I meant.'

'So?'

'Not everyone can deliver a room-service tray in one piece. Open a bottle of champagne. Speak English through the whole transaction.'

'They don't want to hear you, I can tell you that. I've not even been there but I can tell you for nothing that the last thing anyone ordering a bottle of champagne in a five-star hotel wants is to be listening to your impeccable accent.'

'I get good tips.'

'To make you go away.' They stopped.

It was tiring. Marcin felt out of practice talking in his own language, being with someone who knew him.

'Are they all still there?'

'Yeah.'

'Any of them ask for me?'

Marcin thought. A week ago he and Tommy had delivered a drinks order to a party in a suite. Tommy had done the charm thing, Marcin had stayed quiet. The tip had been large. In the lift on the way back down Tommy had asked him, 'You still see that mate of yours? What was his name?'

'Artur?'

'Yeah, him.'

'Not in a while.'

'Awful porter,' Tommy said. 'Dreadful. Complete clown. The fucking yap out of him. He never shut up. I don't know how much he cost me.' Marcin didn't speak. 'No offence, like,' Tommy said, and smiled at himself in the lift mirror.

'Not really,' Marcin said to Artur, hoping he'd pick up on his tone and realize there was something more to be dug out.

'Look at this,' Artur said. Marcin turned around. Two girls were walking towards them. Sort of similar. Both good-looking enough but it was easy to see which one was Artur's as she came towards them smiling, her friend half a pace behind. Part of Marcin wanted to walk out the door.

'Hello,' he said.

'This is Katja,' Artur said, 'and this is Basia.'

'Hi,' Marcin said.

'Hello.' Basia sat beside him, then didn't say anything.

There was a moment of silence. He didn't really feel up to this. 'So what do you do?' he said.

'I work in a café in Maynooth.'

'And do you like it?'

'It's okay. And you? What do you do?'

'I work nights in a hotel.'

She nodded. 'You look like someone who does that,' she said.

'Why's that?'

'You just seem very tired.'

'Really? I thought I was doing okay. I spent the past two days in bed.'

'Doing what?' she asked.

He laughed. 'Sleeping.'

'Oh.' She seemed disappointed.

'Well, I enjoyed it anyway.'

'So if you work nights, when do you go out?'

'In the mornings.'

'Really?'

'Yeah, well, you know, there are pubs that open early and I go with the guys I work with.'

'In the morning? You drink in the morning?'

Marcin became aware that the other two were listening to them. 'Sometimes. It's like our evening. We finish work, we go for a drink.'

'At what time?'

'Half seven.'

'A.M.?'

The other two were laughing at him now.

'Not every day.'

'You've started drinking with Ray and Tommy and those?'

'Sometimes.'

'Who are they?' Katja asked.

'They're the bunch of alcoholics this guy works with. And apparently drinks with.'

'They're not alcoholics.'

'Really?'

Marcin thought. Tommy. Ray. George. 'Well. Not just because they drink in early houses.'

'Despite that, then?'

'Yeah.' Marcin laughed. A little tug in his stomach at the minor disloyalty.

'What kind of people are there at that time?'

'Other night workers.'

'Night workers? You mean prostitutes? Thieves?'

'No, I mean postmen and bakers and other porters.'

'Are there women there?'

'Imagine the kind of women in these places,' Artur said. 'I wouldn't say we're talking beauty queens.'

'You're right,' Marcin said to the girl. 'There aren't many women there.'

'So if these are the places you go to socialize . . .'

'I wouldn't call it socializing so much . . .'

'If these are the places you drink, how do you ever meet people?'

'I ring him,' he said, pointing at Artur.

Later on, back in Artur's house, the four of them were in the living room. Marcin was lying almost flat out on a couch and Basia was beside him. They were passing a joint around and talking quietly, music playing in the background, lights off, with an orange glow in the room from the street-light outside. Marcin was full of the bonhomie of several pints, a couple of shots to drink to home, being away, working and meeting these lovely girls. Andrzej and Basil were gone for the night. Everything was good. If there was a bedroom spare upstairs he thought he might make it.

'I'd like to see you again,' he said to her.

'You're still here.'

'Yeah, but another time. I'd like to meet up with you and do something.'

'I'll set my alarm.'

'No, I'm going to get something else. Something that lets me sleep at night and get up in the day. I'm sick of working like a fucking . . . badger.'

'This guy's drunk,' she said across the room, to the other two coiled up together on an armchair.

'He's a lightweight,' Artur called back.

'They're nocturnal,' Marcin said. 'That was the point.'

'Too sophisticated for me,' she said.

'I did archaeology in college. I know a lot about the impact of animals doing things in the night.'

'You look like you should be an archaeologist,' she said, pushing his hair off his face. 'In some old dusty room. Like a mad professor. Dressed in black.'

'It's not mad. It's normal. He had his cut the same way until he came here and got all . . . tough. Shaved head and working out.'

'Just working,' Artur said.

'Yeah, whatever. Army chic.'

'You're just jealous.'

'I'd come over there and kick your arse if it wasn't for the girls.'

'Yeah, right.'

'You're lucky.'

Basia pulled his face towards her and kissed him.

'We're going to bed,' Artur said, as if on cue, and Katja and he stood up and left the room. Marcin lay on the couch, Basia on top of him. He put his hands under the back of her T-shirt and felt her skin, smooth and soft. It had been a long time since he'd really touched anyone.

And then he was waking up and it took him a moment to realize where he was. The room was still bathed in orange light and he badly needed to piss. He was alone. He tried to remember what had happened, but after his hands on her back there was nothing. Above his head, a rhythmic thumping kept going at an even pace. He looked at his watch and saw it was four o'clock. The thumping above got faster and he heard Katja yelping. He thought about going to look for Basia but, really, he needed to piss and there was no way he was going upstairs. He wandered into the kitchen, picked up a bread roll and found the key to the patio doors. He went out on to the grass and stood there, eating the bread and pissing. When he threw the stale end of it to the bottom of the garden the neighbour's security light went on. He went back in quickly and locked the door. He saw now that Basia's jacket and bag were gone from the kitchen table where she'd left them when they'd arrived. He thought about getting a taxi, but at four in the morning, drunk, half stoned and sexually frustrated, he didn't trust himself to get out of the estate. He lay on the couch and tried to sleep, using a small rug as a blanket.

He woke again slowly. Somebody was tapping his face. He thought it might be Basia come back. When he opened his eyes he jumped.

'It's alive.' It was Andrzej or Basil. 'Just about. Fucking hell, boy, you don't look good.'

'Yeah, I don't feel great.'

'Are you back? Because you'll still have to pay us rent for that couch.'

'I'm not back. I was out with Artur and some girls.'

He knew that Basil was the smaller one but without the other around it was hard to tell which this was. There was no scar. It was Andrzej.

'What did you get up to?'

'Not much,' Artur called from the kitchen. 'He didn't score with Basia.'

'I didn't know that was possible,' Andrzej said. 'Are you gay?'

'No, I'm not,' Marcin said, sitting up now.

'Because that girl will fuck anything. What's wrong with you?'

'There's nothing wrong with me,' Marcin said.

'He fell asleep,' Artur said. 'We left them on the couch getting cosy, and twenty minutes later she calls up to Katja to tell her that this guy's passed out and she's getting a taxi home.'

'Too drunk?'

'No. I was just tired. I'd worked ten nights straight.'

'Ah, work. For Christ's sake, are you a man? I work seventy hours a week and I'd still fuck a girl any time if the opportunity was there. And Basia is always that opportunity. I'd hang up my cock if I were you. You obviously don't need it.'

'He needed it at four o'clock when he had a piss in the garden.' Artur came in bringing a coffee to him.

'I have to say,' Marcin said, 'this is a nightmare way to wake up.'

'Where's my fucking bread gone?' Andrzej called from the kitchen. 'Ask that scarecrow if he ate it.'

'I'm going,' Marcin said.

41

Agnieszka bought a second phone, exactly the same model as her own. She stuck a small silver star on the back of it so she would be able to tell them apart. If Victor ever found the two together she would say she had inadvertently picked up someone else's at work. It was an easy mistake, a cheap popular phone. She saved Julia's number on it without putting in her name.

She was still in bed in her own place one afternoon when the call came. Julia gave her the address, the contact name and hotel-room number. The client didn't use a mobile but was a regular, and was reliable, safe and clean. A good-looking guy, according to Julia. Liked foreign girls. Didn't drink. Urbane and charming. But very private.

'I'm very private too,' Agnieszka said.

'We all are,' Julia said, 'but this man in particular. Don't ask him anything. I'll give you a call to confirm he's there five minutes before the time. It's usually around midnight.'

'Okay.'

'And then you ring me when you arrive, just to let me know that everything's all right.'

'Yes.'

'You walk across the lobby, take the lift to the fifth floor and knock on the door. If anyone tries to stop you or asks you where you're going, say you're looking for Ray and he'll take care of you. Nobody will, though. We've never had any problems in this place.'

'But what do I do if there are?'

'There won't be.'

'But if there are?'

'I'm telling you. There won't be.'

The patience in Julia's tone annoyed Agnieszka. 'I need more than that,' she said. 'If something goes wrong I have to know that there is a plan to help me. You must take me seriously on this. I'm going into this hotel on my own. I'm vulnerable. Just because this man has been okay before doesn't mean he always will be. I don't want to be a lesson for you. If I'm going to do this job you have to look after me properly.'

'I'm sorry,' Julia said. 'It's just that this man is very nice and respectable and really doesn't want to cause a fuss. But of course if anything goes wrong we'll be able to help you.'

'How? What do I do?'

'Ring me.'

'And what will you do?' There was a pause for a second. 'Julia?'

'Sorry. I missed that.'

'What will you do if I ring you?'

'I will have the hotel staff at the door in a couple of minutes. I have a mobile number for Ray. He won't let anything bad happen to you. I promise that.'

'A couple of minutes?' Agnieszka said.

'Listen to me. If you're in this business there is always going to be a chance that something might go wrong. Just as there is in every job. You could be working in an office and one of your co-workers might attack you. I can't tell you that there is zero risk because that's not true. What I can tell you is that there has never been a problem. It's highly unlikely that this man will ever do anything to bring attention to himself. And if, despite that, something does go wrong, I can have someone with you in a few minutes' time. It's a matter of probability. I know you're concerned but, really, there won't be a problem. Do you understand what I'm saying?'

'Yes, I do,' Agnieszka said.

'He's a lovely man by all accounts. You might even enjoy yourself.'

'Okay,' Agnieszka said.

'I'll talk to you later, darling.'

At a quarter to twelve Agnieszka was in a taxi on the way to the hotel. She was dressed tidily, respectably, more as if she was going to a work event than a night out, as she had been instructed. Her phone rang as they stopped at traffic-lights.

'He's there now, waiting for you,' Julia's voice said.

'Okay. I'll be a couple of minutes.'

'Lovely. Thanks, pet. Good luck.'

They turned into the driveway and drove through gardens that felt almost tropical in the damp warmth of the evening. They pulled up outside and she paid the driver. The lobby area seemed to be empty. She opened the door, felt the cool-ness of the air and saw the lift doors straight ahead, twenty metres away. She walked towards them, head down, steady and not too fast. She didn't look to either side but was aware of music playing and thought she could hear people talking quietly off to her left. She arrived at the lifts and pushed the button for up. A bell dinged and in front of her doors opened. She saw herself in the mirrored wall of the lift, pale and unhappy. As she stepped in someone crossed the lobby without turning in her direction.

On the fifth floor she came out into a landing and saw in which direction she had to go. She walked along the empty corridor, phone in her hand, feeling sick. In an hour she would walk out of here and nothing in the world would have changed. Nobody would know what had happened except her and a man she would never see again. She would go home, have a shower and a large drink, and in the morning the only thing that would be different would be the amount of money in her bag. A week's salary from nowhere. She'd forgotten plenty in her life. She could forget this. Outside the room she stood for a moment and then, before she could think again, knocked twice.

The door opened and a tall, clean-looking man stood smiling at her. 'Hi,' he said. 'Had you any trouble finding the place?'

She was exquisite, this one. Sylvester felt the smile spread across his face when he saw her, sheer joy at what he knew was coming. He stood back and let her pass into the room. Watched her tight arse under a black skirt.

'Can I take your jacket?' he said, and helped her as she shrugged it off.

'Thank you,' she said.

'What's your name?' he asked.

'Anneka,' she said.

'Is that Scandinavian? Swedish or something?'

'No. From Slovakia.'

He cocked his head at her.

'Really?'

'Yes.' She seemed nervous. He never knew why questions about where they came from unsettled them. The whole exchange was based on lies anyway. There was nothing to worry about.

'It's just I've been in Slovakia quite often. In Bratislava. I do a bit of work there,' he said.

'Ah.'

'It's a great place. Underrated.'

'I didn't like it,' she said. 'I'm glad I'm not there any more.'

He laughed at her. 'Fair enough,' he said. 'I'm sure you have your reasons.' He ran the back of his hand along her cheek. Her skin was tanned and her dark hair, almost black, was cut in a way that framed her face beautifully. 'You are something,' he said. Delicate bones in her face. He could see the shape of her neck from where he was standing. She was long-limbed and thinner than he would usually like, but there was something in the way that she was looking at him, something latent that he thought augured well. It could go either way, and if he had to take charge he would.

'I have to make a call,' she said.

'Be quick.' She walked into the bathroom and dialled a number in the darkness.

'Hi,' she said. 'It's me. I'm here. Okay.'

She came back out and walked over to where he was standing. She looked up at him but didn't speak. He bent to her face and kissed her, opening her mouth with his tongue. After a second she began to kiss him back. He stopped thirty seconds later, afraid he might fall over.

'Is that okay?' he asked, smiling close to her.

'Whatever you want.' She said it with something close to contempt.

'Get on the bed,' he said. She sat there in front of him and then, unasked and with no showmanship or ceremony, began to unbutton her shirt and lifted it over her head. She stood, unzipped her skirt at the side and pushed it down until it fell at her feet. She kicked it away and sat again.

'Let me look at you,' he said. He knelt between her legs and put his hands on her thighs. 'I'm going to fuck you into next week,' he said, and when he saw the expression on her face it turned him on in a way that felt new.

An hour later he got up from the bed.

'You've got to go,' he said. She dressed quickly and went to the bathroom to check herself in the mirror. While she was there he took out his wallet and counted the fifties on to the bed. She came back in and saw what he was doing. As she watched he counted out an extra hundred.

'For your trouble,' he said. She nodded. He picked up the money and handed it to her. 'Don't talk to anyone on the way out. Just get away from here as quick as you can.'

'Yes,' she said. 'I know.'

She left, and after a minute Sylvester lay back on the bed and looked at the ceiling, replaying everything he had just done.

42

The room-service phone rang when Marcin was in the kitchen loading glasses into the dishwasher. He ran, trying to answer before anyone at the front desk could get it. When he said hello there was silence, then a man's voice ordered six bottles of beer. Slurring. Mix of officiousness and politeness. Marcin checked the room number on the computer. The guest was alone. He went to the bar, got a tray and the beer together, then took the lift up to the man's room. He could hear the television from down the corridor. When he knocked nothing changed. He knocked again, louder, and the sound stopped. Nothing happened. When he was about to go the door opened.

'Oh,' the man said, looking at Marcin, squinting, swaying slightly. 'Oh, yeah. Excellent. That's great.' He was wearing suit trousers and a jacket but no shirt or shoes. He stood back and Marcin stepped into the room. The desk was covered with napkins.

'Where should I put it?' he asked.

'Anywhere. Put it on the floor.'

'Yeah?'

'No problem. Right there.' Marcin bent at the knee and set the tray on the ground. When he stood up the man was staring at him. He was very drunk.

'Okay,' Marcin said.

'So what . . . em . . .'

'Yes?'

'What happens now?'

Marcin smiled. 'Do you want to sign for it?'

'How much is it?'

'Thirty euro.'

'I'm never going to drink all these.'

'Put them in the fridge. Have them tomorrow.'

'Nah. Do you want a couple?'

'I'm fine, thanks. Do you want to sign now?'

'I'll sign.'

Marcin moved towards the door. The man handed him back the docket. 'I'm on my own now and the others aren't coming.'

'That's okay,' Marcin said. 'You'll be fine.'

'I hope so.' He reached into his pocket, pulled out a note and handed it to Marcin. It was a twenty. 'You've been very good to me.'

'That's the job.'

'No. Come on. Take it.'

Marcin took it.

'Good night,' he said, and closed the door.

He laughed to himself in the corridor, putting the note into his wallet and waiting for the lift. He was thinking he would tell the others, but that it would be a ten that the man had given him. The lift stopped on the fifth floor. Marcin assumed it would be one of the others, but it wasn't. It was a dark-haired girl, maybe in her mid-twenties. Good-looking, he thought, as she passed, but it was very quick. She stepped in. 'Ground floor?' he asked.

'Yes. Thank you,' she said.

He stood beside the door and she was behind him. It was only ten seconds but the silence felt like a long time. When the doors opened he let her go out first. As she passed he looked at her but she didn't notice him. She walked across the lobby in a straight line towards the door. Marcin hesitated, as if he had forgotten something, then realized what it was. He smiled and followed her out through the revolving doors and down the drive towards the main road. She was walking faster now and Marcin ran a little to catch up with her. She didn't turn around.

'Sorry,' he said, when he was near enough. 'Sorry. Excuse me.'

'What do you want?' she said. 'I have to go. I'm late.'

'Agnieszka. I'm Marcin Duda. I was the year behind you in school.'

'Please leave me alone. I have to go. You go back inside.' She spoke in English. She was still walking but turned to him now, then slowed down and stopped. It was her. There was no mistake. He knew her well. Even if he hadn't talked to her very often. Even if it was ten years since he'd seen her.

'Sorry. I don't mean to hassle you. I just wanted to say hello.'

'I have to go,' she said. 'I'm really late.'

'Okay,' he said. 'I just realized it was you and I thought that was so weird. I haven't seen you in years.'

'Yeah. I remember you. How are you?'

'Fine. You know.' He was suddenly aware of his uniform. Standing in the street with the hotel rising up behind him. 'Doing this. It's not the best job but I'm trying to find something else. How about you?'

'Good. Everything's good.'

'Are you working here?'

She hesitated. He saw now that she really didn't want to be there talking to him. They were standing on a street in Dublin in the middle of the night, nobody else around, two people from the same town a thousand miles away and she just looked like she wanted to run away.

'I'm working, yeah.'

'You have to go,' he said. 'Sorry again. I just wanted to say hello. It's good to see you.'

''Bye,' she said.

He turned back towards the hotel. Why had he thought that chasing after her was a clever idea?

She spoke suddenly behind him, closer than he would have thought. 'Marcin.'

'Yes?'

'Can you not tell anyone you saw me here? I mean people at home. I haven't been there for a while and it's just difficult. I'd prefer it.'

'Yeah. Sure,' he said.

'Thanks.'

'I should have let you go. I shouldn't have come out and frightened you. It was just the surprise.'

'Sure. I'm sorry I didn't recognize you. I was surprised too.' He smiled at her. 'I haven't been there in years. Really years.'

'Where did you go?'

'I travelled around. What have you been doing?'

'Went to college. Came here. That's it, really.'

'Okay. I'd better leave. Thanks, Marcin. It was nice to see you.'

'And you.'

He went back inside. Tommy had been watching him through the window.

'Do you know that girl?' he asked. Marcin didn't know what to say. He thought and then thought again. 'It's not a complicated question,' Tommy said. 'I don't really care.'

'I kind of know her. I've met her before.'

'Fine thing.'

'Yeah.'

'She looks like she'd be a bit of fun. You should start saving up. It'd be money well spent.' It took Marcin a second to work out what he meant.

43

In Prague it was all business in the buildings during the day, looking at plans and asking questions that Marek answered with confidence. Sylvester stood back and let him do his work. They talked to architects and builders, then into the car off to a meeting in the bar at the Four Seasons with some planning official who told them exciting, surreptitious things they shouldn't know, but friends of Mr Soldán were entitled to a little extra. Marek sat smiling at the show he was delivering. They were all smiling now, moving silently towards an understanding that things were going to happen.

But at night it was tiresome. Sylvester could do it. Deliver the spiel, stay on message, ask the questions. He could listen to the long, shapeless answers that only ever communicated the speaker's desire to be heard. He could slap the backs, laugh the laughs, tell the jokes and talk about money in the right kind of terms with knowledge and detail but, above all, with respect. He pitched his tone right for the laddish vibe, the steak and potatoes in deep-pile restaurants with curtains that swooped and glass that sparkled and waiters that sneered.

More booze than anyone could handle. The loudest table everywhere they went. Would you do that at home? Sylvester wondered, as he watched one of them hop a bread roll off Breen's head in the best restaurant in Prague. But that was hardly the point. They were away. Into the limos after this and off for some fun. God, it was tedious.

When his energy dipped, when he realized that the night was still young and hours would pass before he'd get to bed, his frustration sought a target and found Dessie. Damn him for not coming. It wasn't just that the workload would have been cut by his presence. Sylvester missed the note he brought to these evenings, the laconic ego-deflating punch lines that somehow never caused offence but kept everybody in their boxes, defining the borders of acceptable behaviour. Little foul-mouthed bursts of sarcasm that were distributed evenly and were accepted with pleasure by the multitude. No smile on his face, just a tremor in his hand that communicated his enjoyment as he brought a small glass of brown liquid to his lips. He was like a goat among cattle, irascible and curmudgeonly, quick to move on any bit of nonsense, but there for the good of the party and appreciated for it. Sylvester didn't know how much he made in tips from these expeditions but it was well earned.

Without him a wildness was developing in the group, and no one to keep a lid on it. Sylvester should have taken on the role. He was sober. Oh, how sober he was. How he would have loved right now to whistle down a waiter and get a bottle of vodka and a shot glass. Knock them back. One. Two. Three. Even by then he'd be in improved form, more relaxed, a willing participant in this journey to carnage, one of the boys, loose and easy, ready for the club and the honey-coloured girls who would bend and stretch and spread. But he knew it wouldn't stop there, that he would keep on going through fun and bravado into bitterness, aggression and mess. He could blow it all. End up anywhere. Better not. Better to stop now, no matter what it cost him.

And what had it cost him? On the plane home two days later he thought of all that he had seen and had to close his eyes. Everything was on the tab and he signed at the end of each evening, in restaurants and bars and strip clubs, handing over his card as quickly as he could before he had time to think. The limo company, first-class train tickets to Bratislava and back again, hotel rooms, bottles of wine ordered and never drunk. Single malts slopped down the back of couches.

How close were they now to the end of it all? How much money was there left in the account? It looked healthy enough. If Helen saw the statements she wouldn't be worried. But he was. He knew what was going out and what was coming in and the gap between the two. The thousands that had been spent in the past few days on the basis of what? A reasonable prospect? The heads on these guys, who nodded seriously when they heard the presentation of projected figures and growth rates? Yes, they'd seemed keen. And as the days had passed they seemed to have arrived at a point where agreement had been reached. But it was an unspoken promise and what value was there in that?

The man next to him, Gerry Something, damp hair on the back of his neck, jacket folded across his big lap, pointed out of the window with a meaty finger. 'There's Lambay,' he said. 'Everything stops there. Not a word to the womenfolk, what?' He laughed uproariously. They had been drinking at lunch, in the airport and on the plane.

'Yes, indeed,' Sylvester said.

'Paddy,' Gerry called, turning in his seat. 'Hi, Paddy,' he shouted. He pointed out the window. 'Lambay rules. Nothing happened. Understood?' Roars of laughter from behind them. Sylvester had no idea what he was talking about.

He could sit down with Helen and, in the course of an hour, explain the situation. That it was a solid idea, that he and Marek had given it a very professional go. But unless this crowd came on board, they would need to borrow more within a few months. Did they want to? Was there any point? Weighing it all up, did it make sense?

This was not a conversation he would have. It was better for all of them that she go on not knowing for certain. That they all go on pretending and not asking questions, believing that if you looked the part and acted as though everything was all right, it would be. Because there was a chance, Sylvester thought, that that just might be true. That the key to surviving the tricky parts of life might be nothing more than a willingness to do a good impression of people surviving the tricky parts of life. This could come good for them. These braying half-wits, sweating out overpriced beers and whiskey that Sylvester had paid for, might be his salvation. He would say nothing to her for the moment.

Around him there was a cheer as the plane touched down.

'We made it,' Gerry said, with a laugh that turned into a coughing fit. Sylvester smiled and felt a glow of affection for the old dope.

44

In bed with Agnieszka early in the morning of a day off, Victor held her from behind and, in a state somewhere between waking and sleep, he talked. It was his vision for the future and she laughed at what he said, not sure if he was serious or joking.

In the northern suburbs of Bucharest, behind gates in a villa that sparkled, bigger than anything that existed in Dublin, they lived a quiet, comfortable life. White stairs and black marble. Plants and light. Polished floors and space. There was a girl, stuck at the age of two or thereabouts. No difficult early days, no vision of where she had come from. He couldn't imagine a face but he could get the mood, the feeling of happiness, solidity and respectability. There was Agnieszka spending her days doing whatever she wanted. There were staff to clean and cook for them, to mind the child, to wash clothes and iron. His mother would be there. He would work and come home in the evenings, and at the weekends they would do things with their baby and he and Agnieszka would go to restaurants and clubs. That would be enough for them. He didn't want to travel the world or to keep on building the business, growing just for the sake of it. Get to this point and that would be enough. They would be happy.

He came to the end and waited for her to say something but she didn't speak. She was lying very still. He thought she might have drifted off and sat up to check. Her eyes were open. 'Are you all right?' She didn't answer. 'Agnieszka?'

'I'm fine,' she said.

'I'm just talking,' he said. 'I don't mean anything.'

'I know,' she said, and smiled for a moment, but he could see that she was gone.

Something would always bring her back. Standing in a lift with a guy who looked familiar and then hearing his surname. She knew his cousin well, had hung around with her in the summer after third year, a pretty fox-faced girl who even then was ready to get beyond their town into something bigger. When bigger seemed better rather than just more of the same. This boy standing on the street, looking at her the way all those young fellows used to. Not hostile or horny or unmannerly. Just as if she was something that had to be looked at. As if the act of watching her satisfied something quiet, natural and private within them. It was not something she had ever wanted.

She had come this far with a past she had rewritten and a present that had been going fine but seemed to have taken a wrong turn and was leading her now into a future she didn't want. Things that should have been simple always became complicated. If that Marcin fellow, slow-moving and smiley, maybe stupid, said the wrong thing to the wrong person, would it make any difference? Did he even know anything? There were things she had to worry about and he was not one of them.

Stay on top of it. She could get this back again. Get the money sent. Get some more together, then go and get Jakub and move with him as far away as possible. Somewhere new that, with him, might be different. Get the money and make the move.

She listened to Victor when he talked about Romania. The house in the suburbs like a palace. His mother knocking around the place. Victor looking after them all. Could she go there with Jakub? Was that something Victor could handle? The vision he had might even be improved with this new consideration. They could all be there together. There could be love and happiness and a normal life, safe and protected and a long way from anything bad. If she thought about it hard enough, put everything else to the side, she could see it for a moment, everything the way it should be. But it was a bubble, beautiful and shining, floating beside her, and at any moment, with a tiny damp noise like a kiss, it would disappear.

45

They drank in a bar down a side-street under a railway bridge. The television was tuned into a news channel, stories quietly ticking away on the bottom of the screen, giving the impression that something was happening. There was a smell of toast. The owner was an old man, drinking tea from a mug and talking about racing with a couple of postmen at the counter. A few people here and there, starting and continuing their drinking, no one stopping. But it was civilized. If it hadn't been for the angle of the light shafting in through the window, the raw overexposure of the early day, it could have been any pub on any afternoon.

The two of them sat at the bar and the owner came over.

'Tommy.'

'Ned.'

'How're things?'

'Not so bad. George was asking for you.'

The man laughed. 'Is that a fact?'

'Have you any message for him?' Tommy asked. 'Can I give him some news? Tell him something?'

'Not a thing.'

'Ah, Ned. It was months ago. He's sorry. He's not drinking the same way now.'

'A new man, is he? Changed?'

Tommy smiled. 'Within reason. He's fucking sick of the other place. State of it. He's been scared straight.'

'I can't do it, Tommy. I'm not going to lose my licence over him. He could kill someone next time.'

'George isn't going to kill anyone.'

'That's it,' the man said, his voice hardened suddenly. Marcin looked up. 'End of story. Now what do you want?'

They ordered.

'It's a tight shop,' Tommy said.

'A what?' Marcin asked.

Tommy sighed. 'Your man. He takes no shit.'

'What's he saying about George?'

'George is a bad drunk.'

'Bad how?'

'Messy.' There was a pause. 'Here, you're not going to get me put out of this place, are you? One too many vodkas, you're not going to start fucking talking?'

'No,' Marcin said. 'I drink quietly.'

'Good man.'

So they drank in silence.

It was after eleven when they moved on to a rougher place. A hard-core group at the bar nodded at Tommy and stared at Marcin.

'Who's this man?' one of them sitting at the counter asked, drunk. They were all drunk.

'Fellow I work with.'

'Where are you from?'

'Poland,' Marcin said.

'Polish, is it?'

'Leave it,' Tommy said. 'He's all right.'

'I wasn't talking to you, Tommy.' He pushed himself up off the bar and looked like he might stand up. The barman walked over. Thinning hair, thick glasses that made his eyes look big.

'Settle down.'

'We'll go upstairs,' Tommy said. Up into a room with another bar and a pool table. Local guys in T-shirts and track-suits, smoking dope, drinking cans and playing pool. People coming and going with bags of stuff. Kids mostly. DVDs and iPods and phones. Porn. Cartons of cigarettes. Every minute or two voices would be raised and it sounded like something was going to happen but every time they faded back down into background noise. Bursts of laughter that made Marcin jump. The two of them played together against two young guys, skinny, wiry, hard.

'You know it's fifty a game,' one of them said to Tommy, a couple of shots in.

'Do you think it's my first time here?' Tommy said.

'It is for your man, I'd say.'

They lost on the black. Marcin gave Tommy twenty-five and they handed it over.

'Double or nothing, you and me,' one of the guys said.

'Em,' Marcin said, turning to Tommy. But he had gone to the bar, talking to the others who were doing some kind of business at the counter. 'Okay.' Is Tommy in on this? Marcin wondered. Is it all a plan to take my money or to beat me or kill me or something? For some reason the fear helped his game. The room went quiet when he got on to the black, and some of them laughed and clapped when the ball went down and he won. He looked at his opponent with no idea of what would happen next. The guy fumbled in his pocket and pulled out a bundle of notes. He peeled off two and dropped them on the table with bravado.

'All right?' he said, and he walked away. Marcin went up to Tommy.

'Nice one,' Tommy said. 'Do I get my money back?' Marcin handed him a fifty.

'The twenty-five will do.'

'I have to get out of here now,' Marcin said.

'One more,' Tommy said.

At midday they drank in a normal bar, propped in upright armchairs in a room of carpets and chintz, among tables of office workers eating toasted sandwiches and soup, drinking tea. Marcin knew that he and Tommy weren't in good shape. The barman stood nearby, watching them.

'I won fifty quid,' Marcin said, suddenly feeling a bit better. 'We should celebrate.'

They finished their drinks and went into a supermarket. They bought vodka and apple juice and got a taxi back to Tommy's flat in a part of town that Marcin didn't know. It was bigger than his bedsit but not much. Messier, but not a happy mess. In the living room there was an armchair and a couch, an ironing-board set up in front of the TV. A clothes-horse with rows of black socks hanging like bats. There was a separate bedroom with a single bed and no window. Behind the kitchen counter beside the sink empty vodka bottles and cans were piled up. Cheap vodka. Cheap beer. Cigarette packets and four dirty ashtrays from the hotel. The carpet was murky and the air was stale, the bin beginning to smell in the heat of the sun. Marcin pissed in the toilet without closing the door because the light was gone. There was a packet of disposable razors on the floor of the shower, a bottle of medi-cated shampoo. The towel he dried his hands on was damp.

When he came out Tommy had turned on the TV and taken down the ironing-board. He rinsed two glasses and sat at the table, filled both glasses with vodka, picked one up, clinked it off the other and downed it in one before Marcin had lifted his. He filled his glass again.

'Hey, hang on,' Marcin said. 'We're supposed to be cele-brating. We should have a toast.'

'To what?'

'To my victory. To my hundred euro.'

'Cheers,' Tommy said. 'Have you any of it left?'

'About ten, fifteen, maybe.' That seemed funny to him then and he laughed.

There were ugly people on the television sitting in a studio talking in an accent Marcin couldn't understand. He was maybe falling asleep.

'Do you know what you should do?' he said, waking up a bit, but drunker now, forgetting what he had known earlier on. Some time may have passed but Tommy was still in the armchair staring at the TV. 'You should put up some pictures. Of your kids or something. This place is okay but, you know, it doesn't feel like you live here.'

Tommy turned and looked at him. 'Do you think that pictures of my kids would make it any better? Seriously, is that what you think? I'm not staying here. It's just until I get sorted out. But, you know, with her fucking scourging me . . .' He stood up now, agitated. 'Do you think I like this? What am I supposed to do about it? It wasn't my fault. It's not easy. You know what I mean?'

Marcin nodded. 'I know,' he said, 'I didn't mean anything bad.'

'It'd take more than pictures,' Tommy said, and sat down again. They went back to watching telly in silence.

When he woke the next time, he was in pain. He saw that it was five o'clock. Tommy was asleep in the chair, his head fallen back and his mouth open. The bottle was empty on the floor beside him. If Marcin got home quickly he might be able to get another couple of hours' sleep before he had to go back in. He thought about waking Tommy, directing him to his bed, but in the end he just left, pulling the door behind him, out into the sunshine and the warmth of the other end of the day, into the middle of the road to stop a taxi.

46

In a graveyard beside a small church with a view of a valley between two mountains Anne's mother was buried. The sky was blue and the harsh sun, almost directly above them at eleven o'clock in the morning, made the graves and pathways seem scrubby and neglected. The air was still and hot. The priest had to shout to be heard above the noise of traffic on the motorway, unseen and half a mile away. Dessie stood at the edge of the grave at Anne's side holding her hand, Yvonne on her other side. Beyond them were an endless number of sisters and brothers-in-law, nieces and nephews and cousins. Old and young. People he didn't like and who didn't like him. Relatives he was sure he'd never met but who still took offence when he didn't know them. There were a few neighbours and five or six women that Anne had worked with before she'd had Yvonne. Saw it in the paper, maybe. There were none of his ex-colleagues or his extended family, but he wouldn't have expected them. Not so much the type to read obituaries as to feature in them.

The prayers went on and on. Call and response. They weren't short enough to ignore or long enough to get lost in. Across the graveyard, standing at a respectable distance, was Sylvester in a dark suit. Dessie had not seen him since he got back. He seemed to have picked up a tan while in Prague. Helen was beside him, looking at the ground and moving her lips to the Hail Marys. He hadn't seen her out in the world for a long time. She appeared older than Sylvester, not much but enough for her to know it. She was pretty in a motherly way that put limits on Dessie's imagination. In general he was glad of this.

When the prayers were finished and Anne was talking to neighbours he walked over to the two of them.

'Good of you to come, Helen,' he said, shaking her hand.

She leaned in and kissed his cheek. An expensive kind of smell off her. 'Of course, Dessie,' she said. 'I'm very sorry.'

'Thank you.'

'Dessie,' Sylvester said. 'I'm sorry.'

'Thanks.'

'How is she?'

'She's all right. I think she'd got used to the idea but still, you know . . . It's her mother.'

'Of course.'

They stood in silence for a moment.

'Good thing I didn't go in the end,' Dessie said then.

'Yes,' Sylvester said. 'It was the right decision.'

'Of course,' Helen said. 'It could have been very difficult.'

'How did you get on anyway?'

'Oh, great. No problems. They enjoyed it. I think they're on board. We'll talk about it again.'

'Yeah. I suppose a funeral's not the time to have that conversation.' He smiled a little grimly and the two of them did the same back.

'Right. I'd better get over to her.'

'Can we just say hello?'

'Yes. Please. Come on.' They walked over together and stood beside her until she was free.

'Anne,' Dessie said, 'I don't think you've met Sylvester's wife. This is Helen.'

'I'm very sorry, Anne. It's a pity to meet in such sad circumstances.'

'Thank you.'

'Anne,' Sylvester said. He held her hand for a moment. 'I'm sorry.' He leaned in close to her and said something Dessie couldn't hear.

'Will you come back to the house?' Dessie asked Helen.

'Yes. Certainly. We won't stay long, though.'

'You'd be welcome,' Dessie said. He watched Anne, who was looking at Sylvester now and nodding. She was smiling at him and both his hands were in hers. Sylvester stepped away and was red-eyed when Dessie spoke to him a second later. 'You're coming to the house, I believe.'

'Are we?'

'You are.'

'Very good,' Sylvester said. He moved a step closer to Dessie and looked around for a moment, then spoke into his ear. 'I know the timing's bad and all, but if you have a moment do you think you could sort out tonight for me?'

'Tonight?'

'It's Wednesday.'

'Oh, right,' Dessie said. 'Yeah. No problem.'

'I hate asking but it's just . . . You know.'

'Yeah.'

Sylvester leaned in. 'Same girl as last time.'

Dessie looked at him. He'd never asked for this before. 'Really?'

'If you can.'

He shrugged. 'I'm sure it's fine. Look, I'd better go on.'

'Thanks, Dessie. We'll see you in a little while.'

In the car on the way back they were talking about who had been there. Yvonne was on the phone to friends of hers who were organizing food and tea and drinks.

'What did Sylvester say to you?' Dessie asked Anne.

'He was very kind. Just very nice and genuine. He said

he was sorry and talked about his own mother's death and the effect it had on him. He was honest, I think. And he said nice things about you.'

'About me?'

'Yes. Are you surprised?'

Dessie smiled to himself. 'Maybe a bit.'

'I was, too,' she said.

47

Quiet night. There were two of them. They looked like the right sort of people for the place, dressed well. Maybe a little too flashy. Victor thought they might be foreign when he saw them at first, could even be Romanian, but when he heard them speaking he realized they were Irish. Some deep part of the country that made it hard for him to understand what they were saying. He had been off having tea and when he came back they were talking with Gareth, who was telling them, not for the first time, that he couldn't let them in, they'd had too much. Victor wouldn't have let them in either. He could see they'd been drinking but it wasn't that. He'd let drunker people than these in before. There was something about them that was wrong. Something unnatural in the way they stood close beside each other, each looking in a slightly different direction as if they were waiting for an opportunity.

But maybe Gareth didn't see it. He chatted with them back and forth, not enough edge that you could even call it banter. Victor stood beside him and tried to smile blankly. No problem. But after five minutes it was getting irritating. They were in the way of other people coming and going. He wished they'd move on. They weren't going to get in. He couldn't see why Gareth was letting it drag on.

'Lads,' Victor said, interrupting one of them mid-flow, 'maybe you should try somewhere else because this isn't going to happen for you here tonight.'

'Oh,' one of them said. 'Oh, now.' Victor listened for aggression in the guy's voice but what he heard sounded more like disappointment.

'We're only having a bit of a laugh,' the other said. 'Do you think we're still here because we're trying to get in? There are a hundred places that would be glad to have us. Delighted to see us and take our money. They know us all over town. They know how much we'll spend. Look.' He produced a wallet with a wad of fifties an inch thick from his pocket and flipped through it in front of Victor. It looked like a couple of thousand.

'So take it somewhere else. You won't be spending it here,' Victor said.

'We weren't even talking to you,' the other one said.

'We're just messing around with our old buddy Gareth and you come along and start getting aggressive.'

Victor looked at Gareth, who shrugged in a way that he didn't understand. 'I'm not being aggressive. I'm just asking you to move along now.'

'Yeah,' Gareth said at last. 'We'd better call it a night. Sure places will be closing in an hour. If you want to get in anywhere you'll need to make a move.'

'We've no problem with you, Gareth. We'll be going anyway. You're sound, but this guy's being a prick and that's not right. He's no right to talk to us the way he did.'

'I'm doing a job,' Victor said. 'I don't need to hear your opinion.' It was a line that some of the others used. This guy was annoying him now. The wounded tone. The fact that the accusation was against him. And what was wrong with Gareth tonight? If you let people stay at the door chatting it always went wrong.

'It's your kind of attitude that makes people hate bouncers,' the guy said now. 'Treating people like they're shit. On some sort of power trip as if you're God almighty when at the end of the day you're just a fucking scumbag acting tough with a whole gang of people to back you up. The big man.'

'Walk away now,' Victor said.

'Or what? Or what?' He stood close to Victor's face, his breath sweet and boozy. Victor chewed gum and looked into the middle distance but he could see everything that this man was doing. 'What are you going to do? Are you going to assault me? I'd break you in half if it was just you and me in a fair fight.'

'Would you?' Victor said, turning slightly. There was a whooshing in his ears and things were suddenly jerky.

'I would, yeah.'

'Well, why don't you, then?' Victor waited for a moment. Looked the guy in the eye, and when he moved, Victor grabbed him by the throat and lifted him across the street. His feet barely touched the ground as they moved. Victor slammed him into the wall and noticed how the back of his head bounced off it. Then pulled him back and did it again.

'Now,' Victor said, 'it's just you and me here. What are you going to do?' He had him pinned, his arm pressed across the man's throat, holding on to the shoulder of his jacket. His face was red and getting darker every second. He tried to break free but Victor wasn't even straining. He could hear shouting around him but all he was looking at was this guy's face, waiting for him to say something else. He flapped at Victor's face and Victor clattered him once on the side of the head. 'Don't fucking make me hurt you,' he said.

'Let me breathe,' the guy said, his voice choked.

'I'm going to let you go now but if you try anything I'll break your face. Okay?'

'I can't breathe. Please.' Victor took his arm away and the man bent in half, hands on his knees. Victor walked back over. The other guy was being held by two of the others.

'Go inside,' Gareth said.

'There's no problem.'

'Just go downstairs.'

Victor went to the staff room and made a cup of tea. He sat letting it brew and feeling his heart begin to slow down.

Gareth came in five minutes later and sat beside him. He lit a cigarette. 'What was that about?'

'Did you not see?' Victor said. 'Did you not hear what that guy said to me?'

'I did. I did. But that's not like you.'

'Why were you letting them stay there? Why did you not tell them to move on?'

'Because I thought they were okay. They were just messing around. Pissed, but they were no problem. It's a quiet night. They weren't doing any harm.'

'It always ends the same way if you let people do that,' Victor said.

'There was no problem, Victor, until you came along.'

'What?'

'Well, there wasn't.'

'Are you blaming me for that? That guy was shouting in my face and he made a move –'

'He didn't make a move. He was shitting himself. Did you see the size of him?'

'He was bigger than me.'

'He was taller than you. But you lifted him like he was a child.'

Neither of them said anything for a minute. The smell of the fruity tea with Gareth's cigarette was like autumn.

'I'm not blaming you. I'm just surprised. You never do that sort of thing.'

'He annoyed me. I thought he was going to do something. I didn't like those two. He could have had a knife. I got that feeling.'

'I didn't think so. It doesn't matter anyway.'

'Are they gone?'

'Yeah.'

'Will there be a problem?'

'I don't think so. We can sort it out. Are you all right, though?'

'I'm fine.'

Gareth looked at his watch. 'Do you want to head on?'

'Yeah,' Victor said. 'I wouldn't mind.'

'Are you in tomorrow?'

'I'm off.'

'Well, have a good day. I'll see you over the weekend.' Gareth left.

Victor finished his drink and went back upstairs. His body was stiffening already. He would have a bath when he got home. Lie in it for an hour. As he walked out one of the other doormen, just newly started, smiled at him. 'You fucked that guy up,' he said. 'That was pretty sweet. Three seconds and it was over. That's the way to do it.'

'Yeah,' Victor said. 'Little bastard.'

48

All he wanted to do was lie down and sleep. Wake up some-where far from anywhere and start again. He was plausible. Good clothes and a nice voice. He could work anywhere as a person. As an idea. He could change his name to some-thing easy and unremarkable and disappear into the middle of America. The Pacific Northwest. Alaska. Arizona. Coffee and orange juice in a bright kitchen with somebody else.

But there was nobody else. The problem wasn't her or them. It was all of it. It came easy most of the time but when he had to think and try, it cost him too much. Ten minutes in the back of the taxi with his eyes closed, counting down from a hundred, remembering to breathe. Trying to ignore the background noise.

'Go on, you cunt. Move.'

'Hey. Come on.'

'This prick fucking up my arse for the last ten minutes,' the driver said, 'and now look at him . . .'

'I know. It's a terrible thing. But please. Can you keep it down?'

'You're like some bleeding . . . I don't know what . . . Buddhist. Eyes closed and all. Are you a Buddhist?'

He would be happy when Dessie came back.

He was having dinner with the family that night, meeting them at the golf club at seven. He had to get out from town and he could feel the compromise and frustration of the evening already. She was right to do it. It was to celebrate the deal, which she had been told would happen. What was his problem? He would start carrying it with him in his shoulders soon. The stoop, the mild slump of a man beaten down by reality. That could be him. No future for that guy in America.

She must have felt it, must have seen how they all were when they were together. Stiff and quiet and every one of them wishing they were somewhere else. Daniel was past the worst of it now, the contempt moving into a purer kind of boredom that was bearable. Jessica had always been easier. Less posturing. Younger and brighter, more comfortable. Or that was what she conveyed to him. An impression of confidence and self-containment. His semi-detached daughter. How much did he really know? When was the last time he'd talked to her? Or to Daniel? Or even Helen?

There were things now that had never been there before and things that were gone. They might come back but probably not. Helen had done a lot for him, bailed him out and stayed when other women might have gone. He owed her for that and he was providing a standard of living for her and them in unspoken payment of this debt. But her sticking with him wasn't entirely selfless. He knew that. She was invested in the prospect that was Sylvester Kelly. So when he was at his lowest point, getting him fixed wasn't just an act of mercy. Like a trainer with a horse lying on the ground she had had to make an assessment. There was still something left that might one day pay off. A vision of the cripple romping home. Put away the gun. There's life in him yet.

He arrived before the others and sat at the bar counter with a menu drinking 7Up. He knew a lot of these people. John, the manager, dressed in black tie because the members liked it – they'd voted on it. He stopped beside Sylvester, leaned in without looking at him and spoke. 'Lovely bit of beef now today,' he said, as if it was a racing tip.

'Is it?'

John threw his head back and blew out. 'Beautiful, beautiful,' and he was gone.

The others arrived together, walking into the room as

he had imagined them, but there was something else. 'Everything all right?' he asked.

'Fine.' She touched her cheek off his. 'Here long?'

'Ten minutes.'

He went to kiss Jessica, put his hand on her shoulder and could feel her stiffen and move sideways away from him. 'You okay?'

'Yeah.'

'And you?' He looked at Daniel, took a step towards him and stopped.

'It'll cost you,' Daniel said, and Sylvester laughed, a black pain jangling at the bottom of his stomach.

They sat at a good table, big and round and near the window, where they could see everything inside and out. The sky was grey and pink and a darkening blue. There was a haze over the water and a few yachts out.

'The beef apparently,' Sylvester said, when they were given menus.

'It was like it had walked from Brazil last time,' Helen said.

'Lean?'

'Tough.'

'It would have to swim from Brazil,' Daniel said.

'Do cows swim?'

'Yes,' Jessica said. 'I've seen them.'

'But not . . .' Sylvester paused '. . . professionally.'

'Professionally?'

'That's not the word. Proficiently.' The others laughed at him. 'The day I've had,' he said. 'I need food.'

During the first course Sylvester spotted David O'Donnell across the room. It wasn't a surprise to see him. This was his world. The land to the north, the housing estates and the new shopping centres around the motorways. He was at a table with a group of six young people, men and women, dressed up and at the court of the big man, laughing at his jokes and performing for him when they spoke. He thought about going over but it seemed like a bad idea.

Later on, though, when he felt a big damp hand on his shoulder he knew who it was.

'How are things?' Sylvester turned, did a phoney double-take and stood up, smiling.

'Mr O'Donnell.'

He was standing with his shirt sleeves rolled up, collar open one button too far. Sylvester came up to his chin. A big man with a lot of presence. If he had needed to fight for everything he had achieved in life – physically to overcome his opponents – it would have been easy for him, Sylvester thought. The idea must have occurred to others.

'Mr Kelly.'

'Good to see you,' Sylvester said. 'Out with friends?'

'Friends, yeah. I've lots of friends.' He laughed a growly laugh that he was obviously happy with. On to his second bottle, Sylvester thought. 'Out with the family?' O'Donnell said. 'Helen. How are things?'

'Hello, David.'

'Haven't seen you in a long time.'

'No, indeed,' she said. 'Quite a while.'

'You look well.'

'Thank you.'

'Too good for the likes of this fellow.' She raised her eyebrows and flashed a tight smile.

'I don't think you've met my children,' Sylvester said.

'Children,' O'Donnell said. 'These are hardly children. Young man. Young lady. Nice to meet you.'

They both grinned up at him.

'Is there an occasion?'

'Not really,' Sylvester said. 'Just a chance to get out.'

'Dessie not with you?'

'No. He's on a break. More a family thing.'

'That fellow should be promoted to family member. Make him an uncle or something.'

'I met someone who knows you,' Sylvester said, changing the subject and taking a step away from the table. The others watched for a moment, then, realizing this was not for them, got back to their meals.

'Oh, yes?'

'He spoke very highly of you.'

'A rare breed,' O'Donnell said. 'Who was that, then?'

'A business colleague. Paddy Breen.'

'Who?'

'Paddy Breen?' Sylvester heard the uncertainty in his own voice as his face began to glow.

'Never heard of him. I should meet him, though, if he's such a fan. Who is he? How do you know him?'

'He's involved in some racing syndicate. They're putting a bit of business my way. He said he knew you. Or he'd met you anyway.'

'You know yourself, Sylvester, I meet a lot of people every day and I remember most of them but some slip through. The name means nothing to me but it could have been late at night somewhere. I don't know.'

'Sure. It could be anything. The number of people around you, I'm surprised you remember anyone.'

'Ah, you have to. In my thing. That's what it's all about. For you as well.'

'And who are you with tonight?' Sylvester said, moving the conversation ahead.

'New staff for a sales office in the west. Bonding over a few pints or bottles or whatever they're having. Telling them they're wonderful.'

'And are they?'

'They're all right. Good form tonight anyway, but then why wouldn't they be?'

'I'd better let you get back to them.'

'I'll see you, Sylvester. Sure we'll catch up again. Stay in touch.'

'I will indeed.'

'Delighted to meet you, young people,' he said towards the table. 'Good to see you, Helen.' The three of them smiled politely and nodded as he left.

'It would be nice,' Helen said, as Sylvester sat down, 'if we could go somewhere without you abandoning us for half the evening.'

'What are you talking about? I was sitting there. He came over to me. Put his hand on me. What was I supposed to do? Ignore him?'

'Who was that?' Daniel asked.

'David O'Donnell.'

'Who is he?'

'He's a builder,' Helen said. 'I'm surprised he came over. He sees more of you than I do.'

Sylvester looked at her and she looked back. 'When things settle down I'll be around a lot more. You do know that, don't you? I'm not meeting all these people for fun. It's for you. For all of us.' Her expression didn't change. 'I'm serious,' he said.

'I know you are,' she said, and touched his hand, then looked over her shoulder for a waiter to clear the table.

49

Marcin had intended to go straight home after work but there was a group checking out at six and by the time the porters had everything down and loaded on to the bus, and the tour operator had herded the people into one place so she could count them, the heat of the day was already enough to make them sweat. Then there was a big tip to be divided among them, so going with the others had seemed like the only option. They got stuck in.

At some point in the pub his phone rang. When he saw that it was Artur, he put the mobile in his pocket and tried to ignore it as it pulsed against his thigh. But later, on his way home, when he listened to the message he felt bad. Artur sounded friendly, normal: 'Just looking to meet up some time. Give me a ring when you get a chance. Hope you're well. Yeah. 'Bye.' Marcin sent a text. 'It's been too long. Meet you tonight?' and that was it.

It was after three when he got home. He set an alarm for seven and left it as far from his bed as possible because he did not want to be late this time. He was fearful of how he would feel when he woke but in fact he was all right. Woozy, but a shower helped. He arrived into the pub five minutes early and was on his second drink by the time Artur arrived.

'Good to see you,' Marcin said.

'And you.' Artur looked him over. 'You're fading away. Have you stopped eating?'

'I eat enough. It's just the work and the hours. Sometimes I forget meals, I suppose.'

'You need to take care of yourself.'

'I do. I know. I do.'

'Have you been here for a while?'

'No. I just arrived. I didn't get much sleep.'

Artur sat. They ordered drinks.

'So, what's new?' Marcin asked.

'Not much. Work is fine. I'm going out with a girl.'

'The same one?'

'No. Someone else. An Irish one. I met her at my boss's wedding.'

'Great. What was the other one's name?'

'Who? Katja?'

'That was it.'

'Yeah, well, she's gone now.'

'Right. And are you seeing someone else?'

Artur looked at him.

'What?' Marcin said.

'You're hammered.'

'I'm not. I'm fine. I've had three drinks.'

'You've had considerably more than three drinks.'

'I'm tired, okay? I'm always tired. Forgive me if I don't hold on to every little detail in a way that you'd like.'

'It's hard to have a conversation with someone whose short-term memory is absent. What did I tell you about this girl I'm seeing?'

Marcin stared at him. 'I don't know. Start again.'

'I'm seeing an Irish girl. I met her at my boss's wedding.'

'Okay. I remember that. Great. I'm happy for you.'

'Thanks.' The barman walked by. He stopped and looked at Marcin, then at Artur. He nodded and went on.

'We're moving in together,' Artur said.

'That was quick.'

'Yeah, well, she was moving anyway and I wanted to get out of where I am.'

'You're leaving the boys?'

'I am,' Artur said, smiling.

'How will they survive?'

'They'll manage. Although they'll miss your visits.'

'Yeah. Me too.' Marcin was feeling better now. Another wave of energy from somewhere.

'So that's what I'm doing. Working and looking for a new place and hanging around with her.'

'Nice girl?'

'She is, yeah.'

'Excellent.'

'How about you?'

'Nobody special. There was a girl in the pub at lunchtime today who laughed at something I said, but apart from that, nothing really.'

'Still on nights?'

'Yes. Still on nights. I'm going to quit soon, though, when I get a bit of money together. Enough to take a break for a bit.'

'Right. You should.'

'I know I should,' Marcin said. 'That's why I'm doing it.' Silence fell between them. 'Do you know who I met?' he said then.

'Who?'

'Agnieszka Nowakowska.' As soon as he had said her name it felt like a mistake. His hand touched his mouth as if it was trying to put the words back in. Artur didn't notice.

'No way. Where? In Dublin?'

'Yeah. On the street.'

'Fucking hell. Whatever happened to her? She just disappeared halfway through sixth year.'

'I know.'

'I thought she might be dead. Does she look the same?'

'More or less.'

Artur laughed out of sheer exuberance, the happiness of

something good in the world. 'What a girl she was. Jesus. And what's she been doing? What's she doing here?'

Marcin felt the wrench. What had he expected? It was stupid to have said anything, impossible to unsay it now. He could stop, though. 'I don't know. I just saw her.'

'You said you met her.'

'Okay, I didn't actually meet her. But I think it was her I saw. It was hard to tell.'

Artur's face was pink at the edges as if he was holding his breath. 'So you didn't meet her. And you're saying now that it might not even have been her?'

Marcin shrugged. 'Maybe. Maybe not.'

'That's a pretty shit story.' He stared at Marcin as if he was guilty of some great crime that Artur could not begin to understand.

'What's wrong with you?' Marcin said.

'What's wrong with me? What's wrong with me? Nothing. I'm fine. But I'm worried about you.'

'Don't be.'

'I am.'

'Why? Because I thought I saw Agnieszka?'

Artur sighed. 'No. Not that. But I have to tell you . . .'

Marcin waited, not wanting to hear. 'What?' he said at last.

'The state of you. You're not in good shape. You need to do something about it. Get out of that job and do something else.'

'I'm doing that anyway. You don't have to keep telling me.'

'You said that weeks ago. And still you haven't.'

'You're very good at knowing what I should do with my life. Giving me instructions. Have you noticed that I don't do the same to you?'

'But I hope you would if things were going badly for me.'

Marcin felt lost. There was nothing for him to say, no smart

206

comeback that would make this seem better. He was too tired for any of it. To listen or argue or defend or fight. To have to think. He'd had enough of it.

'You worry too much,' he said, and stood up, stumbling as he got off the stool but steadying himself quickly. He walked straight out, thinking that Artur perhaps might come after him, out into the sticky evening and the blurred jangle of colour that was the summer street, but he didn't.

50

They were supposed to meet after work on the Thursday but she rang that afternoon saying she was feeling sick and going home early to bed. Victor asked if he should come over, if he could bring her anything after work, but she said she'd be asleep and that was all she needed.

She met him for a coffee in town when he had a break on the Saturday evening. She seemed all right, maybe a bit washed-out but in good form. They arranged that they would meet the following night and spend all of Monday together because they were both off. But then he got a text message saying she had been called in because someone else was sick and she needed the hours. She said she'd come over on the Monday morning.

He came into town for no real reason and dropped in to his work. Things were quiet. He chatted with some of the guys there and thought he'd go for a coffee. He headed for a place he liked, then realized that Symposium was just around the corner. Had he known he was going to do this? He didn't think so but here he was, on a Sunday evening, alone in town.

Three of the Albanians were on the door.

'The Italian,' the biggest of them said, when he saw Victor. 'Agnieszka's Italian boyfriend. Where is it you're from again? Bucharest? Transylvania, is it? Dracula the Italian.' They laughed among themselves.

'I wouldn't be telling anyone about it if I was Albanian,' Victor said.

'We're proud of it, though. That's the difference between us and you. Fucking "Italians".'

'Is she here?' Victor asked, taking things down. He wasn't sure if this was just slagging.

'I haven't seen her.'

'If I'd a girl like that I wouldn't let her out of my sight,' the big guy said, smiling.

'Yeah, well, over here you're not allowed to keep women in cages. Where do you think this is?'

They called after him as he walked inside in a language he didn't understand but he knew what they were saying.

He looked to see if Agnieszka was behind the counter, but there was no sign of her. One of the girls came over to him as he stood at the bar.

'Is Agnieszka here?'

'Sorry?'

'Agnieszka?'

'No, she's off.'

'Is she?'

'I can check but I haven't seen her.' She went down to the end of the bar and disappeared through a door. A minute later she came out, followed by a short, bald man.

'Are you Victor?'

'Yeah.'

'I'm Gavin. Agnieszka's told me about you.'

'She's told me about you as well.'

'How are you?'

'I'm all right,' Victor said.

'Listen, she's not here tonight. She was supposed to be but Mr White called earlier and said she wouldn't be in.'

'Who?'

'The owner.'

'Did he say why?'

'No. Sorry.'

Victor stood there, trying to think if there was something else he could ask. 'Okay,' he said.

'If I see her will I get her to give you a call?'

'That would be good. Thank you.'

'No problem,' Gavin said. 'Take care.'

'And you,' Victor said.

He left.

'Have you lost her?' one of the Albanians said, as he passed. Victor said nothing.

51

Dessie parked by the kerb outside Sylvester's house and waited. The taste of the first cigarette of the day was beginning to turn bad in his mouth and he contemplated getting out and lighting another. But Sylvester would be out in a minute. There was no point. He stayed put.

Apart from a message the day after the funeral thanking them for their hospitality, Sylvester hadn't been in touch during his two weeks off. There were times when Dessie didn't know where his phone was. Occasionally he would check it, wondering would he find a missed call or a text message. After one week he rang his own number from the house just to be sure it was working and, after an initial moment of delay, it buzzed into life. He hung up and looked at the display. One missed call. Home. He cleared the screen, put the phone down and went off to see where Anne was.

This first day back he had told himself he would be patient. He had business to discuss later and he would not jeopardize his prospects by being irascible now. After ten minutes had passed, though, he was beginning to wonder. Had he got the day right? He checked the date on the car's display and realized it meant nothing to him. It could be any time of the year, any time of the day or night. He had forgotten what he was trying to remember. When he looked up he saw Sylvester walking towards him, only a few feet away.

'There you are,' Dessie said, when he got in.

'Good to see you,' Sylvester said. 'How are things? How was your break?'

'It was all right.'

'Missed you around the place.'

'I'm glad to hear it. So, where are we going?'

'Into town. You can drop me at the Green. I've a meeting at eight and a load of copying for you so if you want to head off and get that done I'll meet you again at eleven.'

'Fair enough.'

They drove in silence for a while.

'How's Anne?'

'She's fine. In good form. Much better.'

'Great.'

They were faced down the hill, looking out across a pink morning sky at a low sun shining in towards them. Dessie put down the visor. 'Has it been busy?'

Sylvester laughed joylessly to himself. 'It has. It's been a nightmare.'

'Work?'

'Everything. It's good to have you back. We really need to start getting on top of things.'

'That's no problem.'

'Good.'

He left it for a while. He had thought the right time might be that evening, when the novelty of his return had worn off. But here, now, inching along the coast road at a rate that was unlikely to change for the next half-hour, it felt like a good time.

Conversations in the kitchen with Anne. It was odd to hear her speak about things that would change because they had to and because she wanted them to. Requirements she would make of him. She was telling, not asking, but he was happy to agree with her. Everything that had been neglected over the two years it had taken her mother to die would now be put right. Quickly. Mercilessly. Dessie sat and listened. He nodded and said, 'Yes,' and 'All right,' wondering perhaps if, as soon as she stopped talking, he should go to the hall and phone her doctor to come and sedate her. But everything she said was reasonable. No. It was an unreasonable thing to expect that so much change could be brought about overnight. But it was at least rooted in reality.

'You're going to sort out your affairs with Sylvester. You're going to start working full-time as a driver using his car. You'll lease it off him and he can deduct the costs at the end of each month from your pay. He can book you for the hours he needs you at the start of each week and the rest of the time is your own. You're going to get the car reconditioned and buy yourself a proper suit. You'll need to borrow ten thousand from him to get everything sorted but you'll pay it back. You get a career that will keep you going as long as you can drive, and he gets a proper chauffeur at no extra cost. You've no credit history so he has to lend you the money. He owes you that much and it's to his benefit anyway. It's the right thing to do.'

Everything she said had been discussed between them. He recognized expressions of his own that he had used when talking about this to her over the past couple of years. But she had put it all together, edited out the talk of injustices and unfairness and distilled it into something that seemed simple.

'You don't have to convince me,' Dessie said. 'I just don't know will Sylvester go for it.'

'He has to go for it,' she said to him. 'It's only fair. He knows how much you do. He'll understand that you need to put things in order. You will both do better out of it. If he wants to be taken seriously as a businessman he should start doing things in style. Even if everything crashes here, people will still want drivers. Uniforms. Nice cars. Funerals. Debs. Weddings. Airport pick-ups. They'll always be needed. He's not going to leave you hanging.'

'I don't know.'

'This arrangement you've had. It's been fine up until now. You've been patient and he's looked after you. Now it's the next stage. He'll do the right thing.'

'I hope so.'

'If he respects you at all, he will.'

Now he delivered his spiel to Sylvester in the hazy pink light of the morning, not glancing in the mirror in case he saw something in Sylvester's face that might put him off. He did it well, he thought. Listening to his own argument, he could see it made sense.

When he finished speaking Sylvester waited a moment before responding. 'Jesus, Dessie. I'll tell you. Your timing is terrible.'

'I was going to talk to you tonight but I thought, you know, while we're here . . .'

'Tonight? What would be different tonight? It's not a matter of hours. Do you not listen to me when I talk? Do you not know what's going on around here? You've been doing this work for me for three years. What made you decide that now would be the right time to come to me for a loan? Do you know how tight things are? If this crowd don't come through I may just have to forget the whole thing. Fold the company up. I've got journalists sniffing around the place, waiting for me to put a foot wrong. Marek isn't answering his phone. I have to get Breen and his friends over to Prague to sign papers in the next two days or this deal falls apart. And you come back after two weeks and decide that now is the time – right now – for us to start formalizing our business relationship? I don't have ten thousand euro to give you, Dessie. If I went to a bank I couldn't even borrow it because I'm up to my neck in debt. But even if I could, I'd like to take my time and work out whether or not it's a good idea. Can we just get through the next couple of weeks and see where we are then? I can't be thinking about this now.'

'Hang on a second,' Dessie said. 'I know you've a lot going on. But you've been saying for years, literally years, that we'll get this sorted out next week, next month, and nothing ever changes. If I have to wait until the perfect time, it'll never happen.'

'Believe me, Dessie, this is different. I don't know how much you know about what's happening –'

'I don't care,' he said, anger rising in him now. 'Really. I'm the driver. That's all. I'm coming to you to try and get myself sorted out. And when I look at you I don't see a man who's struggling. What I see is you travelling to Prague with a party of six and staying in the Four Seasons. I see you working for the multi-millionaire David O'Donnell. I see you getting punters in and selling ten flats at a time. How can you tell me that things are going badly?'

'But it's all show. If I brought people over on Ryanair and put them up in some dosshouse, I don't think I'd sell too much property. I don't know if this deal is going to happen. Do you understand? And if it doesn't, even the work you've been doing will have to stop. I'm close to the edge here and what I need you to do is to get the fucking copying done and drive me where I need to be and to take your envelope at the end of the week as you've always done until I get this sorted out. You talk about uncertainty and formalizing our relationship but I've never seen you say no to the cash I've given you. I'm on the record. I make my returns. I have to deal with all that paperwork. You take your envelope and good luck to you. For all I know you could be getting three hundred quid a week from Welfare or working forty hours a week for someone else. You could be on full disability. I don't know. I don't care. That's your business. But we came to this arrangement by mutual consent and either of us can end it any time we see fit. It suits me just fine for the moment. I don't need a uniformed driver or an official chauffeur or anything like that. If you want to change things now, right now, then I'm telling you I can't do it. If you want to wait until everything settles down and talk to me then, that's fine. But I can't promise anything. I can tell you that I have no money to give you. I have no money to lend you or to invest in your business. I might in the future or I might not. I'm all over the place at the moment. If you think that this is what I wanted to hear from you on your first day back then you're mad.'

Dessie said nothing. He thought he could stop the car right then and get out of it. Hop over the wall and walk out across the shining sand to the water, past the oystercatchers and the gulls, sand between his bare toes, to the edge, take off his clothes and wade in until he was up to his neck, then dip his head under and drop.

From the back Sylvester sighed. 'I'm sorry. I'm tired and hassled and I don't know why Marek isn't answering his fucking phone.'

Dessie didn't hear him. He was standing at the water's edge now, his hands around Sylvester's neck, holding him down in two feet of water.

'Dessie?'

'Yeah?'

'We'll talk again.'

He nodded but didn't speak. He was thinking now of all the things he'd seen over the past three years. The money that had been spent, the trips they'd gone on and all the deals that had been done. He remembered nights out with O'Donnell, and Sylvester's endless meetings with clients and potential clients, politicians and planners. He thought of the world Sylvester lived in and of the envelope that was handed to him every Friday with a smile and a nod. Fifteen euro an hour. He realized then that he didn't believe what Sylvester was telling him, and once he'd come to that realization, it was hard to understand how he ever had.

52

Victor was awake in bed when the doorbell rang at eleven. He put on a pair of jeans and went down. It was Agnieszka. She stood there, two supermarket bags in hand, and smiled at him when he opened the door. 'Hello,' she said.

'Hi.' He walked into the living room and sat on the couch. She followed him in, took off her jacket and sat beside him.

She put an arm around his neck and kissed him beneath the ear. 'Are you all right?' she asked.

'I'm fine. Yeah.'

'Are you tired?'

He nodded and looked away from her. 'What's the problem?' she asked. 'Why are you being so strange? Have I done something wrong?'

'I don't know,' he said, turning back. 'Have you?'

She said nothing for a moment. Then, 'What are you talking about?'

'You don't know?'

'No, I don't. It would be easier if you just said what your problem is.'

'Where were you last night?' He thought something was there when he said this to her, some flash of doubt or fear that passed across her face, and he didn't know whether he wanted to get in there and pick at it. She hadn't said anything yet. 'Is it hard for you to remember?' he asked.

'I was at work,' she said.

'Were you?'

'Yes.' It pained him to hear her say it, not because it meant she was lying but because of what he would have to say next. The sentences that would come out of his mouth that would lead them into unknown territory. If he could have smiled and pretended that there was nothing else – 'Oh, really? How was it?' – he would have. But he half knew something and he couldn't stop there.

'Because I went to your work. I wanted to see how you were doing. I was in town anyway. And the man. I can't remember his name. He told me that you weren't there. That you hadn't been working. That your boss had called to say that you wouldn't be in.'

The expression on her face barely changed. There was

another long pause before she said anything but when she did he knew they were in a fight. 'Were you following me?'

'No.'

'Were you checking up to see if I was where I said I was?'

'No,' he said. 'Come on. You know that's not something I would do. I wanted to see you, that was all. And you weren't there.'

'No, I wasn't,' she said. It seemed like it was coming now but she didn't say anything else.

'So, can you tell me where you were?'

'I was doing something for my boss.' She stood up and walked across the room to the mantelpiece. There were cigarettes there belonging to one of the others, and she took one out and lit it.

'What was that?' Victor asked.

'Just a job. I was doing some extra work for him.'

'Okay,' Victor said. 'What kind of work? Where?'

'In another club he owns.'

'Which one?'

'I can't remember the name of it.'

'Well, where is it?'

'Down near the river.'

'I didn't know he owned anywhere there.'

'I don't know where it was,' she said. 'God. Enough questions.' She paused. When she spoke again he could hear that she was close to crying. 'You can't expect to know everything I do, okay?'

'What were you doing last night?' He could feel the panic rising in him, filling him up, about to overflow.

'Just wait,' she said. 'I have to tell you this. There are whole parts of my life that you know nothing about, Victor.'

He stood up. 'You're scaring me now. What is going on?'

'Listen to me.'

'Tell me what it is,' he said, in a voice that was getting harder. 'What did you do?'

'I'm trying to tell you. Just. Let me.'

His hands were on his head and he was moving back and forth close to her, agitated. If he had been calmer he would have seen she was scared.

'I did something,' she said.

He looked at her now and suddenly it seemed clearer. 'Did you sleep with your boss?'

'No,' she said. 'Not him.'

'Not him?' Victor shouted. 'Not him? Then who?'

'I don't know,' she said.

'What happened? Who was it?'

'It was a guy. I don't know who.'

'You slept with him. You had sex with someone.'

'Yes,' she said.

'Why? Why would you do that?'

'Because I needed money,' she said. He stopped still and stared as if he didn't recognize her. Then swung his arm and hit her, easy and open-handed, across the face, and a moment later, because once seemed to lack the conviction that such a serious step implied, he hit her again. He was shocked by how loud the sound was, how it echoed in the room around them. That was his answer. She straightened up and looked at him in absolute shock. He took a step towards her without speaking and she ran out the front door into the street and was gone. He stayed standing in the same position, his hand glowing, for what felt like a long time, and then sat down. Her jacket was on the couch beside him. He picked it up and went outside to see if there was any sign of her.

53

After he had left Dessie in town Sylvester began to feel better. He had spoken to Marek and nearly all of the deposits had been lodged to the various accounts. He had spoken to Breen and everything was fine at their end. The contracts had been drawn up and were ready to go. When the clients arrived everything would be ready for them. They would each sit in Marek's deep leather office chair at his enormous desk and sign the document.

'It's a done deal,' Marek said.

'Not until they sign,' Sylvester said.

'You should relax,' Marek said. 'Whatever happens happens. Worrying won't change anything.'

'If you knew the amount of energy and time and anxiety I have spent on this project you wouldn't be saying that. My worrying has been responsible for every positive thing that has happened. It's keeping this show on the road.'

'I don't think that's true. Or very healthy.'

'I know it's not healthy,' Sylvester said, 'but it's how it is.'

It was after midday when Breen rang him, looking to meet. He had something for him, he said.

'Is it important?' Sylvester asked, fighting to stay patient. 'Just because, you know, I'm going off in the morning and there's an awful lot to be done today.'

'I have to meet you,' Breen said. 'Sorry, but that's all there is to it.'

'There's nothing wrong, is there?' He heard his own voice, like that of a fifteen-year-old talking to a girl who was out of his league.

'Nothing wrong. I just need to see you before you go.'

'You're not in town by any chance?' Sylvester asked.

'No, I'm not. I'll be at Newlands in an hour. Meet me there, will you?'

'Of course.'

Sylvester rang Dessie but he was way out on the north-side delivering the photocopied papers and there was no chance he could get back in and drop off Sylvester by the time he was supposed to meet Breen. 'I'll have to get a taxi,' Sylvester said.

'Don't be giving out to me,' Dessie said. 'You sent me here.'

'I'm not blaming you. It's just a complete pain in the arse. When you get finished come and pick me up.'

The taxi got him out on time. There was a convention on a lunch break in the lobby, hundreds of people eating sandwiches and drinking tea. Sylvester wandered through them, feeling hopeless. He was in the wrong frame of mind to be meeting what was still a prospective client. His phone rang. 'I'm outside,' Breen said.

'This place is a madhouse.'

'Yeah. Come out to me. I'm in my car. It's a silver Lexus. I'm in the far left corner.'

Sylvester walked out, blinking, into the sunshine and across the car-park until he saw Breen, who smiled and lifted a hand in greeting. He relaxed a little. Breen pushed the door open for him. 'Are you all right?'

'Grand, yes,' Sylvester said. 'Did you see the state of that place? Who are they all?'

'Pharmaceutical reps,' Breen said.

'Really?'

'I've no idea who they are. Who cares? Fucking people.' He turned to Sylvester and contemplated him for a moment. 'You look hassled.'

Sylvester laughed. 'Never better.'

Breen put a hand on his shoulder. A rough, manly gesture that Sylvester could have done without. 'You're sure?'

'Absolutely. No problem. A busy day ahead but I can't complain about that. Looking forward to getting this deal done. It's very close now.'

'Yes, indeed.'

'So, what can I do for you?' Sylvester asked, as breezy and upbeat as he could manage.

Breen reached behind his seat without looking. He pulled out a plastic Marks & Spencer bag and handed it to Sylvester.

'What's this?'

'That's for you. Fran wasn't able to get the deposit across to Marek in time so he's asking you to deliver it for him.' Sylvester opened the bag and looked in. There was a yellow Jiffy-bag inside.

'What is this?' he said again.

'Look. Fran just had some problems getting the money together in time and he couldn't get the transfer set up so he needs you – we need you – to give that to Marek. The account is set up over there. There's no problem at that end.'

Sylvester felt the weight of the packet on his knees. Not heavy, but there was something in it all right.

'Is this cash?' he asked.

'Yes, it's cash.'

'Oh, Jesus.'

'What's the problem?' Breen said. He was totally cool.

'What's the problem?' Sylvester said. 'Is this the one hundred thousand?'

'Yeah. Well, one hundred and four.'

Sylvester laughed without meaning to, a hollow, breathless cackle. 'And what do you expect me to do with it?'

'We expect you to get it to Marek. I spoke to him a little

while ago. He knows all about it. Fran wants to be a part of this deal. This is his share.'

'Why can't he just get a bank draft? Or do an electronic transfer?'

Breen smiled. 'No, that doesn't work. Not for Marek and not for us.'

Sylvester looked at him, eyes fixed. 'Come on, Sylvester,' Breen said. 'You know what's going on here. How much did David O'Donnell pay per square metre for the Vienna Park development in Prague?'

'He paid the going rate.'

'Are you sure about that? Because Marek says different.'

Sylvester looked at him. 'I don't know what Marek's been saying to you.'

'Oh, for fuck's sake, will you give it up? We're all on the same page. How much did you make out of that deal, then? Can you tell me that?'

There was nothing Sylvester could think of in response. He could not move, as if the bag on his lap had stopped his legs working.

'We know all about you,' Breen said then. 'Everything. You take risks. It's an admirable thing. That hotel stuff. You just do what you want. We don't look down on you for it. All of us, we understand how these things work. Not everything that we've done has been one hundred per cent by the book. That's the way of it for everybody. Everybody. You don't need me to tell you this. It's just pragmatism. A small chance to take for such a nice reward. But if I can be frank with you, you need to get some fucking balls and do your bit. We're ready to go. All of us.'

Sylvester hesitated before speaking. 'I can't carry a hundred thousand euro across Europe. Do you know what they'd do to me if I got caught?'

'What?'

'They'd arrest me. They'd want to know where the money came from and what I was doing with it.'

'You're a businessman. You can explain it.'

'Yes, but this isn't how business is done. Bags of cash in carry-on luggage? Come on. You're not that stupid. I can't do this.'

'No. We're not stupid,' Breen said. 'But you will be able to do this. It's not going to be a problem.'

'How do you know?'

'Because it's highly unlikely that you'll get stopped. And if you do you'll come up with something. Talk to Marek. He'll help you out. One way or another you need to get that money to him by tomorrow. Because if Fran isn't involved in this I'm afraid none of us will be. It's a deal-breaker, really. We all want to be in this together.'

'This is serious stuff. You know that, don't you? I want to do business with you, Paddy, I want things to work out for all of us, believe me. But not enough to take this kind of a risk.'

'You've taken risks before. You're not a cautious man.'

'No,' Sylvester said. 'But I'm not foolhardy either.'

'Then you'll do the right thing here. Have you ever been stopped on your trips to Prague? Have Customs or the police or anyone else looked twice at you? You get on the plane and three hours later you get off. That's it. Marek will be at the airport. Hand the money over and you're finished. We'll be out in a couple of days and we'll have a drink together to celebrate. Seriously. You're doing a favour for a potential client. That's all. You'll be able to talk your way out of it, if it comes to it. You're a clever lad. I'm telling you, this is the only way it can be done. We've all talked about it and it's the simplest, safest way to do it.'

'Why can't you bring it? Why doesn't Fran do it himself?'

'Because the money has to be there tomorrow or else it all falls through. And neither myself nor Fran can travel tomorrow. You're our agent. We're asking you to do it.'

Sylvester closed his eyes. He couldn't feel the packet on his lap any more. He had never been stopped, never even seen a Customs official. Without this there would be nothing left. He opened his eyes and saw that Breen was looking at him, a calm half-smile on his face.

He felt his head clear. By this time tomorrow it would be over. It had to be done. There was no option. Without this he had no idea what path he would take.

'How do you know I won't just pocket the money and disappear?' he said, meaning it as a joke but unable to smile.

Breen laughed. 'You take chances, Sylvester, but I don't think you're so thoroughly fucking stupid to risk everything you have ... Everything,' he said again, smiling gently, 'for that kind of money.'

'No,' Sylvester said. 'Probably not.'

They sat in silence for a moment.

'So if you can give that to Marek,' Breen said, 'he'll make the lodgement and we'll see you at around noon on Wednesday.'

'All right,' Sylvester said. 'I'll see you then.'

'Good man. And for Christ's sake be careful with that.'

'I will.'

Breen started the car. 'I'd give you a lift but I'm headed up North.'

Sylvester opened the door. 'That's okay. Dessie's coming out for me.'

'Good stuff. I'll see you on Wednesday. Have a safe trip.'

'And you,' Sylvester said.

When Breen's car was out of sight, Sylvester rang Dessie. 'Where are you?'

'I'm stuck in fucking traffic on the M50. Where else would I be?'

'Okay. Well, can you get out here as quick as you can?'

'Did you not hear me?'

'Please, Dessie.'

'There's not a lot I can do about it. This is just going nowhere. It could be an hour before I get to you. The whole of the south-side is bollixed.'

'Why?'

'I don't know why. You should just get yourself on a bus and you'll be in town in half an hour.'

'No,' Sylvester said, bag tucked tight under his right arm. 'I'll be here. I'll be waiting for you.'

54

She would leave that day. She would go home and get Jakub from her mother. Together they would go somewhere else. By the time she had him she would know where she was heading.

It had come from nowhere, it seemed, but it must have been in him all along. Better that it happened before they had gone any further. He had done it so easily and with such fluency that it was hard to say, when he'd taken that step towards her, what he was planning to do next.

On the road outside his estate she stopped a taxi and gave directions to her apartment. While they were driving she realized that her cash and credit card were in her wallet and her wallet was in her jacket and her jacket was on the couch in Victor's place. She thought she had some money in the flat, maybe enough, but she couldn't be sure. As they drove towards town she rang her work to see which manager was on and was told it was Karen. Her face burned as she spoke. She put her hand against it and checked her reflection in the rear-view mirror. But there was no blood, nothing broken, she thought. She redirected the taxi to Symposium.

There were a million lies she could have told him. She'd always had an excuse ready for him if she'd met him by chance on the road. When he'd asked the question, she could have said she was at home sick in bed or that the boss had asked her to work in a friend's place or that he wanted her to meet some business colleagues who were opening a new bar. There were a hundred things she could have told him. But still when the time had come there had been nothing she could think of to say, frozen by fear in front of him. And then she had thought it was better just to let him know. If they were going to continue together the truth would have to come out. Let them see if he could handle it. He couldn't. There was no them. He'd hit her. That was all.

The taxi arrived at Symposium and she asked the driver to wait. The place had just opened. Besim and a friend were standing just inside the door, talking to each other. 'Hi,' he said. 'What are you doing here?'

'Is he in yet?' she asked.

'Who? White? No.'

'Where's Karen?'

'She's in the back,' Besim said. 'What happened to your face?'

'Nothing,' she said. Besim put a hand on her shoulder and stopped her. 'Don't,' she said.

'Sorry.' He took his hand down. 'But that's bad. That eye is going to close. What happened? Is it our friend?'

'Yes,' she said, and she was glad when she said it. 'That's exactly who it was.'

'He hit you?' Besim's friend said. 'He hit you?'

'I have to find Karen,' she said, and left the two of them talking to each other.

She found her down in the basement office.

'Hey,' Karen said. 'What are you doing here?' Then she saw her face. 'Are you all right?'

'I have to leave tonight. I need to get paid. Can you sort it out?'

'Of course.' She took the roster off the wall and, with a calculator, worked out how much Agnieszka was owed. From the safe in the corner she got the money and counted it out, then folded it up and put it into a small brown envelope. 'So you're going?' Karen said.

'Yes. Can you tell Luke?'

'What will I say?'

'That I'm finished.'

'That's all?'

Agnieszka smiled. 'That's all.'

'I'll sort it out,' Karen said. 'Can I do anything else for you?'

'Nothing,' Agnieszka said.

Back upstairs Besim came over to her as she was leaving. 'Where is he now?' he asked.

'Who?'

'Our friend.'

'I don't know,' Agnieszka said. 'In his house maybe. It doesn't matter any more.'

'Where are you going?'

'Away,' she said.

'That's good,' Besim said. 'Home?'

'Maybe, yeah.'

'Do you want us to sort him out?'

Agnieszka thought for a moment. 'I don't care what you do. I'm not here any more.'

'We'll look after it. I promise you that.' He put an arm around her as if he was going to hug her, but lost heart and ended up patting her on the back. 'You were a nice girl,' he said. 'You will be missed.'

'Thanks. I don't think anyone's going to notice,' she said.

'They will.'

'No,' she said. 'They'll have forgotten that I was ever here in a few days. And that's fine by me.'

On the street outside she paid the taxi driver and counted the rest of her money. It wasn't enough. She needed more.

55

There was a bottle of vodka he kept for those days that he couldn't sleep. Sitting up in bed and taking it out of the freezer, one good belt, and lying back down. Did he use to drink this much at home? It was different here. This was how they did things. There was a reason why all the porters were the way they were. Which came first? The job, the messed-up lives, the drinking? When he finished up it would be different. He was strangely confident of that. A clean break could be made.

But now he woke up and he knew what he had to do. It was the only way he would be able to get out of bed. He took the bottle and put two good slugs of it into a glass and knocked it back, cold and hard, like life itself. While he ironed his shirt and half watched the news on the television he had a couple more, only because it made him feel better.

The walk in was comfortable. Every night was warm and close, and he didn't know if this was unusual or if people here just talked about it all the time because there was nothing else for them to say. By the time he arrived he was sweating. He thought about having a shower but he had no towel and somebody had pissed all over the floor. He washed his face in the sink, then went upstairs, out across the lobby floor towards the porters' desk. He saw Ray watching him as he came.

'Are you all right?'

'Hmm,' Marcin said. 'Don't know about that.'

'Come in here for a minute,' Ray said. He stepped through the door into the hot, airless room, full of things, that was their station. He pulled Marcin in after him by the arm. 'What are you fucking doing?'

'What?' Marcin said. 'Nothing.'

'You're pissed.'

Marcin laughed. 'I don't know why you would think something like this. It's just so, so stupid.'

'They'll fire you tonight if they see you. You know that? They won't think twice. Is that what you want?'

'I don't know,' Marcin said. 'I need a break.'

'They'll give you a break, all right.'

'I'm okay,' Marcin said. 'I'll be fine.'

'Take the Hoover. Go into the second function room and start in there. Don't talk to customers or staff and keep away from the front desk. Do you hear me?'

'Yes.' Marcin went to leave.

Ray grabbed his elbow. 'Not another drop,' he said.

'Every one of you,' Marcin said. 'Every night.'

'Yeah, but we don't end up like this. And we certainly don't start out like this. Stay out of the way for the next couple of hours. You'll be fine.'

'Okay. Thanks.'

'You fucking eejit,' Ray said, but he was laughing now.

Marcin worked slowly, back and forth, across the floors.

One function room after the next. It was mindless, but inside his head he sang as he worked and he got into a rhythm. He finished there and crossed as quickly as possible to the restaurant. That was a big job and by the time he was finished it was half eleven. He came out and saw that the whole reception area towards the lounge was empty. His head was beginning to pound now. He could see no sign of Ray so he plugged the Hoover in where he was and kept going. How had he come to work this evening? he wondered. Had he walked? Got a taxi? And where had he been earlier when he was drinking? It was a blank, but not something to worry about, he thought. Because he was here doing what he had been told to do. That much he knew.

56

Sylvester was lying on the bed in the room. This would be a quick one, he thought. Everything else – all the anxieties of the day – stayed where they should be, outside, beyond these walls, but he couldn't deny that his body was feeling the strain. Stiff in the shoulders and neck. Maybe the girl would have learned massage and could do something for him. It was worth asking.

He'd asked Dessie to set this up, and when it was all arranged, he'd nearly cancelled. With everything going on and the flight in the morning it had seemed like it might be too much. But lying here now, he knew it was what he needed. A distraction. A good end to a bad day. Turn the brain off and let his body have a turn. He was glad to be here.

The knock on the door came. He stood to open it and there she was. He smiled and let her pass into the room, then closed the door and kissed her cheek. She stiffened and that surprised him. Too late now to be getting coy with him.

'How are you?' he asked.

'I'm fine.'

'Seeing you is the best thing that's happened to me today,' he said. 'I swear to you, the day I've had. You've no idea.' He flopped on to the bed and lay back, shirt collar open, hands behind his head. 'I've been thinking about you all week.' She smiled, tight and edgy, and sat down next to him. The light in the room was dim but he saw the shadow of something on her face. She turned from him as he sat up.

'What's that?'

'Nothing,' she said.

'That's not nothing.' He touched the side of her face and gently pulled it towards him. 'That's nasty. Are you all right? What happened?' She looked at him and didn't say anything. 'What happened?' he said again.

'I got hit in the face by a ball,' she said. 'I was crossing a field near where I live and there were kids playing and that's what happened.'

'Jesus. It looks sore.'

'I'm sorry.'

'So am I,' he said. 'For you, I mean.' They sat for a moment in silence. 'We don't have to do anything tonight,' he said.

'No, it's fine.' She stood up.

'Seriously. It suits me anyway.'

'I have to go home,' she said. 'I mean to Poland.'

'Poland?' he said.

'Tomorrow. I'm not coming back here. I need to finish tonight and I need the money. So we can do whatever you want but I have to get paid.'

'Relax,' he said. 'I'll pay you.'

'I'm sorry,' she said, and started to cry. She was still

standing in front of him. He reached out and held her hand.

'It's okay.' He tried to imagine her life beyond here – pimps or boyfriends or other clients – and couldn't. She didn't seem the druggy type. He realized then that he didn't want to know anything else about her. 'Somebody hit you,' he said. 'And you're going away.'

'Yes,' she said.

'You're not in trouble, are you? I mean really in trouble? You don't need help with the police or anything?'

'I don't think so,' she said. 'But I have to go tomorrow.'

He stood and walked over to the desk chair. His jacket was slung over the back and there was a plastic bag underneath. He picked it up and sat on the bed again. She sniffed a couple of times and stood above him with folded arms. He took out an envelope and from that produced a small wad of notes, then counted out her money, the full amount, on to the bed. Then paused and counted out the same amount again. 'That's a bit extra. I hope you'll be all right,' he said.

'It's a lot,' she said. 'Thank you very much. It's more than you need to give me.'

'I know that, but either I can afford it or it doesn't matter so . . .' He shrugged. 'You may as well. You seem like a nice girl.'

'And you're a good man,' she said. 'I don't know you but I promise I need this to get home. It's for nothing else.'

'I believe you,' he said. She stood, uncertain, in front of him, then reached out her hand. He shook it, looking up at her uneven face.

'Thank you again,' she said.

'That's okay. Good luck with everything.'

'All right. 'Bye.'

And then she was gone. Sylvester lay back. By this time tomorrow he would know if he'd managed to get away with it. If he had, this would seem like the right thing to have done. He would be in another hotel in Prague tomorrow night and there would be cards with girls' numbers on them put under the door of his room. He could make a call without leaving his bed and get one over and do what he wanted, knowing that everything was all right in the world. It was a happy thought. The stiffness in his neck didn't seem as bad now. He was comfortable just lying there with his eyes closed.

57

Gareth was over. They were sitting on the couch, drinking and laughing at some stupid comedy, and that was exactly what Victor needed. The memory of what had happened earlier that day was already fading. It would still be there tomorrow but by then he would be better prepared to deal with it. A clearer assessment could be made.

After Agnieszka had left he'd stayed sitting on the couch. He didn't know where his housemates were but he was glad to be alone.

He shouldn't have hit her. He regretted it, and if he could find her and talk to her he would tell her that. It was wrong. He wouldn't say anything else. There were explanations that he could give her – that he had been shocked and frightened and hurt. That his reaction had been something instinctive, uncalculated, visceral. He hadn't hit her hard and it wasn't meant to hurt. It was a response to a stimulus, a reflex action for which he couldn't be blamed. The job was getting to him. It was too much to take in. But that was for later. He was sorry. That was all he would say to her if he had the chance, nothing else.

There were questions, of course. How long had she been doing this and how often and with whom and where? As he thought about it, the things he wanted to know multiplied and subdivided and lost their shape in a mass of images of places and people until he had no sense of what the questions really were.

He had stayed in the living room for a couple of hours, standing up every so often, ringing her number, but her phone was turned off. He sent a text message that said, 'I am sorry,' knowing she couldn't get it. Beyond that there was nothing else he could think of doing. Going after her, checking her house or her work, seemed like a bad idea. He had hit her. She was entitled to stay away from him for as long as she wanted. If she rang or came back, he would tell her everything and they could talk about it. If she didn't, then he would have to accept it.

But sitting there on his own was doing him no good. He'd thought about ringing home, but all the plans he'd made were too much a part of his conversations with them. At five o'clock he'd called Gareth to see if he was free.

'Is Agnieszka working?' Gareth asked him.

'No. She's busy. Something on.'

'Well, what do you want to do?'

'Do you want to come over and have a drink? Watch a DVD? Get a pizza, something like that?'

'We could do that,' Gareth said. 'If you don't want to go into town.'

'I don't,' Victor said. 'We had a fight, Agnieszka and I. So I don't feel like doing anything much. But I'm bored.'

'And you want drink and company.'

'Yeah. That's exactly what I want.' Victor almost laughed.

'I'll be there in an hour. Do you need me to bring anything?'

'No, I can get everything. Thanks, Gareth.'

He'd gone to the village. Bought cans and vodka and took out three films. By the time he got back he was hoping she wouldn't call him that evening. Give him a chance to do this. Have a drink. Relax. Tell himself that things could be all right without her, before considering whether or not that prospect was something he would have to deal with.

58

Dessie sat in the Merc in the underground car-park waiting for Sylvester and looking out across the dimly lit space. Slumped against the far wall a stray rubbish bag was being filleted slowly and surreptitiously by at least three rats. He had been there for more than an hour and it was coming up to midnight. There was a metallic taste in the back of his mouth that he thought might be the start of an infection. He would get no lie-in the following day, no chance to recuperate. In only a few hours he would be crossing town to get Sylvester to the airport for a midday flight to Prague. The following day he would be out there again at seven to collect the hero, returning in triumph.

His hand reached down and turned the key. He switched on the lights and revved the engine. The rats vanished. He put the car into drive and accelerated out, the wheels screeching as he came to the top of the ramp. He spun the steering-wheel as he left the hotel and drove straight out on to the main road, quiet at this time. He stopped at a red traffic-light, had a quick look, then drove on through. Two minutes later he pulled in at a twenty-four-hour shop and double-parked the car. He bought a cup of tea and smoked a cigarette on the pavement alongside a group of taxi drivers who were complaining about the heat. He lit a second cigarette off the first, dumped the cup in a bin, got back into the car and drove on. Through the docks and over, out along the sea, the air-conditioning off and the windows open, the warmth of the middle of the night giving him comfort. He still wasn't sure what he was going to do.

He turned off the lights and cut the engine as he rolled up at the kerb outside the house. Only the porch light was on. He sat there for a moment, then got out, closed the door quietly, locked the car and unclipped the key from his bunch. He walked across the lawn towards the house. Then, as quietly as he could, he posted the key through the door. There was no sound at all. Walking away from the house he tried not to think too much, down streets he had only ever walked with Sylvester in the direction of the sea and the main road back into Dublin. When he was sure he was far enough away from the house he took out his phone, scrolled through his address book and hit dial.

'Dessie,' the man said, on answering.

'Yeah. How did you know it was me?'

'Your number's in my phone.'

'You people,' Dessie said. 'Jesus Christ.'

'Well, you've my number too, haven't you? You're the one calling me.'

'I suppose I am,' Dessie said.

What can I do for you?'

'Here, do you want to meet me?'

'When?'

'Now.'

'It's pretty late.'

'I know what time it is. Do you want to meet or not?'

He heard the fellow yawn.

'I'm assuming this isn't a social thing.'

'No,' Dessie said. 'It's not.'

'Are we going to talk? Have you got something to tell me?'

'I don't know. Yeah.'

'And it can't wait until the morning?'

'I'm not sure I'll want to talk to you in the morning.'

'All right,' Hennessy said. 'Where will I meet you?'

59

Marcin was hoovering the lobby when the doors of the lift opened and Agnieszka walked out. She stopped for a second when she saw him, then kept walking.

'It's you,' Marcin said, and looked at her again. 'What happened to your face?'

'I have to go,' she said, as she passed him. Two businessmen were drinking in the lounge and they glanced over in their direction at the drunk porter and a beautiful girl. She picked up her pace and walked towards the exit. Marcin went after her.

'Hey,' he called. 'What happened to you?'

She stopped. 'Marcin. Please. Just let me go. I have to get out of here.'

'Can I help? Can I do anything for you?'

'No. Go back to your work.'

'Do you need a taxi? Or some money?'

'No. I'm all right.' She seemed very agitated. 'I can look after myself.'

'Every time I see you you're running away,' he said.

'Why do you think that might be?' she said. 'Have you any idea?' He looked at her the way he always had. The way all those young guys from home always did, as if at any stage she would say something that would answer the only question that ever mattered to them. It drove her mad.

'Did he do this to you?' Marcin asked then, and she paused for a moment, surprised. 'Was it him?' he said.

'How do you know him?' she asked.

'That fucker,' Marcin said. 'That fucking bastard.'

'I have to go,' she said. 'Really, I just do.' She walked out of the door and Marcin could hear her heels clicking quickly across the marble of the porch, then silence. He walked back in and went behind the reception desk. There was no sign of the manager and Marcin didn't know or care where he was. He sat at a computer, took a card out of the drawer and validated it. He got up and walked quickly across the lobby to the lift.

'Here,' Ray called after him from somewhere. 'Where are you off to?' The doors of the lift opened and Marcin got in. He pushed the button and went up.

Straight in, he told himself. No knocking, no listening, just straight in. It might be too late anyway. The lift doors opened and Marcin skipped soundlessly down the corridor. But when he came to the room, he stopped outside it. It was silent. Was he sure this was the one? It always was, wasn't it? He said the number over and over in his head. He stuck the card in the slot, saw the light turn green, opened the door and went inside.

The man was asleep on the still-made bed. He was slighter than Marcin remembered, seemed almost to be floating on the bed's surface, and his face was boyish, babyish even, in its blank, sleeping calm. He held his tie in one hand and the top two buttons of his shirt were open. Marcin saw his jacket draped across the back of a chair. How would he wake him? Was it fair to call his name, then batter him as soon as he woke? Or did he even deserve that much of a chance? Marcin moved closer and stood above him, watching his chest rise and fall.

'Hey, Fuckface,' he said, but the man didn't stir.

He took another step towards the bed and at that moment noticed the Marks & Spencer bag on the floor. There was a padded envelope sticking out of it, and sticking out of that was money. He could see a lot of money. Without moving his feet he hunkered down. His knees clicked like twigs breaking in the dim humming silence of the room and he looked up at the man, but nothing had changed. He moved his head and bent to see into the envelope, his body swaying, head throbbing. It was full of folded wads of fifty-euro notes. He felt light-headed from holding his breath. He checked the man again and, concentrating for a second, thought about who he was and where he was and what he was doing there. Then he stopped thinking. He lifted the plastic bag by the handles. The envelope slid to the bottom with a quiet crinkling sound and Marcin felt its weight. He stood up, took two paces back towards the door, watching the man as he went, turned the handle and stepped out into the corridor. The door clicked closed behind him. For a moment, five seconds maybe, he stood there listening and waiting to see what would happen next. What he would do. Then he ran. The air whooshed in his ears as he pounded down the corridor.

He pressed the button for the lift but decided against taking it and used the stairs instead. Around and down he went, as quickly as he could. He kept on going until he got to the basement, then headed for the staff room. There was nothing unusual about what he was doing. He was carrying a plastic bag. If he had met any of the others they wouldn't have noticed anything out of the ordinary, apart from the fact that his hair was standing on end, his face was chalk-white and he had lost the power of speech. In the staff room he went to his locker, got out his backpack and stuffed the bag into it. There was nothing else in there that he would need. He went up the stairs, walked through the kitchen and out the back door, meeting no one as he went. He ran around the side of the building and was heading for the gate when he saw the box at the entrance and remembered the security guard. He stopped where he was. Could he jump the back wall? He turned and looked up at the barbed wire and roller fencing. The easier way was better. He walked down the drive and past the box. The guard nodded at him as he went and pushed back the glass sliding window.

'Half-day, is it?'

'I've had enough,' Marcin said, smiling.

The man laughed. He was very young. 'See you later,' he said. 'Good luck.'

'Take care.'

And then he was on the road. There was a bag on his shoulder with more money than he had ever seen in his life. His head clouded at the thought and he stopped for a moment, holding on to the railing beside him until his head cleared and he was steady enough to continue. Think about nothing, he told himself. I am going home. He walked on, but after ten minutes was in unfamiliar territory and realized that this was the wrong direction. He would have to turn and pass the hotel again. Pass the security guard who, even now, might have been alerted to the crime that Marcin had committed. He stepped into the middle of the road. Fifteen seconds later a taxi came around the corner at speed, braking sharply when the driver saw Marcin standing there with his hand in the air. He walked to the door and saw the man looking at him through the open window.

'Rathmines,' he said.

'What are you doing? Do you want to get yourself killed?'

Marcin remembered then that he didn't have the fare. He could get it out of the bag but that didn't seem like a good idea. 'Sorry,' he said. 'I forgot. I've no money.'

'Fucking idiot.' The taxi drove off. He walked to the other side of the street and stayed tight to the wall as he passed the hotel, not looking, not turning his head. He crossed the main road. It was too exposed here. If a police car came along he would start running even though he knew he shouldn't. He headed for the lanes and in there, hidden and unseen, he began to relax.

60

Declan Hennessy was sitting at the counter drinking coffee when Dessie walked in. It was quiet and bright and the place was mostly empty. Just a few couples at tables and groups of friends bunched up together in the booths, squeezing the last moments of enjoyment out of the night with hot dogs and cheeseburgers.

'There you are,' said Hennessy.

'All right?' Dessie said, sitting beside him and turning off his phone.

'Can I get you anything? Strawberry milkshake? Banana split?'

'Are you trying to be funny?' Dessie said.

'No, I'm not,' Hennessy said. 'What do you want?'

'Tea,' Dessie said.

The girl brought a mug with boiling water and a teabag still in it. She was uniformed, black and white, trousers that meant her arse was the first thing you noticed.

'Nice,' Hennessy said, after she'd gone.

'What kind of a place is this?' Dessie asked.

'You're the one who wanted to meet in the middle of the night. What do you want to tell me that can't wait until tomorrow?' He took out a small silver box and put it on the counter.

'What's that?'

'I'm going to record this.'

'Do you have to?'

'It's better all round. So we can be clear on exactly what you've said. I won't be misinterpreting you afterwards.'

'I don't know,' Dessie said. He looked around. 'Do you think I can smoke here?'

'Why would you be able to smoke here?'

'Because it's the middle of the night.'

'The law's still the law. Look. You don't have to be nervous. This is just between us.'

'It's not about being nervous. It won't make much difference anyway. He'll know where this is coming from.'

'What do you want to tell me?'

Dessie looked at the recorder on the counter in front of him, green light glowing. 'I don't know,' he said.

'Why don't I ask you a few questions and you answer? If there's anything else that occurs to you, even if it seems irrelevant, just go ahead and say it.'

'Okay.'

So they began. Hennessy knew a lot already, the names of developments and people they had met. Money that had been handed over and bills that had never been paid. Dessie's role was mostly to confirm. Yes. He was there. I remember him. Yes. The full amount. In cash. All those trips and days driving, sitting in the front, not really listening but still picking up enough. The conversations he'd sat through over dinner.

Dessie couldn't tell him anything about Sylvester's days as a councillor or what dealings he'd had with O'Donnell back then.

'So when did you meet him first?'

'Who? Sylvester?'

'O'Donnell.'

'We went to Prague, the three of us. Sylvester was trying to get the company going and O'Donnell said he'd do him a favour and have a look at a few places.'

Hennessy laughed. 'Is that what he said?'

'Yeah. Here, you obviously know all about this trip. What are you asking me for?'

'You tell me what you know.'

Dessie shrugged. 'Marek set it up. There was this new block of apartments he had and O'Donnell looked at them. They were top quality. He was very interested. So he bought twenty.' He laughed at the memory of it. 'Marek got him a deal on them. He was in early and I think that saved him a lot.'

'Do you know how much he paid for each of them?'

'I think it was fifty thousand.'

'That was a good deal. Those apartments launched at a hundred thousand.'

Dessie nodded. 'He was in flying form that week, all right.'

'And how was Sylvester?'

'Like a two-year-old. This was the start of it for him.'

'What happened next?'

'Nothing. We had a couple of nights out and that was it. We came home.'

'And what happened to those apartments?'

'O'Donnell sold them about a year later.'

'Do you know how much he got for them?'

'Sylvester told me. I think it was about a hundred and twenty each.'

'So, O'Donnell did very well out of it.'

'Yeah.'

Hennessy nodded. 'Do you know about the rest of the money he might have paid to Marek?'

'No. What money was this?'

'The other fifty thousand per apartment that Marek would have got, under the table?'

Dessie looked at him, trying to work it out. 'I don't know anything about that,' he said.

'Do you really think that a guy like Marek would sell something half-price to anyone?' Hennessy asked.

'You seem to know more about this than I do.'

'You didn't think it was odd?'

'I thought there might be something going on,' Dessie said, 'but I wasn't paying too much attention. Wasn't my job.'

'Right,' Hennessy said.

'So he paid more for the apartments than they said. What's the problem? Surely that's his loss.'

'Not really. He went to the Czech Republic and, on paper, spent a million euro on property. Then a year later he sold it and came back with two million. A million euro profit. All nice and shiny and legit.'

'Okay.'

'One hundred per cent profit in a year? Sounds great,' Hennessy said. 'But in fact he paid Marek the full price. He just swapped a dirty million for a clean one.'

Dessie let this sink in. 'And you know all this as fact or are you just guessing?'

'Somewhere in between.'

'Would Sylvester have known about this?'

'Who cares? I imagine he did, but he's only a bit-player. His three per cent or whatever isn't really the point. I'm not especially interested in Sylvester. I mean, if he let himself get dragged into all of this, I'm not going to cry for him if it ends badly. But he's not the main event. Now, is there anything else you want to tell me?'

He didn't know about the girls. The weekly meetings in Room 538. It would come out anyway. If Sylvester was exposed somebody somewhere would talk.

'No,' Dessie said. 'That's all.'

'Right,' Hennessy said. 'Thanks for that.' He turned off the machine and nodded at the girl to get the bill. 'Which direction are you going?' he asked.

'West,' Dessie said.

'I'm going south. Can't help you, I'm afraid.'

'That's all right. I'll get a taxi.' They stood up.

'Can I ask you,' Dessie said, 'why do you people hate him so much?'

'What people? Who are you talking about?'

'I don't know. The press.'

Hennessy laughed to himself. 'Well, I can't speak for everybody in "the press". But I don't hate him. He's a nobody. I can tell you that I think he embodies everything that's negative about a certain type of person who gets involved in public life in Ireland. He's corrupt, unprincipled, in it for himself. He's drawn to power as if he's entitled to it, despite the fact that he's not that bright or capable and has no core beliefs. He's a small-time crook, happy to facilitate the big-time operators, turned on by the idea that they need him. He's prepared to sell himself for his own personal short-term gain and doesn't give a damn what the consequences of his actions might be for others. He's a nothing person. Believes in nothing. Means nothing. Good for nothing.' He smiled. 'Since you ask.'

'You're wrong,' Dessie said, shaking his head. 'That's not him at all.'

'No?'

'No.'

'So what are you doing here, Dessie? Why the change of heart?' Hennessy said.

'Oh, I don't know,' Dessie said.

'Seriously? What is it? Guilty conscience?'

Hennessy stood smiling at him, as if all of this was just a bit of harmless fun. There was no way of taking back the things he'd said. Words preserved in that little silver box. Words that would line up on a page and change everything for them all. Sadness came to Dessie, sudden and heavy. 'He let me down,' he said.

'Fuck,' Hennessy said. 'I wouldn't want to cross you. With friends like that ... I'll be in touch. Thanks again.' He left without looking back.

Dessie sat down for a moment and took a cigarette out of his pocket. The girl shook her head at him and pointed at the sign. He stood to go and realized that the bill was still in front of him, unpaid. He left a fiver on the counter and wandered out to look for a taxi.

61

A car door slammed and Victor woke with a jump. The television screen in front of him was blue and he saw Gareth sitting at the other end of the couch, asleep, chin resting on his chest, a beer can still in his hand. From outside he heard voices. He thought it might be one of his housemates arrived home with friends but the sound was wrong.

'Gareth,' he said.

'What?'

Victor got up and walked across the room in darkness to the front window. Besim and the other Albanians were standing beside a black BMW parked in front of the house. There were at least four of them.

'Oh, fuck,' Victor said.

'What is it?'

'I'm in trouble here.'

Gareth came to the window and looked out.

'Who are they?'

'Albanians.'

'What do they want?'

'I don't know. Nothing good.'

'Why? What did you do?'

'I hit Agnieszka. She's obviously gone to these guys.'

'Oh, Jesus.'

Besim was walking towards the house now with something in his hand. He saw Victor looking out at him and, without slowing, pitched a brick straight at him. Victor and Gareth ducked down as the window came in around them.

'Right,' Victor said, as he stood. He went into the hall and opened the door.

Besim stopped and looked at him. 'You fucking bastard,' he said.

'What's it to you? It's none of your business. You don't know anything about it.'

'I know what you did.'

'No, you don't,' Victor said.

'Are you going to come out?'

'Well, there's five of you and there's two of us. That's hardly fair.'

'I'll do you on my own,' Besim said. 'And I'll dance on your fucking head.'

'Okay,' Victor said, and ran at him. He was stronger, he could feel that straight away. He got a hand to Besim's shoulder and a foot behind him and brought him to the ground. They grappled there for a minute as the others stood around in silence, and then Victor was on top, his knees pinning down Besim's arms. He had one hand on his throat and slammed his elbow into the middle of Besim's face hard three times in a row. 'Enough?' he said. 'I have you now. You tell me when to stop.'

'You're fucking dead,' Besim said.

'Knife, Victor!' Gareth called from somewhere, and Victor looked up. Behind him he saw a blur of movement and felt a sting in his back twice. It didn't hurt but it frightened him. He got up off Besim and ran a couple of steps back towards the house. The Albanians were moving away now, dragging Besim with them to the car. They got him into it and took off. Victor reached around and felt the dampness on his back.

'How bad is it?' he asked Gareth, who was beside him now, pressing his jacket against Victor's back.

'I don't know,' Gareth said. 'It's not good.' With his other hand he was dialling the emergency number. Victor sat on the front step. His breathing was clogged now, rasping and hard to find. He spat blood on to the ground in front of him.

'I thought there'd be more,' he said, looking at his hand as the light began to turn grey at the edges.

62

On the street outside she thought about what she would do. There was a chance that he was at her place, waiting. There was nothing he could say or do that would change anything. She was going now. Or maybe he wouldn't even want to apologize. Maybe he would feel he needed to punish her for what she had done even though he knew nothing about any of it. It was unlikely but, then, she would have said that his hitting her was unlikely. She came to a junction and saw a taxi rank in front of her. At her building she got the guy to wait for her outside. There was no sign of anyone on the street. She couldn't see Victor's car anywhere. She went up to the flat, let herself in, and just as she was about to open the door of her bedroom had a moment of panic. He could be in there. One of the others might have let him in, not thinking anything of it. He could be standing on the other side of the door, waiting to grab her and beat her into the floor. There were no notes in the hall for her, no messages to say that Victor had been by.

There was nothing else she could do. She was ready to scream as she opened the door and saw her room, empty and exactly as she'd left it that morning. She put her stuff into a suitcase. There wasn't much she needed. The rest she would leave behind. She counted out a month's rent and left it on her bedside table. Then, as she was leaving, she went back and took it with her.

'Early flight, isn't it?' the driver said, when she got back into the car and asked to go to the airport.

'Yes.'

'What time is it at?'

'Six. But I want to get there early.'

'Jesus, you'll be out there for hours. Where are you going?'

'Home,' she said.

'Where's that?' She kept her gaze out the window and didn't answer. The driver didn't ask again and neither of them spoke for the rest of the trip. There was nothing about here that she would miss, she thought. Wherever she went in her life, wherever the next phase would be, she would never come back here. A hard place.

When she arrived at the airport she checked the boards and saw that there was a flight to Wrocław at seven. From there she could get to her mother's house in three hours on the train. She talked to a staff member, who told her that the check-in crew could sell her a ticket, then wandered across the terminal building taking apart first one phone, then the other, dropping the SIM cards in different bins.

She sat with her bag between her feet against a wall in Departures. There were bodies sleeping around the place, backpackers mostly, saving taxi fares or the cost of a hotel by spending the night there. She should sleep herself but didn't feel tired enough. Her face was sore. She rested her cheek against the cool marble behind her head. There were cleaning staff with buffing machines and bored security guards, who wandered around hoping that nothing would happen or maybe that something would. Every few minutes an announcement blasted through the building about only smoking in designated areas. She began to get cold, the air-conditioning too much for the empty halls at night, and went outside, dragging her bag behind her. She sat on a bench in the warm still air. The sky was already brightening in front of her. By the time the sun went down again she would be with Jakub. She had time enough to think about where they could go next, what they would do and how they would manage it. Nothing had changed. All the things that had made her leave in the first place still held. But she would be with him and for a while that would be enough.

63

Sylvester woke and, for a moment, had no idea where he was. The light was on and he could see the room but just for a second he didn't recognize it. There were no clues, a blank canvas of bed, table, chair, television without history. Words. Then it came to him and things started to move very quickly. He sat up, looked at his watch and saw that it was half four. Why was he still here? What had happened? Had the girl drugged him or had he been attacked? He slapped his face with both hands and tried to think.

They hadn't done anything. She was hurt. He'd given her some money and she'd left. Then he lay down and now he was here. Where the hell was Dessie? He went and got his phone from his jacket pocket. His head hurt as if he was hung-over. He rang Dessie's number and it went straight to message.

'Fuck,' he shouted, and his voice scared him, way too loud in the eerie quiet of the hotel room at night. He hung up, then dialled straight back. Whispered into the phone: 'Dessie, it's Sylvester. It's half four and I'm in the room. I don't know why I'm still here. I'm coming down now. See you in a minute.'

He put on his jacket and saw himself in the bathroom mirror. There was a ghost looking back at him, pale and scruffy and disturbed. He turned off the light and was opening the door when he thought about the bag and the hundred thousand. His heart stopped and his body went rigid. It was a good-sized room but from where he was standing he could see most of it and there was no sign of the bag. He dropped to his knees and looked under the bed. Nothing. He crawled across the floor, checking under the bedside table, the desk, the television unit. It wasn't there. He stood up and stripped the covers off the bed.

'Where are you?' he screamed, into a pillow held against his face. Back into the bathroom. Not in the bin, in the bath, in the toilet, in the shower or in the cupboard above the sink. He rang Dessie's phone again, and again heard the scratchy low growl of his message. 'I'm in trouble here, Dessie. If you get this come up to me. I don't know what's going on.'

He sat on the edge of the bed and tried to think. Had the girl come back? Would she have done this? She didn't seem the type, especially not after what he'd done for her. But she was a fucking prostitute. What was he thinking? He could ring the company, whatever crowd it was they used, and then he realized he knew nothing about any of it. Dessie did it all. There was a member of staff who arranged everything for them here, who kept the room free and clear, made sure that they were never disturbed and that no one ever saw them, then cleaned up afterwards. It didn't cost much for all that he did. What was his name? If Sylvester had ever known he'd forgotten it now. He looked at the phone beside the bed and tried to work out if there was anything he could do. Any call he could make to Reception. I'm in Room 538. Do you know about me? Can you help? I'm not supposed to be here and a prostitute has stolen my client's money.

He would go to Dessie, tell him everything, and he would be able to sort this out. Get his man involved. Get on to the whore company and get the money back. He went through the room one more time, knowing that the bag wasn't there but thinking maybe he could jolt reality back to where it should be by playing dumb. It didn't work.

He opened the door and looked down the corridor. Nobody was there. He left the room and made his way to the stairs, then went down, down, down into the basement and into the underground car-park. He was trying not to run, desperate to get to the next stage when they would be able to do something but trying to be quiet. When he turned the corner he saw only empty space. There was no car. There was no Dessie. He put a hand across his mouth and felt his hot breath pulsing against it. He walked as far as the next corner. There were cars here and there but none of them was his. He kept going until he came back to his starting-point. Dessie was gone. There could be no doubt. His ability to make sense of what was happening was breaking into pieces and floating away. He walked slowly up the concrete ramp to outside and tried Dessie's number again.

'Where are you?' he said, and left it at that.

Sitting on stools behind the porters' desk, Ray and Tommy watched Sylvester on the security camera as he wandered aimlessly up the ramp from the underground car-park.

'What the fuck is he doing?' Tommy said.

'I have no idea.'

'Where's Dessie?'

'I don't know. Gone, I suppose. No sign of him.'

'Should we do something?' Tommy said. 'Should we see if he's all right?'

'No,' Ray said. 'Dessie's always said to ignore him. Pretend he's not there. That's the way he wants it. That's what he pays for.'

'So that's what he gets.'

'That's what he gets,' Ray said. Sylvester turned left at the top of the ramp and disappeared from the picture. 'If he needs anything he'll come in.'

Ray headed off towards the kitchen, then stopped and called back over. 'Where's Marcin?'

'Haven't seen him. Somewhere around.'

'If he turns up will you tell him to get the breakfast cards?'

'Will do,' Tommy said.

Sylvester walked along the driveway in front of the hotel. He looked up at the entrance, glowing in yellow light, and knew what it would be to walk in there and feel the blast of coolness, to smell the flowers and hear the water-feature. Above his head the trees met and birds were beginning to sing. He passed the rockeries and flowerbeds and came to the entrance and the security box at the gate with a guard sleeping in his chair, head lolling back, and kept walking. He turned right and saw in front of him a huge sky full of yellow and pink and blue in the approaching dawn, the air completely still and clear and silent as if the day itself was holding its breath. He stood there not moving, watching this, and believed for a moment that everything had stopped. That he was alone in this beautiful world and that if he wanted he could stay standing there for ever and that nothing would ever change.

64

It was three o'clock when Marcin woke from a dreamless sleep into the pain and confusion of a hangover. He lay there feeling poisoned in the half-darkness, trying to remember why he felt so bad, and then it came to him. He sat up, threw his pillow across the room, and the bag was there, where his head had been, looking back at him as he stared. He sat on the edge of the bed and took the money out, then looked at it all for twenty minutes, stacked in neat piles. It baffled him. He tried to contemplate the options that were in front of him but in the presence of all these notes, with their smell filling the room, it was hard to keep focused. He looked at his phone and saw that there were no missed calls, no messages. He checked the news on the television and saw nothing of relevance. Nothing had happened yet.

It was not his. That thought kept occurring to him. He had no right to rob anyone, to take something simply because it was there. Who the money belonged to or what it was for didn't alter anything. It did not belong to him. He could find a way to give it back. Be honest and say that a moment of weakness overcame him, that he had done the wrong thing and that, on reflection, in sobriety, in the cold light of the mid-afternoon, he was ashamed of his behaviour. He was sorry and here was the money back. Untouched.

Or he could say nothing. Find the man's address somehow and take it to his house in the middle of the night. Put it in an envelope, leave it for him in the hotel lost-and-found and call him from a public phone. 'I am a friend. There is something important for you waiting in the hotel. Good luck.'

He put the money back into the bag and took it into the bathroom with him while he showered. He got dressed and packed his rucksack carefully, set the alarm on his phone, then lay on the bed with his eyes closed. He thought about what might happen, allowed himself to be optimistic and felt himself drift. When the alarm went off he thought he was ready. His phone still had not rung. There were no messages for him.

He left the flat with the rucksack on his shoulder and rang Tommy's mobile as he walked towards the bus.

'It's me,' he said.

'How are you?' Tommy said.

'I'm all right. And you?'

'Grand.'

'Any news?' Marcin asked.

'No news here. Have you anything for us yourself?'

'I'm not coming back. If that's news.'

'Not really.'

'I just . . . I can't do it any more, you know.'

'I know,' Tommy said.

'Will it be all right?'

'I'll tell them.'

'What'll they do?'

Tommy laughed quietly. 'They'll get someone else. It won't be a problem.'

'Thanks, Tommy.' Was there something else he should say? 'I'm sorry.'

'Don't be. It's fine. Listen, I have to go.'

Marcin heard the splash of water and the background sound of people laughing, ordering, being served. 'I'll see you around.'

'Good luck.'

The bus brought him to the centre of town. He walked along the quays towards the sea until in front of a bank he saw a crowd of people and the colours of the coach company. He wandered among them, people saying goodbye and loading bags into the bottom of the bus, smoking cigarettes and hugging each other. The driver asked him how far he was going and he said to Warsaw. 'You're in for the long haul,' he said.

'Yes,' Marcin said. But he didn't think he was. The bus would go through Wales and England, then take the boat to Holland and travel on through Germany to Poland. He could get off anywhere, go anywhere. Disappear into some small town for a couple of months away from all of this until he got his head together and his story straight. And when he knew what to say to people, how to explain everything that had happened to him and all the things he had done, he could begin to think about going home.

Acknowledgements

Thanks to Brendan Barrington, Marianne Gunn O'Connor, Richard and Sue Ogilvy, Magda and Marcin Gajko, Cormac Kinsella, my parents and Sarah.

Loved
this book?

Meet someone who loves
what you love too.

Go to www.penguindating.co.uk
and discover your next chapter.

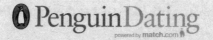

He just wanted a decent book to read ...

Not too much to ask, is it? It was in 1935 when Allen Lane, Managing Director of Bodley Head Publishers, stood on a platform at Exeter railway station looking for something good to read on his journey back to London. His choice was limited to popular magazines and poor-quality paperbacks – the same choice faced every day by the vast majority of readers, few of whom could afford hardbacks. Lane's disappointment and subsequent anger at the range of books generally available led him to found a company – and change the world.

'We believed in the existence in this country of a vast reading public for intelligent books at a low price, and staked everything on it'
Sir Allen Lane, 1902–1970, founder of Penguin Books

The quality paperback had arrived – and not just in bookshops. Lane was adamant that his Penguins should appear in chain stores and tobacconists, and should cost no more than a packet of cigarettes.

Reading habits (and cigarette prices) have changed since 1935, but Penguin still believes in publishing the best books for everybody to enjoy. We still believe that good design costs no more than bad design, and we still believe that quality books published passionately and responsibly make the world a better place.

So wherever you see the little bird – whether it's on a piece of prize-winning literary fiction or a celebrity autobiography, political tour de force or historical masterpiece, a serial-killer thriller, reference book, world classic or a piece of pure escapism – you can bet that it represents the very best that the genre has to offer.

Whatever you like to read – trust Penguin.

 read more
www.penguin.co.uk